CAMEO

Squadron Leader Andrew Halford is on leave in London during the grim days of the Blitz. His parents have sought safety in the country and he goes to check their London home. During the confusing hours of the black-out, Halford drives up the wrong bomb-damaged street and enters the wrong house. In the bedroom he finds a semi-clothed woman seated before a mirror. Staring at him.

The mistake he has made leads Andrew into a complex network of treachery and deceit. And on the track of a sadistic murderer.

In *Cameo* – the action of which takes place in a single week of April 1941 – Winston Graham brilliantly evokes the tension of wartime London; the reckless bravery of airmen who live only for today; the discovery of young love. A masterly thriller, written by a master storyteller.

WINSTON GRAHAM

CAMEO

COLLINS
8 Grafton Street, London W1
1988

William Collins Sons & Co. Ltd
London · Glasgow · Sydney · Auckland
Toronto · Johannesburg

BRITISH LIBRARY CATALOGUING IN PUBLICATION DATA

Graham, Winston, 1909–
Cameo.
I. Title
823'.912[F]

ISBN 0-00-223356-8

First published 1988
© Winston Graham 1988

Photoset in Linotron Aldus by
Rowland Phototypesetting Ltd
Bury St Edmunds, Suffolk
Printed and bound in Great Britain by
William Collins Sons & Co. Ltd, Glasgow

Author's Note

In 1942 I wrote and published a suspense novel called MY TURN NEXT. I have written CAMEO on the same theme, but time has given a historical slant to what was a contemporary tale.

W.G.

Friday Night

I

When you find the dead body of a woman in your bedroom on the first night of your leave it is disturbing to the mind and the stomach – even if you are as used to various forms of sudden death as he was.

It had all begun really on the way home, in the small hours, three o'clock in the morning to be exact, on the way home from a night-club called The Bamboo, in Frith Street. The date was Friday 17 April. Perhaps it should have been Friday the 13th.

He had been careful with his car, the way he drove it, careful to keep to the left of centre and pretty skilful in double de-clutching and not grating his gears. That was as it should be: man on leave, with rank, ought to set a good example. He was not, of course, drunk, just careful with his car.

The first day had been a long one, but not bad, considering. Bit of a blow-out tonight, and why not? Witold had got a bar to his DFC. Good man, Witold. Great big chap, noisy, clumsy; you'd not guess to look at him that he'd be so good at the fairly delicate business of flying a fighter plane. Pale, absent-minded eyes and a wide mouth with irregular teeth that his lips closed over reluctantly. Anything but handsome, yet the girls fell for him in a big way. His parents and two sisters had been killed in the siege of Warsaw.

The other Pole, Stephen, *his* great friend, was quite different; a quiet, pleasant young man, fair-haired, blue-eyed, slight blond moustache; handsome enough and spoke English well. He had lost a brother in the *Orzel*, and another was serving in a bomber squadron. Titled Cracow family; Stephen had been studying medicine at the outbreak of war.

A day and half the night, first supping at the Savoy, going on after to The Bamboo. Three Scotsmen, two Poles and an Englishman. Fair mix. When the party broke up, the Scotsmen had gone off singing and supporting each other; the Poles had grabbed a prowling taxi, the last heard of them was decreasing decibels of noise as the taxi turned out of Frith Street.

Would they go to their hotel? Seemed unlikely. Too dull. Girls? Probably. He had thought of joining them. Flying Officer Witold Poniatowski, Flight Lieutenant Stephen Radziwill, Squadron Leader Andrew Halford.

Better to have stuck together, at least as far as a bedroom door, but his father, evacuated with his Government department to Bath, had asked him to look in at their house at Northcot, see how it was going on. His mother, after expressing distress that he was not going to spend most of his brief leave with them, had added: 'I am enclosing a short list of things we weren't able to bring away when we were over in January, and it would be kind of you, dear, if you would parcel them up. If they won't go in the boot of your car you could leave them with the Farrants next door and I'll ask the GWR to call for them.'

So his idea was to pass the night in the house, just to satisfy them both. He knew his father wouldn't let his mother come up on her own, though what the difference in risk was between London and Bath floored him. But it was Government thinking; no one except those in the flying business had yet come round to the realization that when you were in the air 100 miles hardly counted.

Bloody nuisance all the same, having to come out here. It was why he hadn't gone girl-chasing with the Poles. Bloody nuisance. Or was it a part excuse? Nothing he'd have liked better than to find a girl he fancied – a nice girl, a friendly girl, a free girl, an oncoming girl; but honest to God he didn't really fancy tarts. Something wrong with him. That poem he'd read at Keble: 'Surely the kisses of her bought red mouth were sweet.' Just the trouble: they weren't. Or not to him. The false 'darlings'. The phoney expressions of desire. The cries of pleasure. The hard eyes with the soft lips. OK. He would have liked something. But, with all deference to Witold's and Stephen's taste, he really needed something a bit different, a bit better. Failing it, he had to make do with nothing.

A black cat streaking across the road made him brake suddenly. And as suddenly, just for a few seconds, he felt himself back in his Spitfire. When you fired all eight Brownings your plane checked, dipped its nose, dropped something like 40 mph in its speed. Then, chances were, if you had aimed right and were *near enough*, someone else's boyfriend, some other parents' son, might not see another dawn. That was the way it was in the air. Jolly but grim. Mortal combat. Quite different from braking a 1½ litre MG to preserve one of a cat's nine lives. But all part of the scene. You couldn't change it.

He'd been to No 9 Vernon Avenue early in the afternoon, hurriedly, to dump his kit and to make up a bed, but it would mean messing for himself in the morning. Not that that would be entirely new: in the dark days of last August, with the Battle of Britain raging at its fiercest, the kitchen staff at the airfield, with the encouragement of their unions, had refused to get up early enough to cook breakfast for the dawn patrol.

But there was a bit too much in the echoing house and half acre of garden to remind him of a pre-war life that was really better folded up in lavender and put away for the duration. He wasn't even sure he wanted it back. Not that life anyway. Peace of a different sort. He'd been reading English Lit, and only in his last year, with Munich imminent, had joined the Air Volunteer Reserve. Lucky old Halford. Just got in in time to be launched unfledged against the Messerschmidts. Somehow it had all worked out, and now at 25 he was a senior officer, a hardened war-horse of fifty fights, long-time

9

member of the Caterpillar Club, a chap a lot of other chaps looked up to. Some of them even saluted.

Nothing much wrong with the house; he'd done a Cook's tour this afternoon. Three bedroom windows at the rear had gone, and most of the slates of the garage roof. But the windows were boarded up, and there was no car in the garage to come to harm. The garden, once his father's pride, was a right mess: last year's rambler shoots straggled and waved across the windows; weeds flourished in the borders and the paths. Odd how quickly nature got back at you for trying to keep it tidy. Nothing in nature was tidy. Everything struggled to live at the expense of everything else. Perhaps that was what war was about . . .

No, he thought carefully. Maybe last time. Maybe other times. Not this time. It wasn't just *lebensraum* that Hitler was after.

Creep through Willesden, take the main Thornwood road. No alerts tonight. There'd been a hell of a blitz last Wednesday, but except for a few stray pencils of light tracing infant markings on the slate of the sky, London showed no special signs of life at the moment. Sky fine and clear, a dusting of misty stars, all free from that fevered flush that had marked it for generations. The city slept – or appeared to. It slept with an ear to the ground and an eye on the skies, really altogether more alert than it had ever been among the clamour and the light.

He laughed suddenly. It bubbled up in him like champagne – maybe it *was* the champagne – Witold Poniatowski spoke his English as he killed his Germans, untidily. When he was sober you knew just what he meant: when not sober it was comic guesswork. Sometimes, now and then, he misunderstood commands issued to him in the air, usually when it was an order to break off an engagement. A man without anger in the ordinary sense of the word, a man without fear, but also without pity. There were a few subjects Witold never joked about. Twice already he had been fished out of the Channel.

Past Thornwood and turn right at the Green. Two special constables were pacing the empty streets. There were a few craters round here, partly filled in, but they had to be negotiated. Made navigation a bit confusing. There was Beach Avenue, then two more, then Vernon Avenue. He yawned so widely as he turned down it that his jaw cracked. Maybe he should be tired. Two missions yesterday – one a dog fight, but the Jerry, a Messerschmidt Emil, had turned up into the clouds and he'd lost him. Frustrating that, all the tension, all the adrenaline flowing, then nothing to show for it. He always remembered that time when he and Cowley had shot up a Junkers 88, filled it as full of holes as an old bucket and still hadn't been able to bring it down. It had gone wobbling and wheezing back to France. When they reported to the CO he said: 'No bad thing. It's worse for morale if a few of 'em get back with half the crew dead, and blood everywhere. Not just a nice clean "disappearance".'

Draw up at No 9; leave the engine ticking over while you open the gates; run the car into the drive. Not much point in using the garage, with half the roof gaping. Hadn't seen the Farrants yet: see 'em in the morning. Both of their sons were at sea, one in a minesweeper. Damned dangerous job.

A glint of light from a curtain further down the avenue. Air-raid warden wasn't doing his job. Touch of late frost in the air; there was a smear of rime on the gates.

Surprising, considering the pasting London had had all through the winter, how few really *had* left their homes. People were fatalistic, shrugged their shoulders, thought it probably wouldn't happen to them. Life went on, not merely in the flesh-pots of the West End but in these great sprawling suburbs whose very area made bombing more difficult to invest with frightfulness.

He locked the car and took off the distributor head – an advised precaution in case parachutists should suddenly arrive. (A less likely event it seemed to him since the air battles of last summer.) Open the door and go in. Laughter

11

again – a bubbling gust – because he thought he was going to have difficulty with the key. Surely not as fuddled as all that. He needed another drink now, but maybe coffee was the right bet. As he finally pushed open the door he thought: 6.30 to 3.30, twenty-one hours. It would take longer than that to unwind – properly unwind. Champagne had left him heavy of foot but sharp enough of mind. He wondered if the Poles would find their girls. Wouldn't be surprised if in the end they thought it wasn't worth the trouble and turned in like him.

Pleasant house inside, built to a more or less standard model of these avenues. His parents had moved in when his father got his promotion to Whitehall. He was seven then, so it spanned most of his life. Square hall with wide shallow stairs which led up to a landing with a big picture window. This had been a headache when the black-out first came in. At the back were a kitchen and a dining room; to the right a large drawing room; to the left a breakfast room; above, five bedrooms. His mother said the house was too big. When they came here they had expected a larger family. Instead only him. Pity. All their eggs in one Spitfire.

He had made up a bed in his parents' room, as this faced south. He went in to the room and picked his way across to draw the curtains. He swore as he caught his leg on a chair which unexpectedly got in the way, then was at the window carefully pulling the material over. His mother must have bought new stuff; it didn't seem long since everyone was combing the shops for black Italian cloth and holding substitutes to the light to see if they made the grade. His mother, whose philosophy in life was never to face the worst until it happened, had been caught out, and every pair of curtains in the house had a different lining. He had been training at Aston Down at the time, and had spent a good bit of his early leaves fitting rods and runners.

Now with safety he could take out his pocket torch and flick it on as he moved across the room to switch on the light. He stopped when he saw that since this afternoon the bed had been moved. Or *looked* as if it had. Maybe in his haste this afternoon he hadn't noticed.

He flicked his torch across the bed again, feeling stupid. Then he went to the door and switched on the light. No light.

He'd been in the kitchen specially this afternoon, put down the main switch. And it had worked because he'd made a cup of tea. So what was this? Silly bulb had fused. Try the bedside light. But who had moved the bed?

He rubbed his eyes, swallowed another yawn. Not sleepy now. Not the time to be sleepy. Something very wrong. You didn't need to be slightly fuddled to know that. But perhaps being fuddled had delayed the signals. Finger-tips, hair, nose, all said something, were saying something he hadn't quite latched on to. He flashed his tiny light about the room.

Two things clear. First, this wasn't his parents' room. Bed at a different angle, chairs of different shape, pictures on the walls. Second, still plainer, still more important. Corner-wise, to the right of the main window, a big dressing-table with three mirrors. In a chair at this dressing-table a woman sat with her head on one side watching him through the middle and largest of the mirrors.

II

Thoughts fly quicker than birds. Confused by the black-out, stop at the wrong house; key sticks; probably front door hadn't been locked. A woman waits for her husband – Home guard or ARP duty – perhaps been out herself on canteen work, combing her hair in the dark not bothering to draw the curtains; he lumbers in. She'd watched his gropings about the room in frozen silence. Lucky she hasn't screamed the house down – yet; or cracked him over the head, thinking him a Fifth Columnist.

'I – I *beg* your pardon,' he got out.

Really, he thought, what a drunken clot. Really.

'This . . . must be the wrong house. Not number Nine. Desperately sorry . . .'

You couldn't decently spot the light directly on her, but he caught the glint of her eyes watching him. She wasn't wearing much either, a bare shoulder gleamed, the other was covered by dark hair. He turned the light on himself, so that the sight of his uniform might reassure her.

'Damned black-out. So sorry.'

The sheets of the bed were rumpled, looked as if they'd been slept in.

In the mirror, she still seemed to be watching him, not in the least reassured. Head on one side and scowling at him in fact. Or snarling, like a wild cat caught in the dark. Get out quick. 'Drunken air-force officer on assault charge.' Why didn't she move or say something?

Provoked, he put the light on her, and the light flickered back through the mirror; couldn't see distinctly. Was it only the light that flickered? Sheet over the wardrobe. Room stuffy. The frost on his fingers outside had turned to dust.

He drew a breath to speak but held it there. He went up to her slowly, sidling up, careful not to frighten her any more. Then he saw she wasn't afraid of him at all. Her tongue was half out of her mouth and bloody. Even before he touched her hand he knew it would be cold and stiff.

III

There was that German gunner in the Heinkel that had crash-landed, most of his face blown away. And there was Cowley, his old friend Cowley, pulled out from under the wreckage of his Hurricane. And others. Plenty of others. After all, you get involved in a war and lose any number of your friends, some of whom you unfortunately see when they are past their best. But it's still a new experience to see a dead woman.

A sharp step back, wipe your fingers down the side of your tunic; the torch fell away and the light made a feeble oval on the carpet.

Shaky, believe it or not, he was shaky. Old iron nerves.

Was this an air-raid victim from Wednesday? Death from shock or fright. Fright might have done it, as the windows weren't broken. But those eyes? That tongue? The battery of his torch was running down, the light yellowing. She seemed to be wearing nothing but a petticoat and high-heeled shoes; one had fallen off, lay at an ironic angle to the twisted foot. His finger-tips still tingled from the touch of her ice-cold hand.

Stuffy in the room too. Time to go. Exit gently pursued by a bear.

Time *was* it? A clock on the dressing-table had stopped at half-past nine. Beside it was a vase of flowers, withered, black, an inch of yellow water at the base of the vase.

Beside the vase a stub of candle; necessary furnishing in these times. Go and leave it all, ring the police. 'Pardon me, I've just come from No 7 – or perhaps No 11 – Vernon Avenue and found the body of a young woman sitting in a chair.'

He lit the candle from a box of matches he'd picked up at the Savoy. After the usual pause, the light grew, began to show up more of the room. Furniture was much like his parents' except this was walnut not mahogany; copy of a Van Gogh on the wall, some photographs, another mirror. Clothes on a chair by the bed. Her clothes.

Something creaked. He stopped very still. How to explain yourself, if found? But who would come to find you? Was this the owner, who didn't change the flowers for a month and then come back to die in a bedroom thick with dust? She was still watching him through the mirror with her bloody, staring eyes.

Must stop her staring. Go over, wipe your finger-tips, set the torch down, put a hand on the dark crisp hair, with the forefinger of the other hand pull down the eyelids. Eyes very bloodshot; dry blood in the ears. Shiver, as you step back. Head was moving; it lolled slowly to one side, then fell forward as far as it could go upon the breast. The body was relaxing.

He picked up the torch and shone it at the woman's neck. There was a deep red line running round and across her throat. Ideas of heart attacks or bomb shock could be written off. Someone had used a cord.

IV

Strange she'd not collapsed before, only slumped on the high chair, head resting crookedly against the back. Rigor mortis, he thought, could set in soon after death or be delayed by as much as a day. Average time perhaps twelve hours. But how long before it passed off? This woman was beginning to smell.

Again that creak. Someone listening at the door? He went to the door and flung it open, flashed his torch across the landing and down into the well of the hall. There might be a man or a woman in any of the shadows but nothing moved within the dim circle of light. Back to the bedroom.

He picked up her coat lying on the bed. An exotic sort of scent one associated with good restaurants, the foyers of hotels, the fashionable *thé dansant*. Coat not expensive, though. Nothing in the pockets. Look for the maker's label. It had been cut out.

So. That was how it was. Drop the coat on the bed, go to the clothes on the chair. Blue two-piece suit, blue speckled scarf, brassiere and knickers, a sort of suspender-belt thing; artificial silk stockings. Same scent.

He picked up the one shoe that was free. Maker's name of a multiple shoe-shop. Under the chair a handbag. Kneel, gingerly stretch for it, feeling that she might lean over and stop him. Bag empty. Totally empty except for one kirby-grip.

. . . He'd messed around long enough, tempting fate. Nearly four o'clock. He picked up the woman's coat again, folded it, lining out, the way he had found it. In doing this his fingers felt something under the thin cloth lining.

Bigger than a bus ticket, more likely a design card with the usual hieroglyphics and the maker's name. He felt again in each of the pockets but no hole. He fished for his penknife, and then saw a small inside pocket to the coat not noticed before. He drew out the ticket or whatever it was, and as he did so the wick in the stub of candle leaned over into the melting grease and went out.

His torch came on again, flickering uncertainly, showed his prize. It was a ticket but no bus conductor had issued it. It was a pawn ticket issued on 14 April, 1941 by J Lewistein, Jeweller & Pawnbrokers, and the advance paid for the gold watch pawned was £4.10.0. That was last Tuesday.

She was no longer watching him, but the swollen tongue still filled her mouth with grimace. The black-out curtains were drawn; they'd have to stay. The rest was much as he had found it, except that his fingerprints were everywhere, and by taking the pawn ticket he'd be robbing the police of their most valuable clue.

He went out, hearing no more creaks except those he made himself, and, as he left, the silence of the house closed down again behind him.

Saturday Morning

I

The Baker family was celebrating. Hilda, the eldest daughter, was marrying Arthur Filey. An eight o'clock wedding, for Arthur was a skilled foreman in an armament factory and could only take a long weekend.

So it was literally a wedding breakfast they sat down to. A bit of a squeeze, seating sixteen in this room. They'd borrowed four bentwood chairs from a neighbour, put cushions on them; had had to push the elderly upright piano with the fretwork front flat against the wall and had added a card table which was an inch lower than their dining table and made a sharp ridge in the table cloth – the young ones at that end.

Mrs Baker looked over her fifteen guests with slight anxiety – as was her nature – but mixed now with satisfaction. You could say that Arthur Filey wasn't much class, but he'd a highly paid job, and Hilda, who was twenty-eight, had missed one or two good chances. There was an element of relief in the whole matter for Mrs Baker; Hilda had been a difficult girl, headstrong, temperamental, thought too much of herself and her position in the world, could never be told; her mother had even been afraid that she might take what she called in her mind 'the wrong track'. (She never used expressions like that out loud; old ways of looking at things were laughed at nowadays.) Yet here after all was Hilda, safely and satisfactorily married and really looking happy about it.

Not perhaps a *handsome* man, Arthur, but a serious-minded one and a pretty steady type for Hilda to line up with. Lack of height was one of his problems – Hilda was so tall – but this didn't embarrass him. As he made his little speech after the cutting of the war-time cake, he was full of assurance and looked down at his bride (who fortunately was seated at this juncture).

As for Hilda, she had chosen pale blue *crêpe de chine* with a small blue hat and eye-veil to match. Her colouring was her best point: such pretty ice-blue eyes, and the pale corn-tinted hair she was always so anxious to assure people was perfectly natural. (Which it was.)

Mrs Baker sometimes thought it odd that her two eldest children should be so much alike in feature and temperament – though Louis was not so fair as Hilda – while her two younger ones took more closely after her. Hilda and Louis were like their father in looks and like him in character, especially Louis. Especially Louis Carl, as he had been christened in those high and far off days of hope and goodwill before the First World War.

She'd been quite surprised to see her firstborn here today. Hilda had asked him to come, but his appearances at home were now so rare that you quite expected the invitation to be ignored. As it was, he'd arrived late for the registry office ceremony and didn't seem to have brought them a wedding present of any sort.

He sat now next to the bridegroom's mother, and his hearty laugh sounded at frequent intervals above the noise of the breakfast. A handsome man, Louis Carl (thirty last month), tall, erect, smart, with short-cropped up-growing hair which tried to curl over his ears, a tight ambitious mouth, opinionated eyes. Mrs Filey (petunia-coloured figured georgette: a bit too figured for her build) evidently thought him good company.

Mrs Baker wasn't so sure – at least she wasn't so sure about the laugh. She remembered it on that evening seven years back when, afterwards, after his hearty jollity, she'd gone up to his bedroom and found him packing. 'I'm off,' he had said, biting at his lips, and to her further questioning had added: 'Oh, I don't know. Catch a boat at Southampton – I've a fancy to travel.' And when she had queried in a rising note of distress: 'But what'll happen to your job in the bank? You were doing so *well*!' he'd snapped: 'Oh, come off it. What's a bank clerk? What's a teller? A cog in a wheel. A dead end. A blind alley.'

'A *safe* alley!' she had hissed. 'All this unemployment. And Uncle Fred went to such *trouble*. You've everything to look forward to. I can't believe you're just going to throw it up! Not just like *that*!'

But nothing would deter him, and the following day she realized, when two grave-faced men called, that he hadn't had all that much choice anyhow. It was only a small discrepancy, about two hundred and fifty pounds, but it had meant Mrs Baker making out a cheque for this amount from her small savings to dissuade them from proceeding any further with her son's clerical errors.

He had soon been back again living at home, once he knew there were no proceedings afoot – found work as a car salesman and then later, developing his undoubted talent for electrical things, had gone into the growing business of wireless and gramophones. Three years ago the police had called and asked him to go with them to the station for questioning about some stolen cars. In the end no charges were preferred, but soon after this Louis had left Wolverhampton and she had only seen him a couple of times since. Louis, she recalled, always laughed when he was in trouble.

He and Hilda had never fitted into the middle-class respectable circles of the town. They had always seemed to feel themselves set apart, above the average, of a superior breed. It was the point of view of Carl Baker when he was alive, and the two eldest children had come most into contact with him and had imbibed his view. Carl's mother had been the daughter of a general and had married beneath her – much beneath her, Carl thought, and at the same time had lost her own distinguished name for a commonplace one. Carl's two eldest resented it just as much as Carl did.

Mrs Baker stared at the sepia photo of her husband in the faded gilt frame on the wall, tall, moustached, square-shouldered, in a double-breasted suit, taken the year before they married. Young then and plenty of charm, but always difficult. Always so touchy. And vain. All right, she thought, my name was Mason, and I can't help that; theirs is Baker, too bad, but it's no excuse for neglecting your business the way Carl did, or thinking themselves too high and mighty to earn an honest living like Louis and, to a lesser extent, Hilda.

The breakfast party was breaking up; a group clustered round the bride and groom and others were admiring the presents, when Mrs Baker's attention was attracted by Hilda's crow of delight.

'Oh, Louis, how *lovely*! Isn't that *sweet*, Arthur! Thanks ever so.'

Mrs Baker arrived in time to see her daughter, made expansive on Empire sherry, fling her arms round her brother's neck.

'It's OK,' said Louis, uncoiling her. 'Happened to see it in a shop – thought you might like it. Couldn't think of anything for both of you.'

The present was a cameo brooch, unusually attractive because of its dark background and the coloured circlet about the Roman head. Mrs Baker warmed towards her son.

'Thanks, Louis,' she said. 'It *was* nice of you to bring it.'

'Almost the first present he's ever given me, isn't it, Mum?' Hilda beamed.

'Maybe,' said Louis with a laugh, 'but I put you on to a good thing last year.'

Hilda's eyes narrowed above the brilliant smile. 'OK. That's finished now.'

'I should think so,' said Arthur. 'You never make anything betting, not in the long run.'

'Oh, this wasn't betting, this was a cert, eh, Hilda?' There was again the harshness, the note of irony in Louis' laugh. Arthur clearly didn't much fancy the implication, whatever it was, and he had a finger inside his stiff collar as he glanced from one to the other.

Mrs Baker sharply interposed: 'Well, it's awfully nice to have brought something, Louis. I felt sure you'd forget. It shows he cares for you, Hilda. A brother of mine never gave me anything as nice as that.'

'I remember when I gave you a mouth-organ, Kitty,' said her only surviving brother, who was present, and the moment passed.

Soon the happy pair were off, to chatter and laughter and the stuffing of confetti into pockets and umbrellas. The day was bright and windy – 'true April weather' – and everybody stood in the doorway and garden, holding on to hats and pushing back hair and waving goodbye. People from nearby houses put their heads out and waved, or peered critically from behind casement curtains. War and its grim realities seemed a thousand miles away. Overcome by emotion, Mrs Baker almost missed Louis, who was slipping out by the back door.

'Going so soon, son?' she asked casually, knowing from experience that any show of affection would put him off.

'Not much to stay for now,' he said, looking over the well-kept kitchen garden. 'Somebody been monkeying with your aerial?'

'Tommy. He climbed up and the pole broke. You don't come to see us these days, Louis.'

'I'm busy.' The family cat came and rubbed herself against his legs. 'Things keep me pretty busy. Who does your garden now?'

'I do most of it. Tommy and Ernie help a bit when I make them.'

'Your early potatoes are doing all right.'

'Yes, we shall be digging them soon. Are you in a good job now, Louis?'

'Yep.' He shifted uneasily, gazing at the hedge in which a

few green leaves were beginning to unfurl. He was never really comfortable in his mother's company; she knew him too well; had known him when he had messed in his trousers and stolen from the sweet shop and lied about the bullying at school. It didn't do with her, the façade he'd built up to impress the world. Why had he come? Some sort of silly attachment for Hilda who didn't care a tinker's curse for *him*.

'It's nice to see you in funds. What sort of a job is it?'

'Estate agent.'

'Go on. On your own?'

'No. A firm. A well known firm.'

'Not had your call-up papers yet?'

'Not yet.'

'That's lucky.'

'I'm doing part-time fire-watching.'

Mrs Baker stared down the street. It seemed a small reason for exemption.

'I suppose there's plenty of scope for estate agencies just now. All this bombing, and people shifting out of London. Does your firm work round here?'

'No. London. Plenty of work there too.'

'I suppose. So you're doing all right?'

'Fine. I'll be off now.'

'Well,' said Mrs Baker, 'it was generous of you to buy that for Hilda. It really was. You saw how pleased she was.'

'Yes. I saw.'

'It must have cost a bit.'

'Oh, it cost a bit.'

'Where are you living now, Louis? You never leave an address.'

'Hilda has it.'

'Well, she won't be here any more. Someone might be ill.'

'Care of the YMCA. That'll always find me.'

'Just that?'

'WC1.'

They walked through the kitchen garden to the back garden door.

'I'll bolt it again when you've gone,' she said. 'That little imp Bill Sanders from round the corner will nip in. I won't let Tommy go about with him if I can help it. Bad influence. His family is a bit funny, like. All the Sanderses are odd, like. You remember them, of course.'

'Tommy's growing into a little tyke,' said Louis. 'He needs taking in hand.'

'Who's going to do it?' asked Mrs Baker, her eyes suddenly watery with anxiety. 'Maybe you if you were home.'

'Well, I'm not home. What's he like at school?'

'Not bad. No worse than you.'

'Tommy Baker!' said Louis contemptuously. 'What a name!'

They stood out together on the pavement for a few moments in the windy sunshine. His car was parked nearby, an old Humber. Louis laughed.

Mrs Baker said suddenly: 'Not in trouble, are you, son?'

'Lord God, can't I ever come home without all this prying? You can't wonder I don't come home more often. In *trouble*! What do you think I am? In *trouble*. Good God!'

His mother noticed that he was biting his bottom lip – always a sign. 'Not money this time, is it?'

She flinched under his look. 'Look, I'm living my own life!'

'Of course you are, dear – '

'What business is it of yours or anyone's what I do with it? Eh? Eh?'

'All right, Louis. All right. All right. I only asked. I'm your mother, and I only asked.'

He breathed out his annoyance and impatience with her.

After a minute he said: 'Forget it. I know you mean well. But you can take it from me, I'm not wasting my time. I've other irons in the fire. The estate agency is OK, and it's paying the rent, but that's not all. You may see the difference in a year or two.'

'You mean when the war is over?'

He shrugged. 'Well, yes maybe, when the war is over

things'll be different in London, in England, you'll see. I shan't be taking orders then, I shall be *giving* them.'

'I shall be glad if it makes you happy,' she said quietly, not really listening, but humouring him.

'It'll certainly make *me* happy,' he said, and stopped, frowning. She always provoked him into saying too much. Not that it mattered, because she hadn't an idea in the world what he was talking about.

'I'm off now,' he said again, and brushed her cheek with his lips.

'So long,' she said, and watched him move away down the pleasant side-street, his long-legged stiff walk, shoulders and broad back turned towards her, shutting her out. Handsome, opinionated, aggressive, it was hard to remember what he'd been like as a child at her breast. For so long he'd been a separate, tight-guarded human being, a stranger, a hard man, bent on going his own ways, ambitious for success without having the enduring resolution to work for it, but determined all the same to make his mark. She only hoped that what he was doing didn't end in some disgrace.

He climbed in his car, started the engine and raised a brief hand as he drove off.

Saturday Morning - Two

I

'For loans of above £2 and not above £5 the Pawnbroker is entitled to charge for this Ticket, 3d. Upon receipt of the pledge for each 5/- or part of 5/- lent, 3d. For profit on each 4/- or part of 4/- lent on this pledge for not more than ONE calendar month, 2d and so on at the same rate per calendar month.

'If this pledge is not redeemed within SIX calendar months and SEVEN days from the day of pledging it, the article may be sold by auction by the pawnbroker. If this ticket is lost or mislaid, the Pawner should at once apply to the Pawnbroker for a form of declaration to be made before a Magistrate, or the Pawnbroker will be bound to deliver the pledge to any person who produces this Ticket to him and claims to redeem the same.'

II

The three opaque globes could only just be seen. The centuries-old sign was becoming less popular in the trade; and Mr J Lewistein liked to see himself as a legitimate jeweller. The block of offices of which this small shop formed a part were soot-dusted and a monotonous grey against the greying sky of noon. It looked like rain. Park Street, Euston, that was what the ticket had said. Not far away you could hear the stammer of an engine as it fumbled its way out of the station.

Lewistein was grey-haired, moon-faced, with a poor skin,

sleepy eyes and fat white hands which had never known the indignity of labour. He had been busy about the shop all morning, scolding Belle, his daughter, for not dusting the counters properly, and looking over some pretty trinkets which had come in yesterday: a brooch with a kunzite for its central stone – pity the diamonds surrounding it were phoney; three sapphire rings in which the sapphires were too dark to be top stuff, a pair of cuff-links from India with star-ruby stones. But more important to him, and making up for the tediousness of business, was an *andante* movement from a Concerto Grosso by Vivaldi, a piece for two violins and a piano he'd heard only for the second time last night. The reedy cadencies were on the rim of his mind, perched where he couldn't quite hold them, yet near enough to tease his memory.

When the RAF fellow came into the shop he let Belle serve him, but the rare advent of a serving officer reluctantly drew his attention back to commercial things.

A slim dark lad with three rings on his sleeve, one narrow between two broader with dark edgings. Could never re-member whether this was a flight lieutenant or a squadron leader; must ask David again.

As he pottered forward, the jeweller saw two wings on the left breast of the customer's tunic, which meant that this was a flyer and not ground staff. A pilot. Young, still in his twenties, no spare flesh, good looking in a sharp featured way, high cheek bones. Alert, vital, you could see that. High-strung. A bit on edge. You couldn't wonder.

'Can I do something for you, sir?'

Belle said: 'It's this pawn ticket, Papa. He has brought it in for the lady. He was asking me – '

'I met Miss Ward last night,' said the young man, 'and when she'd gone I found she'd dropped this ticket. But I don't know her address and can't read the address on the ticket. Is it 45 Latimer Street?'

Mr Lewistein took the ticket and pushed his spectacles up his nose.

'No. Excuse me, sir. My writing is poor. That is Gaskin Street. 45, Gaskin Street.'

'Ah,' said the young man. 'Gaskin Street.' He looked at Belle. 'Is that far from here?'

Belle said: 'I don't think so. Isn't it just off Mornington Street, Papa?'

'It's north of here. You cross Hampstead Road.'

'Thank you.'

Belle said: 'Do you want to redeem the watch?'

'Er – yes,' said the young man. It hadn't occurred to him. 'Yes, I suppose so.'

'Very well, sir. If you will kindly sign your name and address and pay the money to my daughter.'

Mr Lewistein brought back a woman's gold wrist-watch with a neat, clear face. He held it in his fat white fingers and seemed reluctant to let it go. Eventually he dropped it into an envelope and flicked the flap across his tongue.

'My boy is in the uniform, sir.'

'Thanks,' said the officer, accepting the envelope. 'The Air Force? What branch?'

'Wireless telegraphy, sir. Music was really his world, though. At the Royal Academy. A beautiful ear. Twenty-one last birthday.'

'Where's he stationed?'

'Somewhere in Gloucestershire, sir. On the ground staff, you understand. A nervous boy. But doing very nicely, sir. Writes such bright and cheery letters. Every Thursday they come, regular as a clock.'

'It's an interesting life.'

'Not everyone gets a scholarship to the Royal Academy, sir. All remarked on his perfect pitch. It was a great shock to us when he had to go. Of course, he's missed the worst raids . . . That one on Wednesday . . .'

Like a pale comely duckling Belle was hovering about the ledger. Andrew smiled at her, showing very white uneven teeth.

She said: 'Miss Ward is lucky in her friends.'

'It's a moot point,' said Halford. 'But thank you.'

Belle blushed, shut the ledger, fumbled self-consciously with the neck of her blouse.

'I always tell David to take care of his hands, sir, as this war won't last for ever. Thank you. Did you give the gentleman his change, Belle?'

'Yes, Papa.'

The officer slipped the package into his pocket and raised a hand to his cap. Then he was gone, and the shop was more drab for his going. With a sense of dissatisfaction Belle re-opened the ledger and made another entry.

Lewistein's mind was wandering back to the Vivaldi concerto, but there was still a small matter to be attended to.

'Belle, I think you were rather forward with the gentleman. I don't like a daughter of mine to be so forward.'

'Squadron leader, that's what he was,' said Belle. 'Squadron Leader Andrew Halford, that's what he put. And he had ribbons as well.'

Her father brought his hairless eyebrows together. 'He was a gentleman, that is for sure. It would be good to be under a man like that. I wish that David should be so lucky.'

III

He'd left his car and was walking. Nice brisk, easy pace. No hint of strain, physical or mental; no obvious sign at all, though the last nine months had not exactly been a Teddy Bear's picnic, to prelude the peculiar traumas of last night. Five hours odd he'd eventually spent in bed at No 9, Vernon Avenue, five hours, it seemed to him, of dozing off fitfully, dropping away into an exhausted sleep when, hell, there was this dead woman sitting at the mirror watching you, and this was your parents' bedroom, the familiar bedroom and it was *their* mirror, and you had to sit up and rub your eyes and curse and realize it was just a nasty memory dragging across your mind.

Still, here was another day. Saturday. A brisk, easy pace.

A man in command of his faculties. Second day of his leave. Plenty of time to relax after he'd got this little problem out of his crop.

He bought a newspaper and leafed through it as he walked. The RAF had been bombing the *Scharnhorst* and the *Gneisenau* in Brest, the seventh time since the German battle cruisers had run for shelter there. It was a small pin-prick of retaliation for the recent raids on London. This was the first day the papers had carried any details of Wednesday's blitz.

St Paul's had got it again, it seemed. A bomb had come through the roof of the north transept and exploded inside the cathedral, bringing down half the roof which by its weight had caused the floor to give way, and the whole lot had fallen into the crypt. The City Temple had been burned out, as had St Andrew's, Holborn. Guy's Hospital and Chelsea Royal Hospital had been badly damaged. Selfridge's had had a direct hit and the roof had collapsed. Maple's and Christie's had been damaged.

Lucky his leave hadn't begun on Wednesday. He'd seen the glow from the comparative safety of Kent.

This was an area of London he hadn't been in before; he'd expected it to be fairly squalid, being near two main-line stations; but not so. The eighteenth century Bloomsbury builders had worked their way up here, and although shops had taken over a lot of the ground-floor space, the three storeys above were of mellowed sooty brick, interspersed with respectable solid Georgian sash windows. Those, that is, that had glass left in them. This was really quite a bad patch, with bomb craters, roped off rubble, and half-torn buildings with beds hanging over precipices and bathrooms exposed like a surrealist nightmare.

Number 45 Gaskin Street had its number painted on a semi-circle of glass above the tall gloomy doorway which was flanked by a sweet shop and a bookstall with handwitten advertisements in the window. He stood in the dark rectangle, peering round for name plates, but none was to be seen so he pulled at a solitary brass bell and could hear it jangling in the entrails of the house. He had time to wonder why he'd come, why he wanted to occupy his short leave poking his nose into some sleazy killing that didn't concern him, why he had not cleaned his shoes that morning and why he hadn't changed into grey slacks and a hacking jacket, as he'd had every intention of doing; then an elderly female with grey hair in curling pins, in a stained art-silk dress with a yellow apron and fluffy pink slippers, was peering at him as if he'd come to collect the rent.

'Sorry to trouble you. I'm inquiring after a friend of mine. Did a Miss J Ward live here at one time?'

Sight of his uniform had softened the gimlet in the old girl's eye. 'Did? She still do.'

'I see. Could you tell me when she was last at home?'

Chapped hands wiped slowly on apron. 'She's at home now, far as I know. Second floor back.'

'In?' He blinked at the landlady as if she were in a bright light. 'D'you think I could see her?'

'So far as I know, you can. Nobody's stopping you. I 'aven't seen 'er go out this morning. It's the back one, furthest from the stairs.'

Clip, clip, his feet went on the worn wooden stairs. So what was wrong? Where was the false link? Dead woman, pawn ticket, pawnbroker, gold watch . . .

He tapped at a door. Nothing. Maybe Lady Godiva downstairs didn't keep too close a watch on her tenants. Likely that Miss Ward hadn't been home last night, or for a couple of nights before.

Another door he'd passed. Try that. Give this one more chance. He lifted his hand to try again, and the door opened.

A thin, pretty, tawny-haired girl with an eager expression. At sight of him her expression changed.

'Oh, I half expected . . .' She didn't finish.

'Sorry to disappoint you. Does a Miss Ward live here?'

'I'm Jennifer Ward. Is that who you mean?'

They looked at each other. A split second of comprehensive inspection.

He felt in his pocket, took out the envelope.

'Is this your watch?'

She took the envelope, opened it, frowned. 'Yes. How did you . . .' She hesitated. 'Come in.'

Small furnished living room. A marble clock between ebony horses rearing, elderly armchairs with knitted antimacassars, a picture of Highland cattle standing in a sombre stream.

She handled the watch, turning it over. 'Where did you get it?'

'I found it.'

'Found it? Then how did you know where I lived?'

'The address was on the pawn ticket.'

'*Pawn* ticket!' She stared out of brilliant brown eyes. 'Do you mean – the watch was pawned?'

She was wearing a buff-coloured print frock, lisle stockings, brown sandals. A very thin girl but splendid eyes, a young, oval face, a light attractive fringe. Her hair was just a warm brown, not tawny, but sometimes the light caught it.

She put her hands through the fringe. 'Do you mean you redeemed the watch?'

'Yes.

'Well, thanks. I'll fetch you the money. Er – how much did you have to pay?'

Halford said: 'Clearly you didn't pawn the watch yourself.'

'No . . . I didn't. Where did you find the pawn ticket?'

'In a house.'

She had been standing by the mantelpiece, but now sat on the arm of the settee, smiled. It illumined the dark room. 'Do sit down. The chair behind you's stronger than it looks.'

He sat down. His business was not with this female.

She said: 'I share this flat with a friend. She was going out with a boyfriend, wanted something special for the occasion, had lost her own watch, asked me if she could borrow mine. But I never *dreamed*. I knew she was short of money – she always is. But it's a bit thick to borrow a thing and then *pawn* it! She *has* a blasted cheek!'

'What's your friend's name?'

Her eyes had been straying to the ribbons on his breast. 'Paula Krissen . . . She must have dropped the ticket! That really is adding *insult*!'

'Paula – Krissen, is it? She isn't in now, I suppose?'

'I haven't seen her since Tuesday. I was half expecting her when you knocked – thought she might have mislaid her key.'

'Ah,' he said.

'By now she must know she's lost the ticket. I hope she's worried stiff!'

This girl was much younger than the one he had found – probably not much more than twenty. Her figure was too slim to be good, but she'd such an unstudied grace about her way of standing and moving and sitting, he found it hard to take his eyes off her.

She smiled at him. 'How did you come to find the thing?'

'I'm on a few days' leave and spent the first night sleeping at Northcot, near Thornwood: my parents' house, but my father's work has been transferred, so the house has been empty. Number Nine, Vernon Avenue. Last night was my first night, and in the black-out I made a bloomer. I got the number right but there're bomb craters in the street – made it a bit confusing, I suppose – and I picked the wrong avenue. Carlton Avenue. It's the next one. Number Nine Carlton Avenue was also empty, and the door must have been un-locked, because I got in without noticing the difference. In the front upstairs bedroom was a woman, but she was dead. Nothing to identify her, nothing in her handbag. The coat pockets had been emptied, but in an inside pocket I found this pawn ticket.'

As he was speaking she went slowly white at the corners of her lips, and her eyes were fixed on him in shock and embarrasment.

'I didn't want to be axle deep in a police case on so short a leave, so I rang them from a call-box without giving my name. But I committed the unforgivable sin of bringing away the one essential clue. From there the hot trail led direct to you.'

'Police case?'

'Any sudden death is a police case. Even in wartime. But this woman I found had been strangled.'

Jennifer Ward got up, went to the mantelpiece, stood there looking rather sick.

'Crikey . . . D'you mind if I have a cigarette?'

He offered her his case and struck a match. At close quarters he already found compensation for using up a few hours of his leave.

She drew at the cigarette as if she had a grudge against it.

'What was she like – this girl, this woman you found?'

'Well, it's a bit hard to judge, the way I found her and the circumstances, only a torch and a candle. She looked tall – thirty to thirty-five, I'd guess – dark hair, quite a looker, well-dressed probably. Sleek black hair. Expensive perfume.'

'That's Paula,' she said. 'That's Paula.'

In the silence you could hear a baby crying somewhere.

'Gardenia,' the girl said. 'She always used it. That's . . . Paula. I can't *believe* it. Honestly! How could it ever have happened to her?'

'Somebody knows – but I don't.'

She kept her head down, staring at the smouldering end of her cigarette. 'What do you want to do now?'

'I planned to tell her relatives. D'you know any?'

'None I've ever heard of. Masses of friends, of course. I've only known her a few months.'

'Enemies?'

The girl made a little face, half grimace, half smile. 'Can't *say*. She would talk about herself by the hour. But most of it was superficial stuff, her boyfriends or her work.'

'What was her work?'

'She was an actress and dancer. In choruses and things, at theatres and night-clubs. She'd had a fair number of engagements, but they'd been drying up recently. She was worried about it – always short of money – the odd night here and there kept her going.'

'And the boyfriends?'

'I hardly ever saw them. Paula fell in and out of love quite easily. This one . . .'

'The latest one?'

'She only met him about three weeks ago. She seemed taken, more than ordinary. That's why she borrowed my watch – wanted to make a good impression – or so I *thought.*'

A picture of Paula Krissen was beginning to come up clear on the screen.

He said: 'I don't think I can decently drop it here without giving the police some sort of clue. Otherwise I really foul up the works.'

'Yes, of course. You must.'

He hesitated. This was where he baled out. He'd never had the least intention of going beyond the first few steps, just to satisfy his curiosity. Well . . . he'd done that. It wasn't too complex now. Paula Krissen had probably got involved in some *crime passionelle.* Or her boyfriend had quarrelled with her and lost his temper.

(Come on, Andrew, he said, it can't be really as simple as that.)

And Jennifer Ward? Did she follow the same career? Wouldn't mind taking *her* out for an evening. A leave well spent. Uh – huh? At least he wouldn't put a cord round her neck, whatever the provocation. Hell, she was thin, but so *pretty.* And so lively – until he tossed a death into the conversation.

'When the police come,' she said, 'I needn't tell them anything about you.'

'Thanks. Especially as I should be the prime suspect.'

She looked startled. 'Oh surely not!'

'Why not? There's no proof of my story. I might have finished her off myself . . . Though, come to think of it, I couldn't. She'd been dead too long.'

Jennifer Ward shivered.

'What's your name?' she said suddenly. 'I swear not to pass it on.'

'Halford,' he said. 'Andrew Halford.'

'There's a call box just round the corner. Or one downstairs. But then Mrs Lawson would be bound to hear . . . I . . . suppose you might not even have to mention the pawn ticket?'

'No. Just give 'em the name and the address.'

There was a pause.

'Are you an actress too?' he asked.

She half smiled. 'Me, no. Just a typist. I work for Beaufort's, the publishers, in EC4. Last week the building was bombed, burned out. So I'm off work until we find new premises.'

The young ingenuous typist and the not-so-young chorus girl with demi-monde habits. Perhaps this one had ambitions to get on the stage too, wouldn't confess them to a stranger. Otherwise, why share the flat? Did Jennifer Ward also go off for the weekend with boyfriends? Perhaps she was even now waiting for some lumpish territorial chap to come rolling round.

She said: 'Won't there be finger-prints, your finger-prints, I mean, on things in the house where Paula is? The police must have got those by now.'

'Finger-prints aren't any use without a man to link them to. Anyway it's a fair risk. I should have gone to them last night. On the whole, I'm glad I didn't.'

She had finished her cigarette, got up abruptly, dropped the end in the grate. Now that you looked around you could see the signs of female occupancy in the room, decorating or softening the awful Victorian furnishings.

He said: 'How come you're sharing a flat with Paula if you've known her so short a time?'

'Same old thing. Part of my roof came off and a friend, Diana, who shared it, had just gone to join the WAAF. I met Paula at a cocktail party; she said, there's room in Gaskin Street. So I came.'

'Just like that.'

'Just like that.'

He still hesitated. 'Does Paula Krissen have an agent, d'you think?'

'A theatrical agent? Oh, yes. It's Frederick Hanson of St Martin's Lane. She was always going off to see him.'

He offered her another cigarette but she shook her head. He noticed she was looking at her watch.

'Are you expecting someone?'

'What? Oh, no. Not at all. I was only thinking.'

'I can cut along now. I expect you'd like a bit of time to mull it over.'

'It isn't that,' she said. 'My face is a trifle red.'

'About what?'

'I don't have four pounds ten to give you at present!'

'For what?'

'For the watch. I didn't get paid this week as the place is a shambles . . . Perhaps you could keep the watch till Friday?'

'Forget it – '

'I can't do that. If you could leave me your address . . .'

'Somewhere in England.'

She smiled. 'But you must have a forwarding address?'

He said: 'I've been thinking too. If I ring the police again now I shall bow out; everything will be taken out of my hands. I don't really think I shall be able to write it out of my life as easily as that. Do you?'

'I've no idea . . . Yes, of course I see what you mean. It's too grim for you to forget or – or ignore. But what else can you do?'

'Well, I've been wondering. Wondering if we might postpone this dire civic duty of going to the police – say just for a single day, or part of a day, while we have a little more time to consider it.'

He met her surprised glance with a friendly frankness as candid as her own.

'What does that mean?' she said.

He ducked the question.

'Well, for instance, can we find out anything more about this man she's recently been going out with? You never saw him? Or heard his name? . . . Or where they met?'

'I know where they met. It was at the Blue Peter – a night-club in Berkeley Square.'

'Someone introduced them?'

'Don't think so. Paula said they got talking at the bar. It's rather a classy place. I've never been, but she went there about once a month.'

'Seeing what she could pick up?'

'Maybe.' There was less warmth in that reply.

'Well, I never knew the lady. I'm only judging from what I'm told. Did she never say anything more about the man?'

'He wasn't badly off. Bought her a nice brooch, I remember.'

The baby was still crying, a passionate sound, without solace.

'If I thought there was a chance of identifying this chap,' Andrew said, 'it would seem a reasonable thing to follow his trail for a bit.'

She went to the window. 'It's still pretty hard to believe what you've told me about Paula. Are you sure she – that she died the way you think?'

'I've never seen a strangled woman before,' Andrew said. 'But there wasn't a lot of room for doubt.'

She put her hands to her elbows as if cold. She came round, thin as a rake, great eyes on him. 'If you don't tell the police at once, what do you want to do?'

'Well,' he said. 'What are you doing today?'

She flushed. 'I have to go to Beaufort's this afternoon, to a temporary office near St Paul's. The manager has found a place of sorts and expects to re-open next week. Nothing else.'

'I have some bits of things from the house that I promised to parcel up and send off to my mother. After that I'm free. Will you have dinner with me tonight? Then we might go on to the Blue Peter.'

The flush faded and she smiled. 'If the police don't catch up with me I'd love to.'

Saturday Evening

I

Smart Mayfair night-clubs do have a membership list even in wartime, but Andrew had been lucky enough to recall that a great personal friend of his was likely to be a member. He was lucky enough too to catch him at his hotel and an exchange of telephone calls did the rest. The name of Count Radziwill – Stephen's father – counted for something still.

They got there about nine-thirty, climbed unaided through the gilt and red plush, found seats and sat for a few minutes listening to the band. Jennifer was in a shortish satin frock of cerise and cream, off the shoulders, with big sleeves. It was not haute couture but it looked right on her. She wasn't thin-bony, she was thin-slim, and her shoulders looked good enough to eat.

At the restaurant she'd told him that on the way back from Beaufort's she had called in to see Paula's agent, asking him for Paula's address while she was out of town. He said he didn't have one, that he'd been trying to get her an audition for a new revue opening soon at the Prince of Wales's, that when she called in last Monday she'd seemed in high spirits and had promised to telephone him Friday. She hadn't telephoned him Friday, so he was expecting a call after the weekend. Frederick Hanson hadn't met Paula's latest boyfriend.

During the afternoon he had telephoned his mother, taken the MG in to have a few minor jobs done (his screenwiper was playing up, and one front brake was binding) and generally occupied himself with everything except the one big question. Maybe it wasn't really a big question at all. He'd wanted a girl; he'd found a girl; and rather a smasher in her ingenuous way; chance had brought them together; it was going to improve his leave no end – certainly the next day or so.

Shouldn't he have gone to the police about the dead woman's identity in any case? Even if the police had called it was likely that Jennifer Ward would have been free by the evening. They couldn't arrest her; she would be a far more innocent party in their eyes than he. So – this dinner might have taken place just the same, without any need to worry about Paula and her affairs. A chance meeting with a nice girl, a dinner, a dance; kiss her good-bye at the end of the evening; or a bit of petting in the car; maybe something more: difficult to tell about a bright young girl living in a shabby flat in war-torn London. Why keep the shadow of Paula hanging around them, with her nasty boyfriend in the background?

Well . . . that was all logic. But there was a high-strung, combative streak in him that wasn't confined to aerial dog-fights. It was still less than twenty-four hours since he had stumbled on the woman, and, in spite of his daily diet of war, it would be a long time before he forgot Paula Krissen's face. It looked as if Jennifer would have come out with him tonight anyway; but a common purpose of finding out if possible why it had happened – bound the evening together, bound them together, would, if the evening went well and he wanted to follow it up, give him a fair excuse for seeing her again tomorrow.

Jennifer said her father had been a not-very-successful novelist who had died two years ago. Her mother had rather smartly married again – 'a nice man, a chemist, but not as important to me'. From Swindon Jennifer had written to Beaufort's, who had published her father, and they had offered her a job as typist with prospects of becoming the managing editor's secretary.

'They pay terribly,' she said, 'but I'm told publishers

always do; they have lots of applicants for jobs because girls think it's a glamorous profession. Knowing my father, I should have know better than *that*!'

'And what did you talk to Paula about?' Andrew asked.

'Actually it was a bit of a Box and Cox arrangement. She was in during the day, and when I came home she was usually off out somewhere. It suited us. Of course we did talk . . . I liked her, though some people might look down their noses at the way she lived. But she was never crude about it. What happened outside wasn't my business, and she didn't bring men into the flat. She took life so light-heartedly that other people took her the same. She was always joking and talking, with her funny bit of an accent and – '

'Accent?' said Andrew. 'What sort of accent?'

He spoke sharply and with the hint of authority his rank had given him; she looked at him, great-eyed, before going on.

'She was foreign. Her father and mother were both naturalized British subjects; one German, the other Hungarian. Paula always had an accent. Why?'

'Don't know.' He had found his concentration diverted by her reaction. 'One takes extra note in wartime.'

'Oh, she was English enough in the way she looked at things! And furious about the bombing. She used to curse and swear and shake her fist!'

'Go on,' he said.

'I've forgotten where I was. You put me off.'

'Well, start again at the beginning.'

'Oh, I know; I was saying how happy-go-lucky she was. Nearly all the time she was in good spirits. Only once in a while she'd get fits of the blues and would hardly utter for a couple of days.'

'Did it coincide with anything?'

'No. Not in the sense you mean.' Jennifer disturbed her floating fringe. 'Come to think of it, there was a doctor she visited two or three times. She had bad headaches, and he'd give her something. Always seemed to put her right.'

'Who was he, d'you know?'

'Yes, because I got a prescription made up for her once. Norley was the name. His surgery was in Shadwell.'

'Shadwell, for Pete's sake! Isn't that miles away, down in the East End?'

'She used to live round there.'

'Was she Jewish?'

'I don't know.'

'Well, we're not getting very far, are we. If I went to see her doctor it's unlikely he'd tell me anything except to mind my own damned business.'

She said: 'You're really interested in following this up?'

He considered. How far should he be honest with her? If she'd been fat and spotty, would he have wanted to carry on at all? When you've been at stretch for a long time and get a few days' leave, you want to measure them out, occupy them, savour them, fill the unforgiving minute. Monday he must see his parents. Should be tomorrow really. But much as he loved them and wanted to see them, a day would be enough. His mother would say he was thinner than ever and would try to put back the lost weight in twenty-four hours. His father would talk – knowledgeably enough – about the war, and knock out his pipe and show him the daffodils, and ask him, hopefully, whether it was likely he might be drafted out of front line combat to become a trainer pilot. And one or two neighbours would have to come in for drinks. What was wrong with that? Nothing was wrong with that. But if you're living most of the time just below the sound barrier you can't suddenly settle for the lower decibels. Five days. Fill the unforgiving minute. Wasn't this – taking a nice and immensely pretty girl out and pursuing the causes of a crime – as good a way as any, and better than most?

'There are still a few people I know in Vernon Avenue,' he said. 'I talked to an ARP warden this afternoon, asked him if by any chance he knew who lived in No 9 Carlton Avenue, as I'd seen an ambulance there this morning and wondered if someone was ill. He swallowed that and said No 9 Carlton

Avenue belonged to a retired bank manager called Hill who'd lost his wife in one of the early blitzes while she was visiting friends and had then shut up the house and gone to live with a sister in the Lake District.'

'I've never heard Paula speak of anyone called Hill.'

'Unlikely he was anything to do with it. A murderer would hardly strangle a woman and leave her in his own house. Anyway, the police will be following that up. This man – the one Paula was going out with – did she ever say that he was foreign?'

'No. As I've told you, he seemed quite well off. Drove a car. Bought her presents.'

'A brooch, you said.'

'Yes, a cameo. And a nice compact. And a scarf.'

'None of which, of course, she could afford to pawn. Otherwise she mightn't have bothered to borrow your watch.'

She looked down at it. 'I still owe you money.'

'Good job this isn't a Victorian melodrama.'

She looked up then, glinted with humour. 'You've still time to grow the moustache.'

'Many of my friends do,' said Andrew. 'They vary from brief shadows on the upper lip to heavy Hungarian things that sway in the breeze.'

'I've never met a Squadron Leader before,' she said. 'When you came this morning I wasn't sure what the rings were, so I bought a pamphlet in a kiosk just off Salisbury Square. But it didn't tell me what the medals were.'

'The medals?'

'The ribbons.'

'Oh . . . one's the DFC. The other's a Polish thing.'

'Why Polish?'

'Well, I was flying with a Polish squadron for a time.'

After they had been in the Blue Peter for a while they danced. This was good. All right, sad about Paula, but it was war-time London. Eat, drink and be merry, for tomorrow . . .

There wasn't much in the girl, but what there was felt

good. She moved against him, slipping into his step, smiling, her frock rustling; she laughed at something he said; a deep sound for her. She used some scent but it was very slight, not powerful, like –

'What was the scent your friend used?'

'What? What scent?'

'You told me this morning. Some flower.'

'Oh, Paula. Yes. Gardenia.' She shivered. 'It was strong but it suited her. That's . . . I suppose that's what clinched it, made me certain there was no mistake.'

When the dance ended Andrew said: 'Let's see if we can pump the head barman.'

The internationally known Henry was a mountain of a man, still young but gross of face and feature, with curly fair hair and pouting lips. There were only two other people at the bar.

'Paula Krissen been here tonight?' Andrew asked as the drinks were slid across to him.

'*Who*, sir?' Henry looked a little surprised, as if being asked to betray professional secrets.

'Miss Krissen. You must know her. Tall, dark, a bit foreign.'

Henry went away, busying himself with the little tasks that even the most distinguished of barmen find to do. Then, having had time to look at Andrew's uniform in more detail through the mirror, he came back. 'Miss Krissen? Oh yes, sir. That is to say, no. We haven't seen her for upwards of a week.'

'As long as that? She'd be in with her friend, I suppose? What's his name, I forget?'

'You mean the tall gentleman? Couldn't say, sir. Rather the stranger to me. I think he's a new member.'

Andrew looked at Jennifer, who was listening politely. 'What's Paula's friend called? I never remember his name.'

She said brightly: 'Was it John something or other?'

Andrew frowned. 'The man I mean is a tall good-looking fellow, youngish, well-dressed, well-heeled.'

'With curly hair and a big laugh, sir?'

'That's the chap.'

'I'll ask Ernesto when he comes back. He served them.' Henry removed his bulk to attend to someone else.

They finished their drink.

'Dance?' Andrew said.

She smiled at him and slid quietly off her stool.

'Curly hair and a big laugh,' he said when they were moving.

'You know, this man still might have nothing to do with her being dead, might have left her somewhere, gone home.'

'An alibi would be needed,' said Andrew. 'And why hasn't he bothered to ring her?'

'So what's the next move?'

'I'm wondering if the old girl in the green dress might have seen him or know something about him.'

'Who's that?'

'The one who answered my ring at your place this morning. Looks like an elderly tart.'

'Mrs Lawson?' She crowed with laughter. 'Our landlady? Have you never heard of Harry Lawson, the comedian? She's his widow. And frightfully respectable.'

'She shouldn't take to curling pins at her age,' said Andrew unreasonably. 'Every curl on her head looks like a fate worse than death.'

'I did ask her about Paula this afternoon, but she didn't seem interested, except about the rent Paula owed.'

The dance stopped.

'Another drink?'

'Thanks, no.' He found her looking at him. She said: 'It's quite difficult . . .'

'What?'

'You'd think me rude.'

'Try.'

'I mean it's difficult sometimes to decide – You must be very young for your position?'

'Not these days. I'm twenty-five. There are a few younger.'

45

He was going to say plenty younger, but in fact not too many had stayed in circulation.

'Well, you look so different sometimes from others.'

'Sure. Who doesn't?'

'I mean . . . you're in authority, aren't you. It's – a big job, and then you look older. But other times – ' She gave him a flashing smile – 'other times you don't.'

'Do have another drink,' he said, 'then you'll be able to read my chracter.'

'And lose my own?'

'Henry will come if I whistle.'

She shook her head. 'Thanks no, I mean it.'

'You may be dead tomorrow.'

'Or wish I was.' She looked at him closely. 'You see, that's what I mean. I can't tell whether you're joking or serious.'

'Always serious about drink.' They got to their table, and as they did so a mountainous figure came soft-footed after them. Thick lips pursed as if in distaste at his own lapse of dignity, Henry said:

'I have just asked Ernesto, Squadron Leader. Miss Krissen's friend, you were inquiring about.'

'Yes?'

'The name is Charles Mason. Ernesto recollected the gentleman's name, and I have verified it in the members' book. He became a member in March.'

'Charles Mason.' They sat down at their table. 'Thank you very much. Very good of you to take the trouble.'

'Not at all. My pleasure.' Henry caressed his bush of glossy hair and prepared to withdraw.

'Oh, and Henry!'

'Sir!'

Andrew hesitated. 'We have only met tonight, and I'm loth to ask a favour. But I assure you it's a serious and important matter . . . If Mr Charles Mason should come in here this week, I wonder if you could telephone me at this number? It's the RAF Club. If I'm not in, leave a message. Or ring Miss Ward. But don't tell Mr Mason what you have done. Would that be possible?' He wrote the number on the back of a club card, and Jennifer added hers.

While they were doing this Henry flipped at his bottom lip doubtfully. Andrew took out his wallet.

'Thank you, no, sir. That is not the problem. Any friend of Count Radziwill – only too happy to oblige. The problem is that I shall not be here after tomorrow night; and I'm not sure how far you could rely upon Ernesto to do this. He's not the most reliable of men. I am sorry to be leaving the bar in his charge.'

'Are you moving your job?'

'Yes, sir, I'm joining the Navy on Monday. But I will certainly pass the message on to Ernesto and impress on him that it is important.'

'Thank you very much.'

They watched him lumber back between tables to the bar.

'That's the trouble with these last two wars,' said Andrew after a silence. 'It pulls in everyone, not just those suitable, but all the odds and ends. Can you imagine him as an able seaman? And yet nobody forced him into the *Navy*. Under all his fat and hair . . .'

'So the man's name is Charles Mason . . .'

'Yes, and it means nothing. Any more than his face, if you saw it, would mean anything. Any more than you can judge the sort of guts Henry has by the way his dewlaps shake when he's mixing his cocktails.'

'But the name. Even if it's false he will have had to use it elsewhere, sometimes. He knew Paula two or three weeks . . .'

'I suppose so.'

'Give up, then?'

Thinking of war, Andrew's mind had been straying. This time last week he'd had a brush with his opposite number, Mike Dancer, of 932 Squadron. They'd been on a combined. op and Dancer had as usual led his squadron too fast. It was splendid dashing stuff, but it usually meant there were one or two stragglers, and then a cloud of MEs could come out of the sun and pick them off . . . And the following day they'd been scrambled in the middle of lunch and gone up on a false alarm and Sergeant Bennett had been shot down by our own ack-ack and landed in a field, writing the plane off and breaking his leg . . . And as soon as he got back there were decisions to be made – not his but radically affecting his future. The situation in Greece was pretty grim, and the squadron might be going with others to the Middle East to replace some in bad need of repair and refit . . . And just now he had had his hands on a slip of a girl with lovely soft hair that he wanted to touch, and a curl of fringe decorating her forehead, and eyes like lamps, and a lissom delicate neck leading to a lissom delicate body. And he could do with another drink.

'Give up, then?' Jennifer said again.

'What? Oh, no. Not yet awhile.'

'I was wondering,' she said after a minute, 'whether I might go to Shadwell, see her doctor. Tell him she hasn't shown up for a week and that I'm worried, and does he know where she is?'

'How long is it since she lived down there?'

'Several years. She left there when her mother died.'

At this moment Andrew glanced over her shoulder and spotted two new arrivals in conversation with Henry at the bar. Perhaps he should have expected it. That telephone call had given it all away. Poniatowski, towering above everyone else, made an odd trumpeting sound that nearly stopped the band. They were soon on their way across, Radziwill, thin and fair-haired and handsome, elegant, flat-footed like a ballet dancer, his enormous companion lumbering behind.

Introductions. Stephen Radziwill bowing courteously over her hand, Witold Poniatowski clasping her hand between his two and uncovering his teeth in a wide, hungry smile. Andrew liked her composure under their interested and admiring glances; it seemed to be a natural un-selfconsciousness without deliberate poise. Perhaps she was still young enough not to be self-regarding.

They sat together for half an hour and talked jokingly at first, seriously after. Andrew expressed ironical surprise that they were on their feet again so soon after last night. Stephen responded that it was only natural Andrew should be mistaken about their condition, as last night he had been so far gone he would probably have mistaken his own mother.

This comment had a sharper edge than Stephen knew. Witold started telling Jennifer a comic story about Starzynski, the last mayor of Warsaw, but it wasn't such a very funny story really because later Starzynski had died in a concentration camp, and the joke began to run downhill. Then the men began to talk and argue together about service affairs. About Spitfire snobbery, and why Hurricanes, admittedly a bit slower, hadn't had their fair share of credit for the victories of last summer. Both Poles flew Hurricanes, but these were due for replacement shortly. And why was the Luftwaffe better at picking up ditched crews than the RAF? The Germans had inflatable dinghies, which the British had not; also they carried a chemical that stained the sea around them yellowish green; and there were high-speed launches ready at strategic points along the French coast.

For a while Jennifer sat there almost unregarded. She noticed that Andrew seemed to have no special resentment against the men he fought, whom he shot down or who were trying to shoot him down. To him it was like a very dangerous sport, something that brought him satisfaction on the highest level of achievement, blood-racing, blood-letting, but of an almost chivalrous nature at heart. There was nothing chivalrous about the Poles. They had lost too many women and children among the charred homes of their own country, seen too many people dive-bombed without mercy by the unspeakable Hun. To them it was kill, kill and fight, fight so long as there was any country or island in the world to give them equipment and harbourage to carry on. It was well known that 303 Squadron had at first been refused permission to fight because so few of the pilots could understand the language of their hosts and instructors; but then one day a

Polish pilot had deliberately disobeyed orders and broken off to attack some German fighters and had shot two down. After that they had been admitted to combat.

There was no language barrier with the quiet-spoken Radziwill. In even, accented English he began to tell Jennifer of his pre-war life, of his father's extravagance and the debts overshadowing their estates near Cracow, of his own decision as a younger son to become a doctor, of his hope of returning to Poland after the war, of his certain conviction that, whatever else, they would need doctors and medical supplies.

'After the war,' said Jennifer, knowing the grim realities behind everyone's cheerful, carry-on-regardless attitude.

'Do you think that we shall never see an end, a favourable end?' asked Stephen, quick to catch the nuance.

'No, of course not! Not since the Battle of Britain last summer. It was Hitler's first defeat.'

'It must be the first of many. England is still alone. But let us think of something happier. Will you dance?'

'Thank you.' With a half-apologetic glint at Andrew, she got up and was led away.

'Nice garl, eh?' said Witold. 'Pret-ty little garl. All right, eh? Hum, hum.'

'You have the mind of a tram-driver, Witold. It runs in well-worn grooves.'

'Ah, so? What is that? How do you mean it? Is she not a nice garl?'

'Very, I think. So not to be the subject of nudges and winks from you, old chap.'

'Andrew, you are a bad faller. Tell us, how do you know this one? Where do you come upon this one since last night? Or was she already up your shirt?'

'Sleeve, man, sleeve.'

'As you please about that. But —'

'How did you go on last night?'

'Well away. Well away. But not like this little garl. Do you know if she has a sister? Another one up your shirt? A nice friendly one who says "heigh-ho" and does not cry for the marriage licence?'

Stephen said: 'In Poland except in the cities we don't have much middle class, so this kind of dancing is restricted to a small number of people. Dancing of another sort, folk dancing, is everywhere.'

'Of course,' said Jennifer. 'The polonaise. And the polka.'

'The polka is more Czech in origin – or Bohemian as it was called then . . .' Stephen looked round at the slow-moving figures about him. 'I do so wish we could dance it now.'

'The polka? Well, I'm game.'

'I believe you are.' He smiled at her. 'I *love* English girls. There is a joy in them.'

'But not in Polish girls? You surprise me.'

'Ah yes. There is much joy. But much sorrow too. That is how life has taught them to live.'

'At present, I'm sure . . . Have you sisters?'

'Three brothers. Or had. Now I have one.'

'I'm sorry.'

He was silent while they passed the saxophonist, who was doing some solo variations. 'I was in Warsaw when the war broke out. I was at the medical academy. It was the vacation, but I stayed on. My eldest brother came up from Cracow to join his regiment. I met him during the August of '39. We knew war was coming but not when. The harvest had been gathered early because of this. My eldest brother had married young, already had four small sons. When I drank with him that night he said to me: "Now I am willing to die because I have sons to carry on the name . . ." His will was granted.'

They danced without speaking.

'I depress you,' he said.

'*No*,' said Jennifer. 'But I can think of nothing to say but how sorry . . .'

'Then let us talk of other things.'

They talked of other things. But presently Stephen said: 'When Germany attacked us they gave no warning, no ultimatum, no declaration of war. The Panzer divisions just invaded the frontiers. And German fliers dressed in Polish uniforms, with their planes painted in Polish colours, attacked our aircraft on the ground, destroyed our aerodromes . . . From all over Poland we sent cavalry to fight the tanks. It was very bad for the horses.'

After a few moments Jennifer said: 'Perhaps soon . . .'

'Yes, perhaps soon. I do not know where my elder brother's children are but I hope they will survive. They have to survive. I remember in those days after Poland had been first invaded the whole country waited for England to keep her word. There were three days of dismay. Then England declared war. Warsaw went mad. People stood in the streets cheering as if we had won the war. England was in, all was well. England would bring France in and together, against England and France, where would Germany be?'

'That *does* make me sad.'

'I was sad – and glad. Sad because I knew England could not help in time. Glad because England kept her promise . . . and may *yet* keep her promise in the end – to free Poland.'

The dance came to an end and the dancers returned to their table, Jennifer with a higher colour than when she had left. They all had another drink together laughing and joking, and then the Poles rose to go, sensing that, although welcome, this was not to be a party.

'Your friend's charming,' said Jennifer as they watched the retreating figures.

'I noticed he was. Oh, yes.'

'He said he knew we'd be here?'

'I rang him this afternoon. They're both grand men to have with you in a fight.'

'We talked a lot,' said Jennifer. 'Seriously, I mean. Among other things he said something strange. He said that Russia was a more permanent danger to Poland than Germany, that the Russians were the worst enemies.'

'He's said the same to me,' said Andrew. 'Maybe he's drawing on folk memories. Or perhaps he sees further than we do. Don't forget that when Poland was collapsing the Russians advanced and met the Germans halfway.'

'He also asked me, he said, why did we specially want to come here tonight?'

'Stephen's a very astute person. Or maybe I let something out in my call. What did you say?'

'I said, we wanted to find somebody called Charles Mason, who was a member here.'

'Did you tell him why?'

'No . . . I didn't feel I should.'

'He asked me why.'

'Did he? When?'

'Just before he left. He said, why did I want to meet someone called Charles Mason? I said, because I thought he'd killed a girl, though we'd no proof. I didn't go into details. Stephen said he'd like to help. I said I'd keep in touch with him for the rest of my leave.'

They danced again a couple of times. The Poles had left the club. Presumably there was not enough unattached female interest to keep them there.

Andrew said: 'What was Paula's father, d'you know?'

'Something in the docks, I think.'

'And he was German?'

'Yes.'

'When did he die?'

'I don't think she knew. He left his wife when Paula was about fifteen.'

Andrew took a firmer grip of the girl's waist, but then the music stopped. That was a bit like life, he thought. The music was always stopping at the wrong moment.

'I wonder if this doctor has a surgery on a Sunday. Did you say his name was Norris?'

'Norley.'

'Doubt if it would be worth a visit. But if anybody went, I ought to go.'

II

They drove home through empty streets, the occasional bus, blue-lit, growling past them noisily in the dark; a few shaded lights where repair work was going on through the hours of the night. The sky was covered with heavy cloud and there were no searchlights up. A few couples cuddled in doorways. A drunk or two, a stray dog; taxis and a few private cars. Not as late as last night. But a longish drive for him yet, out to Northcot. That is, unless she invited him in.

He knew she wouldn't. Not yet. Not in so many words. He would have to play it by ear – and keep that ear sharply attuned to changes in her choice or attitude.

They sat in silence for a few moments after stopping outside 45 Gaskin Street.

'Thanks, Andrew,' she said, 'for a terrific evening. Paula was my *friend* – but you can't help enjoying yourself. You're pulled two ways. I'm distressed about her; but it's been *lovely*.'

He stared up at the unlighted windows, and those with the faintest of glows behind the black-out blinds.

'It's not healthy living here, you know. Look at the next street. It's been flattened.'

'Oh, yes, that wasn't Wednesday; that was about a month ago. I suppose they were aiming for the railway stations.'

'As they might well do again. You can't hide railway lines on moonlit nights.'

'Oh, well . . . We're all in it, aren't we.'

'You could live out a bit,' he said.

She shrugged. 'Isn't it really a question of taking your chance? Anyway I don't know what will happen now Paula has gone. I'll have to find someone else to share the flat. I can't afford it on my own.'

He leaned over, turned her face quietly to his, and kissed her. Her lips tasted fresh, young, innocent, like petals newly

54

opened. He kissed her again and stroked the softness of her face.

'Tomorrow,' he said, in a matter-of-fact voice, but speaking against her face, 'I'll call to see Dr Norley. No harm done, is there?'

'No harm at all.'

'In the afternoon it will be a good enough excuse to call and see you and tell you about it. Are you free in the afternoon?'

'Yes.'

He kissed her again, began to stoke her neck and shoulders.

'Come out in the car with me,' he said.

'Tomorrow afternoon?'

'Yes.'

'Would that help the mystery in any way?'

'Depends which mystery you mean.'

'Suppose there's no solution?'

'OK. It's my leave. If *you* don't mind.'

'*I* don't mind,' she said.

His hands had found their way inside her coat and stroked her naked shoulders. But they made no attempt to go beyond the limit of the dress.

'I'd like to come out with you,' she said.

'I'd like it too.'

'Thank you.'

Reluctantly he let her go. She fumbled with the door catch, got it open.

'Don't get out,' she said, and then: 'Take care,' her eyes finding some reflected light to glint at him in the black-out.

Perhaps in wartime it was an odd remark. Perhaps it had a number of meanings.

He did get out, but only stood and watched her until she had unlocked the door and was inside.

Then he drove off.

Neither of them had paid any attention to another car which had stopped a few doors behind them on the other side of the street.

Sunday Morning

I

It was just before 10 am when Louis Baker called at a café in Piccadilly and asked if Mr Armitage had arrived. The waitress said no, so Louis ordered coffee and sat down. While he waited he chewed at his bottom lip as if there were an unpleasant taste in his mouth.

Mr Armitage arrived thirty-five minutes later, a rather shabby, stout, elderly, fastidious man with small self-confident eyes and smooth black hair spreading down from a bald dome. Mr Armitage was not his real name, though Louis did not know this. A wide circle of friends and distinguished acquaintances called him Walter Gissing. This was not his real name either, but the wide circle of friends and distinguished acquaintances did not know this either.

'You said ten,' Louis observed sulkily as the newcomer sat down.

'You might have had to wait longer,' said Gissing.

'It was the arrangement we made.'

Gissing looked cautiously round the half-empty café. He had made sure the Kardomah was open on Sundays before fixing the venue.

The waitress came, and he ordered China tea with lemon. Then he busied himself taking off his gloves and scarf, folding them beside him on the table.

Louis said: 'Something delayed you?'

'In a manner of speaking, yes.'

There was a pause. Louis was uneasy in the silence. This

was the first time they had met for three weeks and since then a great deal had happened. Louis wanted to talk.

'Have you brought the envelope?'

'All in good time.'

'It was a promise,' Louis said. He was using his aggression like a shield.

'If we were satisfied.'

'Fifty down and fifty when the job was done.'

'Yes.' Gissing nodded and said no more. The silence persisted.

In exasperation Louis said: 'Well, it was *done*. The job was done. Do you want me to tell you about it?'

'Certainly not.'

'So what's wrong?'

'You know she's been identified?'

Louis' cup rattled. 'What d'you mean? Who says she has?'

Gissing shrugged but did not answer.

Louis said: 'Have the police found out?'

'Someone else did. He telephoned the police but did not tell them who she was.'

'Did he know?'

'He must have done.'

'I don't see how he could have.'

Gissing frowned and pursed his lips. 'The instructions, you know; complete removal of identification.'

'That's what I did!'

'Why were you so casual and careless?'

'I tell you, Mr Armitage – '

'Pray keep your voice down.'

'I tell you, Mr Armitage – '

The older man put up one fat finger. 'Let me tell *you* something, Louis. The fact that you were chosen . . . exceptional esteem. I expect to receive a special commendation for you as a result. That's regional, but when the full report is seen by our masters . . . At the conclusion of the war – '

'That can't be too soon,' said Louis.

'Amen. But in order to establish your claim to a position of real authority . . . an absolute regard for carrying out your orders *to the letter.*'

'My orders were *vague!*' said Louis.

'You were not told to make a *friend* of the woman!'

The tea came – no lemon – and Gissing lifted the lid and peered suspiciously inside. Then, muttering about the poor quality, he poured a pale stream of liquid into his cup. Louis watched the retreating figure of the waitress.

'Was *I* watched, then?'

Gissing took three lumps of white sugar from his overcoat pocket and dropped them into the cup. He did not explain that when novices undertook their first big operation they were always watched.

'How else,' said Louis, 'could I have done it – except by getting to know her?'

'In Art, in Law, in anti-Law, it is essential for the participant, the combatant to remain detached. You know. A barrister doesn't identify with the client he's defending. Does he? Neither should a man in your position . . .'

'What?'

'Have allowed himself the pleasures of involvement – '

'Pleasures!' Louis drank his coffee noisily, spilling some in the saucer. 'Have you tried it yourself, Mr Armitage?'

'Tried what?'

'Doing what you asked me to do.'

Gissing's small eyes, which looked as if they were more familiar with balance sheets than sulky criminals, still had enough steely content to stare Louis down.

'I don't like your tone . . .'

Louis said roughly: 'It was *easier* that way.'

'What way?'

'Having her! Then doing what I had to do.'

The older man considered this. 'Really?'

'Really.'

'You were thinking of disguising it as a sex crime? . . . But you didn't rape her?'

'Oh no,' said Louis with satisfaction. 'Not on your life. She was ready for it.'

'But not for what followed, I presume.'

'No . . . But it puts you in the mood.'

'In the state we're going to build – no room for moods.' Gissing shook his tonsured head distastefully. 'If you aspire to giving commands – you must know how to obey them. Clinically. Unemotionally. Why did you not set fire to the house?'

'What?'

'The house you left her in. It would have been simple enough to do.'

'There was no raid that night,' said Louis. 'If you'd told me I could have waited another day. As it was, all the fire services would have been round in no time, *fighting* it! That would have drawn *attention* to her. For God's sake! The way I reckoned it, the house was empty. The owner was in Windermere and was trying to let it. How many people are wanting rented accommodation in the suburbs of London these days? I can tell you: I know: damn all. With luck she could have been there three months before she was found!'

'Yet it has been only three days. *And* identified. That's the crux of it all.'

'I don't see how I could have done more. It was the luck of the draw.'

'Or lack of resolution at the end.'

Louis laughed – the first time this morning. 'That's one thing you can't blame me for – lack of resolution!'

'It's what I argued on your behalf. So I have brought you the envelope, as promised.'

He unbuttoned his coat, from which one button was missing, fumbled in an inside pocket, took out a handkerchief, a newspaper cutting and a box of matches; then a sealed envelope which was passed to the younger man, who cradled it between his fingers before stuffing it in his own pocket unopened.

'There were expenses,' Louis said. 'You told me you'd meet expenses. I've made a note. D'you want it?'

59

'The other, the greater award,' said Gissing, 'may yet come through. At the moment, though . . .' He paused as some people passed the table; he put the handkerchief, the cutting, the matches carefully away.

'Pretty nearly thirty pounds,' said Louis. 'There was hire of the car and other incidentals.'

'At the moment, though, there may still be things for you to do.'

Louis' mind was on the extra money he could claim. Then abruptly he came up against the dark statement, like a wall, square across his path. It was something in the other man's manner more than the actual words.

'What d'you mean?'

'Calm yourself.' Gissing eased his stout body on the uncomfortable chair. 'Nothing yet. But the error – or omission – it has left loose ends. May have to be tidied up. We shall know soon.'

'Know what?'

'What has to be done.'

'I don't follow you.'

'So we shall have to meet again, quite soon. Say nine o'clock tomorrow evening in the Piccadilly Underground. The Bakerloo line.'

Louis was struggling with worms of doubt. The new notes rustled in his breast pocket.

'Nobody's more keen than I am to see things through,' he said in a grating voice. 'But – '

'Incidentally,' said Gissing. 'Don't be out late tonight.'

'Oh? . . . Oh, I see.'

'I hope you do. Let us look forward to the days when we shall no longer need to meet in secret,' said Gissing without enthusiasm. 'In the meantime – '

'When all this is swept away.'

'In the meantime think of and remember your ancestors. Implicit obedience is the watchword that will bring us victory. Remember it well. There is no compromise.'

For some time after Walter Gissing's plump and respectably

shabby figure had disappeared up the steps into the street, Louis sat on, playing with the coin with which he would presently settle the bill. In spite of the irritation and the alarm, Armitage's words had injected stiffening, tonic matter into his brain. Now and then he raised his head to stare with arrogance at people passing his table.

He'd expected a better meeting than this – expected praise, not sinister criticism, implying that there was more to do. Acting as he had done had been a long way out of his league. You don't suddenly graduate that high without feeling dizziness after. Praise was what he had wanted.

All the same, there'd been a thrill in it at the time. A horrible thrill, mind stretching. You'd felt a cruel angry joy, coming up behind her when she was sitting in that chair admiring herself in the mirror. Blinding nerves but blinding dominance. She hadn't even looked up at him as he took out the cord. In silencing her for ever he'd reached a peak, a second orgasm of conquest which had carried him right away, so that afterwards he'd stood over her swaying like a drunk, drunk with triumph.

But it hadn't lasted. Covering his tracks, the mundane, petty things, they brought him down to earth. And once down there was no way of climbing to the peak again.

In the days since then he'd thought quite a lot about it. It was no visual nightmare that troubled him, it was the noise she'd made – it was as if a chain saw had struck metal; he'd no notion any woman, any human being, could make such a noise. He'd pulled and twisted, pulled and twisted till his hands were cut deep with the cord, trying to stop it. Perhaps it had only lasted a few seconds but it had seemed like minutes. God, how he'd tried to stop it!

All that would take time to forget. Not long, but a little time. In a week, in a week or two, it would all go.

He *had* to remember who he was. A man of achievement now among inferiors. A man of mounting achievement, a man who would be worthy – and would be seen to be worthy – of his ancestry.

He thought of his time in the bank. Just a clerk. A nonentity. Spoken to as if he was dirt by that fat little crud who called himself the manager. He thought of his time as a car salesman, trying to ingratiate himself with the loud-checked, loud-mouthed gilded youth who came to try his cars. And at school. And at other times. Those times would never come again.

Armitage might be treating him very much as an inferior still. But this was in an altogether different cause.

Sunday Morning – Two

I

The surgery was off Dellow Street. Andrew parked his car a couple of hundred yards past, on a corner opposite 'The Old Pie and Mash Shop', and walked back over the cobblestones which had made his car rattle so much, past a cluster of houses and then through an area of devastation, with palings drunkenly leaning, the serrated edges of blackened walls, and ribs of rafters like half-cooked skeletons from which the flesh had been scorched away. Yet the fresh seaweedy ozone of the river followed him on the breeze, mingling with the charcoal smell of burnt wood; and only just out of sight were the derricks with elbows sticking up like grey herons feeding among the shipping of the docks.

A well-polished brass plate incongruous in a wall of white-washed brick; the heavy pine door, half ajar, was pitted with shrapnel marks. Inside was a dark waiting room with chairs, of which only a few were occupied, on the walls the usual posters: 'Careless Talk Costs Lives', 'We are not interested in talk of defeat'.

The patients were ushered in by a tall, thin, acidly good-looking receptionist of about thirty-five, with a virginal walk. She was very neat and clean in a white overall; you couldn't have found better in Harley Street.

When there was only one elderly woman with a tea-cosy hat between himself and the presence and no one else had arrived, Andrew said:

'I suppose Dr Norley is generally busier than this?'

The old woman eyed him up and down in a gloomy but

not unfriendly manner. 'It's Sunday, see. Not many of his regulars come Sunday. Don't encourage 'em, for one thing. But it's my knees. They've been cruel all week. Tried to wait till tomorrow, but no. He won't give me enough killers at a time, see.'

'Killers?'

'Pain killers. Says it's dangerous. Come off it, I says, what do it matter to an old body like me? Comfort, I need.'

'Are you a new patient of Dr Norley?'

'Cripes no. Been coming ever since I opened me shop. And that's six years or more.'

'He's a good man, I'm told.'

She shrugged her wool-wrapped shoulders. 'I reckon he's better'n most. But there's none able to cure my knees, mister. You in the services?'

'Yes.'

'Fighters or bombers?'

'Fighters.'

'Wish you could soak them buggers. Over they come, night after night. Last Wednesday was a right bugger. Went on seven hours, it did. Hope they're getting tired. I know *we* are!'

'Did you say he was attached to a hospital?'

'No, I didn't say nothing of the kind. But he is. You mean Dr Norley? Yes. He's at the Commercial Dock two days a week. Biggest round here. He works hard, he do. All these cas-ualities – '

'Yes, please,' said the receptionist in a far-from-East End voice.

Andrew stared at the Christmas – Christmas '39 – number of *Punch* until the old lady hobbled out again.

'Hope you shoot down plenty of them buggers,' she said as she passed.

'Yes, please,' said the receptionist.

A square-built sharp-faced man sat behind a desk in a large consulting room. A couch, with a folded tartan run on it, weighing machine, angle-poise lamp, printed sight-tester,

64

filing cabinet, framed diploma, photograph of a dumpy woman with a child and a small dog. Like the receptionist the place looked clinical and clean.

'Well, young man, what can I do for you?'

Andrew stared back at the exploratory and professional gaze. He supposed the chap might think he was coming to him about something he'd picked up from a tart. Norley looked puffy under the eyes, as if short of sleep.

'I'm not here about my health,' Andrew said. 'I used to live in this area but I've been abroad for a while until I joined the RAF. I came to call on friends yesterday but they'd moved. Then someone said you might know something because they thought the daughter was still your patient.'

Dr Norley raised his eyes towards the ceiling. 'What was the name?'

'Krissen. A Mrs Krissen and her daughter Paula.'

The eyes came down and the doctor picked up a pen as if ready to write a prescription. His fingers were stained with nicotine.

'Mrs Krissen is dead.'

'So I hear. A pity. What about Paula?'

'She left the district years ago.'

'Yes. But hasn't she continued as a patient of yours?'

'As a matter of fact, yes.'

He stood up and went to the filing cabinet. 'I don't have her latest West End address. She has dropped in and seen me but has always paid for her consultation on the spot. I believe she moves about a lot. She's in the theatre, you know.'

'She always wanted to go in for that.'

There was a pause.

'Next time she calls, would you mind giving her my address and asking her to write me?'

'Certainly, I'll do that for you, Wing Commander.'

'Squadron Leader,' said Andrew. 'I was once fond of Paula. A boy-and-girl attachment, you know.'

'Ah, I see – But she must have been older than you.'

'Not that much. At that age it didn't seem to count.'

'She's an attractive girl.'

'I remember she used to suffer from headaches and depression,' said Andrew. 'I remember that. She was quite young at the time, but often it was two or three days before she was her old cheerful self again.'

'Well, women do have that sort of trouble.'

'Does she have depressions now?'

'I'm afraid I'm not at liberty to answer that. But if you locate her, perhaps you'll be able to cheer her up yourself, my boy. Eh?'

'Very likely,' said Andrew.

Dr Norley looked up at the ceiling again. This was a nervous tic, not anxiety for the safety of the roof. Andrew wrote his name and forwarding address on a sheet of the doctor's writing paper.

'I'll put it with her file. Have you a long leave?'

'Two more days. I was hoping to locate her before then. Leaves have been rather infrequent this last year.'

'Quite so. Quite so. You are one of those young men,' said Dr Norley, 'to whom we owed so much in the Battle of Britain. The country is very proud of you.' He tapped his teeth and waited for his visitor to go.

'It's the bomber crews who need a boost, not us.'

'Well, I suppose it's a job of work. We none of us do it without remuneration. I suppose you'll get five or six hundred a year . . .'

Andrew got up. 'I never met Mr Krissen. He was a German, wasn't he?'

'I'm sure I don't know.'

'It occurred to me,' said Andrew, 'that Paula might be worried about the war. With her parentage she might, as it were, be pulled both ways.'

'My dear Wing Commander,' said Norley wearily, 'aren't we all worried about the war? Do you realize that Hitler controls *all* Europe. Those countries that are not actually conquered exist only on his sufferance. The might of his Panzer divisions, his dive bombers, the massed ranks of a united people behind him – who can stand in his way? Only you men of action can escape the depression that envelops the rest of us.'

'It's a point of view – '

'For my part, I see no daylight anywhere. It really depends how long people can keep going. Most of this winter I have been on the go fourteen hours a day, and I'm one of many. No country can keep on like that for long. I see the strains that other people miss. One doesn't need mixed parentage to be worried these days.'

'Thanks for your assistance,' Andrew said. 'I was lucky to find you in.'

Norley said: 'I'll not forget your message.' He turned back towards his desk before the slim receptionist had ushered Andrew out.

Andrew climbed into his MG in the mean street outside, put in the ignition key and drove off. He felt that a brilliant and successful detective had not been lost when he joined the Air Force.

All the same, his visit had not been without result.

Sunday Afternoon

I

He called at two. He'd found a tweed jacket and flannel trousers and his only apparent connection with the RAF was his tie. She met him with her wide, slim-faced, brilliant smile. When he was away from her he wondered if she might be holding something back from him about her friend's death, but when he met her such doubts seemed absurd.

'Super day!' she said. 'Where are we going?'

Red sandals, good stockings, a coral-coloured woollen frock which buttoned up the front to a roll collar, a red beret on her jaunty brown hair, to which the sunshine again gave a tawny glint.

'Wherever you like.'

'Wherever *you* like. It's your leave.'

'Most of the coast's prohibited. We might go north.'

'Let's go north.'

'Buckingham perhaps, and then Oxford if we've time.'

'Lovely.'

They climbed in the car and he was about to turn the engine on when she spread out a newspaper before him.

'Have you seen this?'

A small photograph on the back page: 'Early yesterday morning the police called at a house in the Northcot district of Middlesex and removed from it the body of an unidentified woman. The house it is understood has been empty for some months. The police received an anonymous telephone call in the early hours of yesterday morning. The woman had been dead for several days, and a description of her is being circulated.'

'Still unidentified,' said Jennifer.

'Unless the police are playing their cards close to their chest . . . I see we've occupied Addis Ababa.'

'Where's that?'

'A bit far away to be very important, I'm afraid.' He gave her back the paper.

'Did you see Dr Norley?'

Andrew told her. 'And you? Have you looked through her belongings?'

'Her suitcases are always unlocked. We shared the same room, of course; but it's hell picking over someone else's things.'

'I hope you overcame your scruples.'

She looked at him quickly. 'Are you getting at me?'

'Not a bit, no!' He smiled as he started the car. 'But let's face it, if we're in earnest we can't afford to . . .'

'Let scruples get in the way? Well I didn't. But I'm just telling you . . . Paul Pry isn't my pin-up boy.'

They drove off, heading towards Wembley and Harrow.

After a few minutes she said: 'There were about a dozen letters, nearly all from men, none signed Charles Mason. Bills. She really did owe money! Three letters from a Canadian at an army camp in the North of England, two from a major who seemed to be writing from the Middle East; two from a married man I remember her talking about in February. There's one other dated January which is from an aunt in Birmingham. Paula spent Christmas with her. I've brought it with me. One or two sentences did strike me as a bit off-beat.'

'There was nothing in any of the other letters to suggest any line we might follow? This married man . . .'

'Friendly little notes; not the sort of answer you'd get to a threat of exposure or anything.'

'Any of the addresses in London?'

'Only the married man.'

'Worth a visit?'

'Both letters were dated February.'

'Ah . . . Anything else in the drawers or the suitcases?'

'A few things. Her father was called Hans Krissen and he was born in Hamburg. Her mother's maiden name was Magda Varkoni and she came from Szeged. Paula was born in Bermondsey in 1910. She went to the council school and then took classes in ballet and won a certificate. She joined Madame Opie's Dancing Academy and later teamed up with a man called Arthur Trimmer and they toured together. They probably lived together too, I think, but he died in 1938.'

He turned a corner and accelerated away up the road. 'You've certainly done your stuff, Jennifer.'

'When I snoop,' she said, 'I snoop real good.'

The bright sunshine flooded the streets, showing up the sightless ruins but also the great areas of undamaged property. Barrage balloons glinted over the city. There was a gusty, healthy wind which pushed round the corners and whistled past the windscreen and the side curtains.

'Like the roof down?'

'Yes, please.'

'It'll be draughty.'

'Yes, please.'

Soon they were off again. He was enjoying himself. He was excited by this girl. Luck after all, he thought, that he'd made that half-drunken error. Without it he would be trying to fill in today with some sort of contrived entertainment. Instead this. He drove with zest, knowing she was young and vital and pretty and unpredictable and a challenge.

'You've told me nothing about yourself,' he said, raising his voice to be heard. 'I know only that you used to live in Swindon, that your father died and your mother married again. Can you fill in a few corners?'

She tried to push some hair inside her beret. 'I'm twenty-one and of British parentage. My identity card is number NBQX 132/5.'

'Where are you registered for wise-cracks?' he asked.

'It's stamped on my ration card. Seriously, Squadron Leader . . . '

'Seriously?'

'Well, sort of. I've no real *past*. Wish I had. So much more interesting, a woman with a past, isn't she?'

'Time'll take care of that,' he said. 'Enjoy your innocence.'

'Is that what it's called?' she said. 'Well, thanks.'

They were through Mill Hill now and making for St Albans.

'Did your mother mind,' he asked, 'you sharing a flat with an older woman like Paula?'

'Well, she didn't really know much about it, except that I'd changed my address.'

'I see.'

'Suprisingly enough,' said Jennifer, 'Mummie is very much in love – more than she ever was, I think, with Daddy. One of those things. So she isn't perhaps so careful about her one ewe lamb as she might be.'

'Sorry about that.'

'No need to be. It wouldn't have raised the earth if she'd known. Actually Paula was OK.'

'I'm sure. It's just the mixture I thought odd.'

'No different from if I joined the WAAF.'

'Did you ever think of it?'

'What, joining the WAAF? Oh, yes. Especially when Diana went. But my job is supposed to be of some national importance.'

'Publishing books?'

'Oh, I didn't tell you. Beaufort's have been more or less taken over by the War Ministry. We printed and published a lot of leaflets and booklets for them.'

'*How* exactly did you meet Paula?'

'I go out sometimes with this man I've known since the Swindon days, Christopher Watson, and he took me one night to a bottle party given by a French actor called Julio Vallence, and Paula was there. The blitz had been at its foulest, and Diana Foster was off to Aldershot the following week. The night before, a bomb had landed in the next street and our windows were blown out. If they hadn't been taped we might have been cut up. Then when it began to rain we realized part of the roof had gone. So somebody told Paula this and she said, come and share with me, I'll be glad to have someone to pay half the rent.'

He changed down and roared past a convoy of army lorries.

'Christopher Watson a beau of yours?'

'Beau? Isn't that a bit old-fashioned?'

'I am old-fashioned.'

'Oh, come on . . . No, Christopher Watson is not a beau of mine. I think he fancies me a bit but I don't fancy him.'

'What does he do?'

'He's quite a lot older than me, more Paula's age. He's in the Foreign Office. And doing a bit of fire-watching. He's been rather busy lately!' She peered at a passing garden. 'Aren't the daffodils great? It's nice to feel they don't have to worry about Hitler.'

'I wonder if they have daffodils in Berchtesgaden.'

'Hope so . . . But what about you? I know nothing about you either – except that you called to see me yesterday with a – with a story that my flat-mate had been murdered. You just had a pawn ticket . . .'

'Wonder you believed me.'

'Yes, isn't it? Perhaps it's the uniform. You know, it impresses.'

'What does?'

'The uniform, of course. But . . . I know nothing more. Nothing else about you at all. What must I do to open the oyster? Is there a password?'

'No password. No oyster. What is there to tell? My life is almost as innocent as yours.'

'Should I give a hollow laugh?'

He laughed instead. 'OK. But it's largely *true*. I was at Oxford, done a year there before Munich, reading Chaucer and Piers Plowman, that lark. I got into the RAF Volunteer Reserve just in time, and when the war came I'd already done a fair number of flying hours, so it was easy from then on.'

They were in open country now, the sun shining through some elms which in spite of being bare had a swelling thickness in the twigs and branches that showed the leaf-buds were not far from breaking.

'I've told you my parents have been evacuated to Bath. I've no brothers or sisters, but I have two aunts who decorate interiors and one uncle who operates on them. For a living now I do a lot of routine flying with bits of excitement thrown in.'

'How did you win your DFC?' she asked.

'Chiefly by staying alive. It was such a free-for-all last summer that you were bound to shoot other people down if you didn't get shot down yourself. I'm good at dodging.'

'*Have* you been shot down?'

'Oh, yes.'

'More than once?'

'Well, three times, I suppose.'

'You suppose. What does it feel like?'

'Like having a baby, I imagine. When it's over you forget the pains.'

'And remember the joys?'

'Well, not exactly that. There's a sort of emergency jiffy when you know your crate is going down and you can't stop it. So you stand up in the cockpit, cross your arms in front of you, be damned sure you've got a firm grip of the ripcord ring, and dive out head first. The parachute jerks your guts when it opens, but then you sail gracefully along, watch your plane hit the ground and go up in flames and hope you'll land on a haystack.'

There was silence between them for a bit.

'Have you ever been wounded?'

'Once in the leg. Once in the arm. Cross-examination over?'

'I won't ask again. But I've never met anyone like you before – at least not been out with them. It's a – it's a – '

'Go on, say it. A privilege.'

'That wasn't quite what I was going to say, but yes.'

'Then don't say it and don't think it. There's been a lot of hero stuff talked.'

'Not true?'

'Let's change the subject. Isn't it lucky we've got something else to talk about?'

They stopped to get petrol in a village. Here in the gardens some of the early blossom was showing. She opened her bag and took out a crumpled letter. As he accepted the envelope he caught the half-faded scent of gardenia.

2, Newmarket Street
Bridge End
Birmingham
12 January

My dear Paula,

It was ever so nice having you to stay last week and really a change for me. I was that sorry to hear you was worried about things the way you said. It isn't fair you should be bothered and bullied with such troubles. You know my advice so it's no good for me to repeat it. The trouble is dear you shouldn't never have *begun*. Kurt and Emmy are nothing to you, and you know what would happen to *you* if you slipped up in any way, it's not nice to think of. I should ignore the whole thing if I was you, I know its easier said than done but honest I don't see what they can do if you do. They cant do anything to you, can they, it's awfully hard to give advice but thats my advice, tell em where they get off. Well I took *your* advice and went to the Prince of Wales's and it was a real good show. It's nice to know that Mr Ellison is a friend of yours. I never in my life see anyone so much like a woman only I wish he hadn't taken off his wig at the end, it was the first time I'd been to a theatre since your uncle died in 1929, he was the one for going about, I like my fireside. Are you short of coal in London? I forgot to ask when you was up. The cold has been something chronic this week, the streets as slippy as ice, though I dont go out much of course. Let me know if anything else happens and dont worry dear it will all come right I am real sure. Much love from your loving

Aunt Nell

Andrew passed the letter back. 'Is that Max Ellison?'

'Paula knew him pretty well – I think he's playing Blackpool at present.'

'By rights we should at least see Aunt Nell. But I've a feeling this isn't something we're going to be able to squeeze into a couple of days.'

'When do you go back?'

'Tuesday evening. I suppose we could whizz up to Birmingham today. "It isn't fair for Paula to be bothered and bullied with such troubles." What troubles? Aunt Nell knows. And who are Kurt and Emmy? Are they the bullies? Again, Aunt Nell will know.'

'If she'll tell us.'

'It's worth a try. Don't you think?'

After a minute: 'It's what *you* think, Andrew. This is *your* leave. You've only two and a half days left. I'm having fun just batting along like this. It's a lovely day and . . .'

'Lovely company,' he suggested. And added before she could reply: 'All right. All agreed. D'you mean do I want to poke around in some shabby street in Birmingham searching for a mythical Aunt Nell when I could be scorching along the empty roads with a young brunette for company?'

She looked at him and laughed. 'I just don't know what you want to do. But whatever it is, please do it.'

There was little on the road; not at all like a peace-time Sunday afternoon. Overhead a few aeroplanes circled and droned, hardly heard above the hum of their own engine and the rush of the wind.

'It must be strange to drive a car after being in a plane,' she said.

'Actually it's much harder to drive a car than fly a kite; you have that much less control over it. You really grow into a plane, become a part of it; then it's a joy to handle, answers every touch.' He cocked a professional eye upwards at three Blenheims droning off towards the south-east. 'Besides, it's going back in every way. It's losing a dimension. In a car you're pinned down like a beetle crawling over a piece of paper. It's like having length and breadth but no height.'

'We're rather a fast beetle.'

'Yes . . . this is very nice . . . If we go to Birmingham we're going to be pretty late home.'

'If we go to Birmingham you're going to use a lot of petrol coupons.'

'Ah, that's one thing they're decently generous with. You don't mind being late back? In that case I suggest we have tea in Stratford. It's not the most direct route but I know a decent place there.'

'Where you used to take your Oxford girlfriends?'

'It was a bit far from Oxford in those days, and I only had a bike. But if you have a better suggestion . . .'

'Sorry, no. You're in charge.'

II

Although the air about them was chill it was not cold in the car. In the country some of the younger trees were half in leaf, and their leaves in the sunshine were the brilliant pale green of watered silk.

Jennifer took a long breath. 'It makes you feel pretty small, doesn't it.'

'Small?'

'I mean, after the worst winter England's ever had, so far as its people are concerned, nothing has changed. Has it? After all the bombing we've been through; the ghastly nights, the days when there's smoke and rubble and wounded people

76

everywhere; it hasn't altered this. Coventry and Plymouth and places have been turned into ruins, but these fields and trees and hills and little streams are still the same. Germany can't destroy them.'

'Only we can do that with ribbon building,' he said. 'I see what you mean, though. I should have liked the popular song better if it had said, "There'll Always Be an England – in the Geographical Sense of the Word".'

'Now you're having me on.'

'Not at all. Only it wouldn't have been such an obvious attempt to cash in on a patriotic mood.'

'Very good, sir,' she said. 'Quite so, sir.'

'Don't be a little monkey.'

'I don't think I could be,' she said, 'in the geographical sense of the word.'

'One more back answer and I'll take you home without supper.'

'Oh,' she said, 'is there going to be supper too?'

They drove on in cheerful silence for a while. They hadn't passed a car for several miles.

'Permission to speak, sir?' she said.

'Say on.'

'There's a heavy bomber on our tail.'

Andrew glanced in the mirror. It was a large black American car, looked like a Buick, and travelling fast.

There was a brief hoot behind them. Halford extended his right hand and waved it forward, at the same time drawing in and slackening speed. The road was perfectly clear ahead but was steeply cambered and none too wide.

The other car drew abreast. There were two men in it; both wore RAF uniform and goggles. Very odd.

'Your Polish friends?' Jennifer asked.

'Lord, no. Not in that bird kit.'

Having almost passed them, the driver of the Buick cut in too soon, as if he was trying to avoid something coming the other way. Andrew shouted and jabbed his horn fiercely and as fiercely braked.

The overtaking car had braked too. There was a squeal of tyres and a crack of metal as the two cars touched. The wheel in his hand kicked like a horse, and they went off onto the grass verge. Beyond it was a ditch. They swung away from the ditch and the two cars again bumped. The MG jumped in the air like a wounded buck; they were on the verge; a tree was flying at them; tilt and they were over; the world heeled; sky and grass and flying mud. Then crash.

Sunday Afternoon – Two

I

A blackbird was chattering in the silence. It sounded rather disturbed. The only other sound was a clicking of hot metal. And there was the smell of petrol.

Andrew moved his hand. That was all right. Yes, but it hurt and there was blood on it. Like the time he'd landed on a fence and the wind in the parachute had pulled him over it, ripping the skin on his arm as it did so. The car was on its side.

'Jennifer!' he said.

'Hullo.'

He gulped. 'Are you hurt?'

'Not much. But you're heavy.'

'Good God.' He was on top of her. He couldn't open his door. That was petrol dripping.

They were deep in the ditch, rather more than half overturned. He could see one of her feet, the dashboard, the steering wheel. He tried to put pressure on the steering wheel and push himself out. She made some sort of a noise.

'*Sorry!*' Obviously he couldn't get out that way. But there was no bloody roof: you just had to *fall* out. Why hadn't they both been thrown clear? Dripping petrol. Would be a pity to get frizzled up in a car after never having had so much as a flash burn before. He reached through the spokes of the wheel and switched the engine off.

'Jennifer.'

'Yes?'

'Can you take my weight on your shoulder?'

'Yes.'

He heaved, she squealed, and he rolled free and fell into the depths of the ditch, which was dry but a mass of dead bracken and bramble. He got to his knees. She was still in the car, not exactly under it but it seemed pinned down by the angle of the car.

No one about, not a soul. Unmistakeable smell of burning rubber. Wires had fused. They would glow red hot and the contact would run along to the fuse box.

He tried to shove the car back but it was immovably stuck. He got his hands under her arms and said: 'Can you wriggle or push?'

'Don't know. My leg's caught.'

He heaved, at first gently, then, as the bonnet of the engine began to smoke, with all his strength. She was coming.

She cried out and said: 'Wait. Not too fast. I think I can get out if you wait. This door – '

He pulled again and she cried out again, but now she had come out as far as her waist.

'Like this. Heave! Push with your legs – '

'I can't, Andrew. It's – stuck!'

'No it isn't! It can't be.' Her face was close to his and looked very pale. He stopped and kicked vainly at the car door. Then he got her round the waist and heaved like an all-in wrestler. She came, slithering and sliding; there seemed a lot of her; it took such a long time until both feet appeared. Then he collapsed with her into the ditch.

He was up on the instant helping her to crawl on hands and knees out of danger as the car burst into flames.

II

She was a bad colour, so he picked her up and stumbled with her along the base of the ditch until they were well away from the heat. Then he put her down and helped her to scramble out of the ditch and into the soft grass of a coppice which ran beside the road. At his urging they went on until they were a hundred yards away and hidden from view. It seemed a reasonable precaution.

She was sitting, grey-faced, eyes flickering; blood from his hand had stained her hair. He wiped his hand on the grass; just a scratch, near the scar left by last September's landing – only then he had been half blind with Glycol.

She said: 'God. I feel queer.'

'Lie back.' He helped her to slide herself towards a tree trunk and she leaned back on it.

'I think my leg's got a bit of a knock,' she said, and then leaned her head back, not fainting but not far away.

He saw there was blood on her stocking. Her skirt was riding high and he pulled at the stocking impatiently, fumbling awkwardly with the suspenders; the back one had seized up. He got it undone, pulled the stocking down to get a better look at the half bruise, half cut about an inch above the knee. Not deep but nasty; the skin was discoloured and blood trickled from the side of it.

He found his handkerchief, folded it into a pad, dabbed at the cut, then left the handkerchief there, wishing there were a stream nearby.

The coppice was quiet. The birds were quiet. Only the wind hummed. The late afternoon sun made zebra stripes among the trees. No sound from the road. The thick black column of smoke had not yet apparently attracted anyone's attention. You'd think you were in the Sahara.

She opened her eyes.

'Feeling better?' he said.

'Did I – go over?'

'You had a little rest.'

'How awful . . . That accident was deliberate, wasn't it?'

'Any pain anywhere?'

'My knee.'

'Anywhere else?'

'No . . . You've cut your hand.'

'It's only a scratch.'

'Where are we?'

'Somewhere between Banbury and Stratford – '

'The car?'

'Gone up in smoke.'

They sat quiet for a bit.

She looked dubiously at her leg. 'I think it was the edge of the dashboard.' She lifted his handkerchief. 'It's almost stopped bleeding.'

'Any pain in your body or head? Not swimmy now?'

'No. It was just the shock.'

'Those bastards.' He had found a second handkerchief and was wrapping it round his own hand.

'Perhaps someone has decided it's my turn next.'

He looked at her quickly. 'Why should you be in danger?'

'That's what I don't know!'

'Lie still,' he said.

'What?'

'Lie still.' He was peering through the bushes. Jennifer craned her neck and now could see what he could see – a car coming from the opposite direction. A black car. The same black car.

It approached slowly. When it got to the blazing wreck it stopped. A door opened and one of the men slid out. He was about to go nearer to the MG when he glanced up the road and quickly got in the Buick again. Another car was coming. The black car accelerated gently away and passed the on-coming car about three hundred yards from the crash. The oncoming car stopped at the wreck and the driver got out, peering into the ditch and then stared after the retreating Buick. Now another car was coming along and also stopped. Soon there were a group of people looking down at the wreck. Clouds of oily smoke drifted before the wind. It reminded Andrew of other crashes he had seen.

He was squatting beside Jennifer. 'What d'you think?'

'About what?'

'Now's the time to go back and make a fuss. The police'll come, take our testimony. They'll talk about a tip and run driver. Word'll go out for a damaged Buick.'

'What choice have we?'

'We can't be far from some village. I suggest you stay here resting your leg and I'll take a recce, come back in half an hour, see what's happening.'

'No,' she said.

'What?'

'No. I'm well enough to come with you.'

'It'll do you good to stay quiet for a bit.'

Keeping behind the bushes, she got up and began to tie his handkerchief round her leg above the knee. That done, she pulled up the laddered stocking and fastened it. She looked over her shoulder at him, hair blowing across her face in the wind.

'I'm not staying here. The gentlemen in goggles might come for a second look.'

'Unlikely now . . . But would you rather go back to the car?'

'It's your feeling not to?'

'Well, at the moment our friends probably don't know whether we're in it. I think it might be healthy to leave them in that state.'

'Then let's go. I can walk – slowly.'

He helped her up, and they set off. There was a mass of thickets among the tall bare trees and it was very easy to keep out of sight of the burning car. Smoke still hung in the sky, marking the spot.

They crossed a lane but kept to what looked like the main road, though the names on the signpost had been painted out. He glanced at her sidelong. She had lost her beret and her hair was a thick lambent mop in the sunshine.

'I must have been a tidy weight in the car,' he said.

'You were.'

'Sure you're not bruised anywhere?'

'Don't think so. I'd tell you if I was.'

'You know,' he said, 'I believe you'd make a damned good pilot.'

'Thank you, sir.'

'Now I know you're feeling better.'

'Would you have me in your squadron?'

'Depends on whether you could obey orders.'

'Haven't I done so up to now?'

'I haven't given you any.'

'How shall I know when you do?'

'I'll blow a whistle.'

I'm damned near *courting* this girl, he thought. Being silly with her and enjoying it. And there's a burning car less than half a mile away, and we might be under it. And there was a young woman strangled in a lonely house. And somebody has been trying to get rid of us. And this is the best leave I've ever had.

In trying to avoid being seen, they'd taken a wrong direction, for the road was becoming more rural. The sun was low above the hills on their right. It flung long itinerant shadows on the landscape from clouds bustling across the sky.

'Here, let me carry you,' he said.

She stopped and shaded her eyes. 'I'm OK. Listen to that lark singing. Can you see it?'

'No. Give me your arm, then.'

She allowed herself to be linked and together, with a rare sense of comradeship, they walked on. A car came behind them but after a moment's slackening buzzed on ahead. A blue Riley.

'Perhaps we should thumb a lift,' he said.

'I was thinking that. But let's get a bit further away.'

The road was straight again now, with a barn on the left and a smattering of Jersey cows. Some sort of an advertisement hoarding reared its head on the distant left.

She sat on a stile, and he leaned beside her against the dry stone wall, picked a piece of grass to chew, rubbed his hand where it was still smarting.

'My father was crazy on motor cars,' she said, 'only he could never afford the ones he wanted. I remember when I was about fifteen we went on a picnic, the three of us. It was a Morris Major, a pretty looking car; but when we were miles from anywhere there was a clatter in the engine and that was that. We had to be towed. They said it was a broken valve spring . . . I remember we all sat on the edge of the road, like this, waiting for someone to come past. I remember it was April and the sun was shining.'

'My car's going to need more than a new valve spring. Damn them for dressing up in Air Force uniforms!'

'That seems to me the least of their crimes. Would you mind less if they'd been in civvies?'

'Yes,' he said, and they both laughed.

'What's that advertisement in the distance?' she asked. 'I can't see from here.'

'What *I* should like to know,' he said, 'is whether that little accident was arranged for my benefit, or yours, or for us both.'

'Well, they can't have been trying to stop us going to Birmingham, since we didn't know ourselves when we set out!'

A cyclist was coming their way. A clergyman, middle-aged, red faced, bald. Andrew raised an arm.

'Sorry to stop you. We've been walking some distance and my partner's gone lame. Where will this road bring us out?'

The clergyman glanced at their clothes; perhaps he thought they'd been rolling lasciviously in the hay.

'White Otterham, young man. I am the incumbent there. A matter of three miles. Cross the Kineton-Gayford road in half a mile, then straight on, taking the left fork at the school. An interesting village with a Norman church. If you look in the niche on the right of the altar you'll see a really beautiful fragment of a medieval St Jerome. And there are brasses . . .'

'Thank you. Would there be nearer villages on the other road?'

'There's Crosby. A little less than two miles if you turn left at the next crossroads. It is very small and distinguished only for the number of its public houses.' The clergyman coughed. 'To the weary traveller that might seem more inducement than my Norman church. We also have good beer at White Otterham.'

Andrew smiled. 'We want whatever's nearest at hand.'

The clergyman fingered the lever of his bell. 'There is an hotel on your left. Not three hundred yards. No doubt you could get refreshment there.'

Andrew thanked him and he rode on.

'A lesson in cross-examination,' he said. 'One finds out the important thing as an after-thought. It's that sign probably.'

It was that sign. 'Marley Manor Hotel. Nine-hole golf course. Boating, fishing, Luncheons, Bar. Open to Non-residents.'

A wide carriage drive showed a corner of a large house among the trees.

'We can get a rest and a clean-up. Maybe they'll have a car for hire.'

'I'll take you up on that cup of tea, if there is one. I've no yearning for beer or Norman churches.'

The old house was warming its mellow stone in the declining sun. Three elderly men in golfing gear were standing at the door, and a couple of cars were in the drive.

The entrance hall was low beamed and filled with settles and brasswork. In one corner was a carefully disguised reception desk lit by low-voltage bulbs and occupied by a pert young female with dyed hair and a dumpy figure. Jennifer collapsed into a chair as Andrew went to the desk.

He explained that they had had a minor car accident and would like tea and the facilities for a clean up.

'Tea's over, sir. We shall be serving dinner in an hour.'

'We'll be staying for that. In the meantime order tea for my friend. And I should like to see the manager.'

She seemed about to argue, but his manner was too much for her and she pressed a bell. A middle-aged, soft-voiced man in a sleek dinner jacket with padded shoulders presently came out. Andrew told his story a second time and asked about hiring a car back to London.

'We have no car here, sir. I could phone Repington, but

the difficulty is petrol. Things have been tightened up so very much of late. Of course if you have petrol coupons of your own . . .'

They were in the car. 'What about trains?'

'You could pick up the branch line at Repington, four miles away, but I'm not sure of the service. I think Sunday trains have been discontinued. I know buses have. Actually, we can accommodate you here if you find it difficult to get back.'

'How far are we from Stratford?'

'Eleven miles.'

'We could pick up a connection there?'

'Oh yes. I think you'd have to change, though. They alter the train services so much, especially Sunday travel. I'll get you the latest timetable.'

There was no vital reason as far as he knew why they should return tonight. Unless Jennifer had other ideas. He didn't much take to the manager; words slipped smoothly and easily out of his mouth like plums from a broken bag; he had polish and suavity and wariness.

'What sort of rooms have you to offer?'

'We have just one very nice double room left on the first floor . . .'

'Singles.'

'Ah, that's a little more difficult . . . No, I see we have two nice singles on the second floor. You're lucky to get them, if I may say so; we have a busy weekend.'

'I must first consult my friend. Perhaps I could let you know a little later on.'

The manager's eye slipped past him, travelled to Jennifer, summed her up with professional coolness. 'Very good, sir; we'll *try* to hold them for you.'

'One other thing,' Andrew said. 'Is there a doctor locally or a nurse who could dress my friend's knee?'

'One of our receptionists is a VAD. She'll be due on in about half an hour.'

'I'd be really grateful if you could let her see it. Thank you very much.'

He went back to Jennifer. 'Tea at once. Then someone's going to look at your leg. Then dinner. Then we'll see if we can get home.'

'Difficult?'

'Very.'

'Well, let's hope we can,' said Jennifer cheerfully. 'I shouldn't want Mrs Lawson to think I'd done a bunk, like Paula.'

Sunday Evening

I

They could hire a car to come out for them from Stratford, where there was a railway connection for Rugby; then if the train was punctual they could catch the 11.05 for London. It meant arriving back in the early hours of the morning, and of course that was conditional on there being no raid in progress. The VAD lady advised Jennifer not to walk too much on her leg for the time being. Maybe she was in cahoots with the manager who saw a bit of extra trade disappearing; but that tipped the scales. They stayed on.

Andrew rang the local police, told them of his accident, said he would see them in the morning.

The Marley Manor Hotel catered for the weekender, the not-too-serious golfer, the honeymooner, the Mr and Mrs Smith-and-no-questions-asked – not even when the names on the ration cards differed. It was a place where people didn't mix much outside the company they came with; a comfortable anonymity existed. Mr Parker, the manager, must have been quite used to welcoming RAF officers and their wives or girlfriends; the only oddity in this case being that the visitors pretended to want single rooms. However, he accepted this eccentricity with a good grace. Andrew found they had been given rooms with a connecting door to which there was no key.

He went down and explained this to Jennifer, who smiled. 'His mind is just as one-track as a Victorian's.'

'Never mind. So long as the food isn't bad.'

The food wasn't bad. Part way through the meal Jennifer glanced round and said: 'People are quite smart for wartime, aren't they. Wish I'd brought a change of frock.'

'If you had it would have been in the car.'

'Along with my toothbrush. Does your beard grow fast?'

'Anyway,' he said, 'your frock's all right. I like it.'

'On the whole,' she said, 'it was a fairly clean accident, wasn't it. Everything has brushed off. I just sorrow for my nylons. They're the only pair I ever had.'

'I'll get you some more.'

'D'you have American friends? They're about the only source.'

'We'll see.'

Conversation petered out while they ate. The enormity of what had happened to them, of what had been attempted, had been slow in soaking through – through the liveliness and the high spirits. Each withdrew temporarily from the other, thinking of the events, weighing them, conscious of a danger they had not thought existed, puzzling, pondering, speculating. It weighed more heavily on Jennifer who, though naturally the more ebullient of the two, was less used to escaping with her life at rather short notice. Privately each speculated a little as to how long it would be before the two men in goggles discovered they were not in the car.

After dinner there was an informal dance. For its conversion into a country hotel from the private days when it had been a small Queen Anne mansion no unaesthetic expense had been spared. The Tudor-style dining hall had a minstrel gallery, ornate leaded windows, pseudo granite pillars. The neo-Georgian games room had tubular steel chairs and brown cord carpet; the vast beflowered sun lounge was strewn with chaise-longues and green linen cushions. Andrew was glad he had a wallet full of back pay.

The dance was held in the dining hall to the strains of a radio gramophone concealed in the minstrel gallery; a great log fire, electrically lit and giving off no heat, blazed in the hearth.

'If you'd like to dance,' said Jennifer after a bit, 'don't let me stop you.'

'Who on earth would I want to dance with?'

'I thought you were eyeing that blonde in the green give-away dress.'

'I come of hard stock,' he said, 'so I'm always suspicious of give-aways.'

'No, seriously.'

'Seriously.'

'All right. What would you rather do?'

'Talk to you.'

She looked at him. 'Now you're having me on.'

'You're a modest girl, aren't you.'

'Didn't think so. Not specially.'

'That watch,' he said, 'which you may say brought us together. It's a valuable one, isn't it?'

'My grandmother's. My mother gave it to me when I was eighteen.'

'You were very generous, lending it to Paula.'

'I suppose so. Pretty idiotic, you may think. Or do you wonder if perhaps I'm not telling the whole truth?'

'When you look at me like that I believe everything you tell me.'

She glinted a little, then glanced away, fingers touching the watch. 'You never met Paula. She was a strong personality. She was a lot older than I am. I suppose I was flattered to be her friend, to share her flat. Does that explain anything?'

'Yes,' he said. 'Sorry.'

'Sorry for what?'

'Putting a question that gave you the impression I was doubting you.'

'It's a free world,' she said. 'Still. Just. Thanks to people like you. If anyone is, you're entitled to doubt.'

'My leave, as you frequently remind me, is privileged. Let's go in the next room. There's a real fire there.'

As they went in she said: 'I'd better ring Mrs Lawson, just tell her I'll be back tomorrow, case she notices.'

He watched her limp slowly away. Somehow her walk was jaunty in spite of its impediment. He picked up a Sunday paper and scanned it to see if there was any further mention of the discovery at Northcot. But all he saw was that things were getting worse in Greece. The Anzacs were fighting a brilliant delaying action; the British had shortened their line to defend Athens; the Greeks were holding out with great courage. It all sounded too familiar. Like Dunkirk over again.

She came back.

'Get through all right?'

'Yes, quite quickly.'

'Anything wrong?'

'She said two men called to see me about an hour ago. She told them I'd be back later, so they said they'd call again tomorrow.'

'What names did they give?'

'None, as far as I know. She wasn't keen to talk long because a raid had just started. I could hear the anti-aircraft guns over the telephone.'

There was a pause. 'It could have been the police,' he said.

'Or the two men who tried to bump us off.'

It was what Andrew had been wondering. 'I doubt it.'

'If it's the police I shall have some explaining to do.'

'Not that much. Just be the innocent.'

Jennifer was fingering the two-inch-long tear in her skirt. The chambermaid had promised her a needle and thread but had apparently forgotten. The seams had broken too under her arm where Andrew had pulled her out of the car. They were minor blemishes but she would have been much more comfortable in the dining room if they'd been repaired. She looked up and saw Andrew smiling at her.

She smiled back inquiringly.

Ducking the implied question, he said: 'I promised to ring Stephen too. I should let him know where we are. And what has happened. I said we'd keep in touch.' He looked at his watch. 'Or maybe I should leave it till morning. Did Mrs Thing say the raid was bad?'

'I think she thought it was going to be.'

'Why wasn't she in the shelter?'

'She doesn't often go. You get blasé, you know.'

'Not a course to be recommended . . . By now Stephen is likely to be out on the tiles with Witold. I'm more likely to catch him in the morning.'

They talked for a few minutes, then she said: 'I think I'll go to bed. If you don't mind, that is.'

'Your knee painful?'

'No. Nothing. It's just a minor cosh.'

'A night cap?'

'Thanks no. The wine was great.' She paused. 'I wonder how long it will last.'

'What?'

'The wine. The *French* wine. We shan't get any more.'

'Spanish and Portuguese might filter through. And a bit of Algerian. It isn't any worse than in Napoleon's time.'

'They smuggled then.' She got up.

He said: 'Shall I give you a hand?'

'Lord, no. I'd rather not make a scene of it, and I got up easily enough before dinner.'

'I shan't be long. I'll knock when I come up and see if you've everything you want.'

'Oh, I shall be OK. Thanks. Good night, Andrew.'

'Good night, Jennifer.'

She reached up and kissed him lightly on the lips. It was the simplest, most innocent-seeming of salutes but it affected him like an electric charge.

Once again he stood watching her limp away.

II

He sat for half an hour having a further drink and keeping his mind carefully on other things.

However well Jennifer might play it when the police came, if *he* became involved he was in the mire with both feet. He'd withheld the clue to Paula's identity, he'd followed ideas of his own without thought to his obligations as a citizen. To say nothing of his special commitments as a senior officer in the Royal Air Force.

The accident of this afternoon put a new blip on the radar screen. This was something bigger than he could tackle on his own. But what else to do? Give up now?

By Tuesday evening different and more familiar patterns waited. He was hoping to try out a Messerschmidt BF 109 which had been captured, after the Boffins had had their sniff around. There were, they said, a number of important modifications. Andrew was no test pilot but he had an ability to fly a plane to what was called 'ten tenths', meaning he could take it nearer to break-up point than most of his fellows.

Well . . . a day and half left. He hadn't even *seen* his parents. So up sticks now, shove Jennifer on the train back to London tomorrow to fend for herself, and make a cross-country trip to Bath, spend the last night where duty and affection called? The last thing he wanted was to be withdrawn from operational duties while this affair of a murdered woman was thrashed out.

No damned car now. He would miss the MG. He'd taken it over from Flying Officer Birtles S J, who had bought it in the early days before Dunkirk. Birtles had now bought it in another sense, though there was a faint hope that he had baled out in time and was a prisoner in France.

Insurance companies notoriously take a long time to settle claims. Would his bank manager wear the extra unsecured overdraft to pick up another car in the meantime? Couldn't call on his father for a loan. Most bank managers you went to to ask for a loan looked like frozen penguins.

Aunt Nell in Birmingham. What could she tell them about Paula? The trouble is dear you shouldn't never have begun. Kurt and Emmy are nothing to you . . .

One question he should have asked Jennifer. He should do it tonight because by tomorrow morning . . .

He dabbed out his cigarette, which had been smouldering unsmoked in the ash tray. The night was still young but he had been near to nodding off. Other short nights were catching up. Plus the shock of the car accident. The tones of the radiogram came unabated from the dining hall. The blonde in the green give-away dress came into the room as if looking for someone, glanced at him in a sultry fashion, went out again. Dear Heaven. One man's meat.

A last half-suspicious glance around the room; then up the shallow polished stairs, past two potted palms whose elegant leaves were stirring slightly in the breeze from an open window. Inefficient black-out again. The second flight was less impressive, and Rooms 22 and 23 were not far from the end. Twenty-two was a pleasant enough room with blue curtains and cream walls, decorated with photographs of Shakespeare productions at Stratford; but one felt the greater indulgences had been lavished on the double rooms of the floor below.

Ignoring the connecting door, he went out and tapped at the door of 23.

'Yes?'

'You all right?'

'Oh, yes thanks.'

'May I come in?'

'Yes.'

This was a twin of the other room, but a pink colour scheme. Pink for a girl, blue for a boy. She was sitting in bed and had been reading a magazine. She'd borrowed a green Shetland bed-jacket from the VAD.

'I brought you some aspirins in case your knee keeps you awake.'

'It's fine now I'm in bed.'

'One question I should have asked you before you left. Did you tell Mrs What's-her-name where we were staying?'

'Mrs Lawson? No, just that we'd had an accident near Stratford and had had to put up at a hotel.'

'Good. I'm glad of that. Keep everyone guessing as long as possible.'

He sat on the edge of the bed. Her hair was coppery now,

in this light, and looked as if it had been well brushed. Which was unlikely. Her normal pallor had taken on a slight flush. He wondered why he hadn't thought her quite as beautiful as this before.

'You kissed me,' he said.

Her eyes widened. 'Yes?'

'Dangerous to trifle with a squadron leader's affections.'

'Oh, it was just sisterly.'

'It didn't feel like that to me.'

'Sorry, sir.'

His glance strayed. It was probable, circumstances being what they were, that she had nothing on except the bed-jacket.

'Do you remember early on this afternoon, when we were deciding how to spend the day, you said something.'

'I don't remember.'

'You said, "I just don't know what you want to do, but whatever it is, please do it."'

'Did I?'

'You must have a fairly good idea what I want to do now.'

'I doubt if I ever said any such thing, but if I did I was referring to – to harmless pleasures.'

'Harmless pleasure is what I'm after.'

He leaned forward and gently cupped her face in his hands. 'Just a brotherly kiss.'

Presently they separated. 'I never had a brother,' she said.

'I'll make up.'

His hands stroked her neck. After a minute, kissing her again, he moved the bed-jacket back, slipped it off her shoulders. There was nothing underneath. His hand went down her arms, moved to stroke her breasts. To his surprise, they were not so small. Incredibly silky and warm –

She broke away. 'Andrew, please. I don't think . . .'

He sat back. 'Feeling shaky?'

'Not *that* way. *Very* shaky another way.'

'So am I. You know, I want you very badly.'

He began to move his hands about her breasts again, with

great gentleness but no lack of instinctive skill. She broke eventually away from him.

'Oh, Christ, stop it! Please, please, please, please!'

'Why should I?'

'Why should you? Because, because, because . . .'

He saw she was genuinely upset. Her great eyes were brimming.

'That's no answer.'

'It wasn't meant to be.'

She sat there, her beautiful young breasts exposed, until he kissed each in turn and then pulled the bed-jacket round to cover them.

'What's the matter?'

'Andrew, I've never had a man.'

'So?'

'Do you believe me?'

'Of course.'

'Really?'

'Why shouldn't I?'

'I'm scared.'

'Of me?'

'No, no, *no*. But of what you think of me.'

'Why should I think worse of you for being chaste?'

'That's not it. I mean, Andrew, I care too much. I'm not – not a one-night stand.'

'Did you suppose I thought you were?'

'Why shouldn't you? I live with Paula. I go to a night-club with you. I come out in a car and am willing to spend the night here. Why shouldn't you think I'm an easy lay?'

'I only have to look at you,' he said.

She half smiled, looking younger and more innocent than ever. He sat back, frustrated, half loving her, half resenting her.

'Perhaps we'd better call it a day, then. It's been a pretty hefty one for us both.' Lightly, to take the tension out of it, he added: 'I shall attempt your virtue again tomorrow.'

She said: 'It isn't my *virtue* that matters, Andrew. For

God's sake. I don't care if I lose it. I don't feel I have any specially to lose. I – I can't explain any better except to say that . . .'

She tailed off. She found she couldn't explain that she was more than half in love with him and suspected that he wasn't even remotely in love with her. She didn't want to get badly hurt; and she didn't want the special affectionate comradeship that had grown between them in two days to end in a casual coupling. She knew it was easy come, easy go in wartime – and had to be: life was nasty, brutish and short, especially for men like him; and to deny him what he wanted for the sake of some old-fashioned dislike of being taken for granted, some sort of prideful, self-doubting reserve, seemed shabby and mean.

He was halfway to the door and she drew in a breath to call him back.

All she got out was: 'Andrew, I'm *sorry*.' Which wasn't the right thing to say.

He smiled at her wryly. 'Think nothing of it.'

Sunday Evening – Two

I

The Blue Peter was unusually busy for so early in the
evening. Wednesday's bad raid had given people the urge
to get out, to celebrate the fact that they were still alive, and
to gamble on the unlikelihood of two such fierce blitzes
coming in the same week. Usually the Hun needed a breather
himself.

Dot Forrest was there and so was Louis. It was a lucky
break for her. She knew he was a member – he'd brought
her here once himself – but after that he'd made excuses not
to bring her again, and she was curious to know why. She
thought she knew why.

So she'd come with Guy Patterson – known to his friends
as Dad, because he was stout and the wrong side of fifty. Dad
was very keen on her and she kept him on a lead in case he
could be useful to her. He had been useful tonight.

Miss Forrest was tall and blonde and striking, with something of the brittle, tigerish, enamelled look of a Hollywood
starlet; a slight American drawl went with it, though in fact
she'd never been further west than Colwyn Bay.

They formed a group at the bar. Among them an undergraduate, somewhat the worse for drink, and a subaltern
from an infantry regiment, were wrangling interminably
with a plump girl in a backless evening frock. Patterson,
whose face was so flushed that it might all have been a birth
mark, was stroking Dot's arm and muttering whisky and
endearments close to her long platinum hair. The under-

graduate was beating time to the music on the counter with a two-shilling piece. Dot was watching Louis.

He stood a little separate from the rest, glass in hand, nodding now and then to show he was with them but taking no real part. One of Armitage's first pieces of advice to him when they had met more than a year ago was: lead a normal life. Behave normally. Never forget you're just an ordinary citizen.

So after Thursday and Friday in a peculiar state had come, the wedding – the invitation picked up from an accommodation address earlier in the week – going home to be surrounded by all the familiar, irritating things. People he'd left behind, never wanted to see again.

But it had worked. Pity about Hilda, that she'd had to take up with a poor specimen like Filey. She deserved better than that. Always fond of Hilda. Been very close as kids. So when this brooch came back to him, so to speak, he'd thought it a good idea to pass it on to her. He'd picked it up in the Caledonian Market three weeks ago. It had been a snip. The revolting Jew boy who'd sold it him was just closing up and for some reason was in a hurry. Maybe, thought Louis, he'd be in more of a hurry in a year's time . . .

So the change had done him good. He'd felt better for it. But meeting Mr Armitage this morning had been unsettling again. What the hell did he mean by loose ends? And another meeting tomorrow. That had never happened before.

So now he was listening to the nonsense they were talking at the bar: about the war, about the blitz, about rationing, about the latest American jazz, just as if he was remotely interested in any of it.

At first he'd been annoyed to find Dot there, and annoyed at the challenging way she had greeted him. But on the whole there was no harm in it – she was here with Patterson so she couldn't attach herself to him at the end of the evening. And she was a hell of a good-looking girl which made everything easier. They had had a bit of a flirtation before the other woman came along. When the memory of the other woman had faded there was no reason why he shouldn't pick up with Dot again.

On the other side of the bar, Henry, on his last evening, presided magisterially, assisted by Ernesto, the slim, young, bedroom-eyed Italian who in June 1940 had turned out unexpectedly to be a Cypriot. Ten minutes ago Henry had excused himself and done some telephoning. First he had rung the RAF club and learned that Squadron Leader Halford was not in and had not been in all day, then he had rung 45 Gaskin Street and been told that Miss Ward was not in and had not been in all day. Finally on his own initiative he had made a third call and had a brief conversation with the man at the other end.

He lumbered back to smile inscrutably at the company and push his mane of hair out of his eyes. Tomorrow, he feared, some of that would be cut. Tomorrow a new life. He hoped he would be sent to the Far East. Singapore or Hong Kong. He had never been East of Suez. It was a challenge.

The band struck up a mournful fox-trot, the saxophone wailing like a distressed air-raid siren. A few couples began to gyrate about the floor, moving like somnambulists through the thin fog of cigarette smoke.

'Come on, Dot,' said Guy Patterson, stroking. 'Let's dance.'

'I wish you'd stop that,' she said, giving his hand a playful slap. 'You're making me go all gooseflesh.'

'That's someone dancing on your grave,' said the undergraduate. 'It isn't Dad at all. Dancing on your grave.' He took up his beat with the two-shilling piece. 'Ti-pom, ti-pom, ti-pom-pom.'

'I thought I'd promised this to Charles,' said Dot. 'Didn't I promise it to you, Charles?'

Louis came out of his preoccupation. 'Oh, give it to Dad. I'm not fussy.'

'If you dance with Dad you'll need new feet,' said the undergraduate. 'I've seen him before. Ti-pom, ti-pom-pom.'

'Don't call me Dad,' said Patterson in annoyance. 'What

are you doing here anyway? When I was your age I was in the trenches! Blown up twice! That *was* a war.'

'The old Blighty stuff,' said the student. 'A long way to Tipperary and all that. Well, Dad, I'm deferred, if that means anything to you.'

'Oh, reserved occupation,' said the fat man with contempt. 'Didn't have any of that in the first war. Any young man with guts – they went.'

The student snorted. 'Not *reserved* occupation! *Deferred*, see? Just till I get my degree in engineering. They reckon I may be slightly more use to the country than square bashing. This war isn't going to be over tomorrow, you can bet your shirt on that. So maybe I'll see some of it even yet – more, even, than I've seen in London already. Didn't get any of that in the first war, did you, Dad? Only a few measly Zeppelins!'

'Charles is in a reserved occupation,' said Dot. 'Aren't you, Charles.'

'What's that?' said Dad, whose face still had its birth-mark colour. 'Another engineer, eh?'

'Wireless telegraphy,' said Louis shortly.

'Charles has got a new girlfriend,' Dot said spitefully. 'Haven't you, Charles. That's why he doesn't care for me any longer. Won't even dance with me now.'

'I don't know what you're on about.'

'I saw you in the Windmill last Monday. Aha, didn't think anybody had spotted you, did you, eh? Nice cosy seats in the back row.'

There was an explosion of laughter, not from Louis, but from the undergraduate and the subaltern and the girl in the backless frock.

Louis drained his glass, stared at Miss Forrest with large cold eyes.

'My sister,' he said.

'Go *on*!' Dot's was a cynical assumption of belief. 'She's not a bit like you, is she.'

'Happens to be the truth.'

'Well, well.' Her wide-eyed astonishment knew no bounds. 'Just fancy petting with your own sister! It's not done, honey. Prayer Book says you mustn't.'

The undergraduate leaned over. 'I must tell you this one. This Irish girl. She went to the confessional and said: "Oh, Father, I'm going to have a baby." The priest said: "Are you sure it's yours?"'

There was more laughter.

'How many sisters have you got?' Dot asked. 'Really, truly.'

'Lay off it, Dot,' said Louis. 'You've made your point.'

Dot examined her paint-bright face in a hand mirror and rubbed her little finger along her bottom lip. 'Well you did promise, you know.'

'Promise what?'

'You said you'd take me to the theatre one night. Remember? You said, "We'll go to the Apollo, see the Maschwitz revue." Remember?'

Louis pushed his glass across the counter towards Ernesto. 'Same again,' he said. 'And same for Miss Forrest.'

'Thanks, honey.' To the barman she said: 'I'll have another Scotch to match this one.' And then: 'You didn't bring her tonight, then?'

'Who? What d'you mean?'

Louis looked across his drink at her, and her bold gaze flickered. She moved as if her shoulders had been splashed with cold water. Then his expression changed and he laughed flatly.

'No, I didn't bring her tonight.'

'She got someone else?'

'It's finished between us.'

'No kidding?'

'She's nothing to me any longer.'

'Thank you, Mr Mason,' said Ernesto as Louis paid him. 'Another beautiful note. So clean. *Molto bene!*'

'What the hell's it to do with you?'

Ernesto looked his surprise. 'Pardon, sir. Nothing, sir. I

did but remark. Since the war we have so much dirty paper; crumpled and stained. I beg your pardon for using the Italian – '

'Forget it. Just give me the change.'

'*Certainement.* Pardon . . .'

'What's he doing, Ernesto?' asked the subaltern. 'Trying to pass you a phoney bill?'

'No, sir. Certainly not, sir. *Ecco.*'

'They'd shoot you in the States for passing a phoney bill on a barman,' said the subaltern. 'It's as bad as cheating at poker.'

Dot put a hand on Louis' sleeve. 'I'm with Dad tonight, as you know. But can we go sometime?'

'Where?'

'To the theatre, of course. It's good, they say. "New Faces". At the Apollo.'

Louis counted his change, put it away. Dad Patterson, who'd been to spend a penny, was coming back and would soon claim this young woman. And two Polish officers had come to the bar. And a bearded old chap with one arm, in a crumpled dinner jacket, who was a terrible bore. There was no one he wanted to talk to here, certainly not those two drunken fools with the girl in the backless frock. Dot was the only one worth looking at. If he'd not done much more than look at her yet, there was still time. His appetite was recovering.

'Next Tuesday,' he said on impulse.

'What, to go to the Apollo? You mean the day after tomorrow?

'Sure.'

'OK.' Her lips twisted with a moment's doubt. 'That'd be wizard, Charles. You won't let me down this time?'

'I didn't let you *down*. It wasn't definite. This is.'

'OK. OK. Wizard. What time?'

'It starts at 5.30. Meet you at five – not later – in the foyer.'

A hand touched her arm. 'Remember me?' said Patterson resentfully. 'This is our dance.'

Dot smiled at him and then, brilliantly, over his head, at Louis. 'It's a deal, pal. Tuesday.'

Someone else had come closer. It was one of the Poles, a great chap with a gaunt face.

'Please,' he said to Louis. 'Please. You have the light?'

'What?. . . Oh.' Louis stared at the cigarette in the officer's hand. He took out his lighter and flicked it a couple of times. A yellow flame lit the cigarette. The Pole blew out smoke, some of it into Louis' face.

'Sank you. Sat is good. Bloody good, you say. Everysink in England is bloody, eh? Bloody this, bloody that.' The Pole laughed, showing teeth like a blitzed graveyard. With contempt Louis saw that the man was drunk. Drink was not one of his weaknesses, and he despised it in others.

'Please do not take too much notice of Witold,' said the slimmer, smaller man. 'He is always so friendly with strangers, and he does not understand the English reserve.'

Louis grunted. Dad Patterson was leading Dot onto the floor. She was taller than he was, even without high heels. Louis was reminded of Hilda yesterday, towering over Filey. He glanced at his watch.

'Zis morn,' said the big officer, putting his glass down with exaggerated care, 'I hear the cuckoo. Yes?'

Louis stared at him expressionlessly.

Witold said: 'In my kon-try, zere it is the omen – the good omen. If der cuckoo calls loud three times above the cottage roof it is der good omen for good luck. Bloody good luck, you will say maybe perhaps yes.'

Louis yawned but didn't reply.

'Permit me to introduce myself,' said the slim fair officer. 'Radziwill – Stephen Radziwill. You must excuse Witold's English but he knew scarcely a dozen words when he came here ten months ago. He makes himself understood, does he not. You are Mr Mason?'

'Who told you that?'

'Henry. I happen to admire the blonde young lady, and he told me also who she is talking to.'

'What is it to you?'

Stephen looked Louis over carefully. 'I believe we have a friend in common, is it not so? A Squadron Leader Andrew Halford.'

Louis stared back. 'Never heard of him.'

'Dear me, maybe I have made a mistake. You are Charles Mason?'

'Yes.'

'That is strange, is it not. Well, well.'

'I understand der English,' said Witold. 'But when I fly off I grow into a rage with the pleasure to kill the Hun, and then der English is forgot. So der crackle-crackle goes and I forget to understan'. But so long as I kill, what matters it? Hey, bloody hell, yes.'

He was leaning closely against Louis while he spoke. Louis began to feel under pressure.

'Are you on leave?' Stephen asked.

'No,' said Louis.

'Ah, the back-room boy, perhaps?'

'You could say that.'

'So necessary in this war. Witold thinks it is just killing Huns – that is all that matters. But there is much more – a secret war – that goes on. In my country there were no Quislings. Other countries have not been so fortunate: Belgium, France, Denmark, Holland. Were you in London on Wednesday last?'

'Yes.'

'We were more lucky. Our leave does not begin until Thursday. But when I drive through London it reminds me of Warsaw. You know? Not so bad, but bad enough, and getting worse. It is not a pretty thing to see.'

Louis looked at his watch again. 'Time I went.'

'Do you go on to another club? Better than this? It is very *early*.'

'I've an appointment.'

Stephen Radziwill glanced at Henry, but Henry was not looking at him. They had come in answer to the phone call, a shot at a venture. All Stephen knew was that Andrew wanted to get in touch with a man called Charles Mason, because he suspected him of having killed a girl. Nothing more than that. Andrew had left word with Henry, but Henry hadn't been able to find him, so had rung Stephen. Where did one go from here? You could hardly keep the fellow in the club against his will in the hope that Andrew would turn up. Stephen didn't like the look of Charles Mason: there was something in the way his hair grew, something self-regarding and self-opinionated about his eyes. But it was one thing to mistrust a man . . .

'Well,' Louis said. 'See you sometime. So long.' He nodded and pushed his way out of the corner. Stephen's sensitive nostrils twitched but he made no move to stop him. Witold took his cue from his friend and allowed his fingers to drop from Louis' sleeve.

Louis nodded good night to the others and crossed the floor. Dot was still dancing with Dad Patterson and made a grimace over the fat man's shoulder. 'Tuesday?' she mouthed. Louis nodded grimly and half smiled. 'Tuesday,' he mouthed back. Satisfied, she turned to her partner. Louis was arrogant and a hard nut, but he'd a lot going for him in her eyes. She'd made a definite step forward in their relationship tonight. There was a flicker of desire for her in his expression which had never been there before.

II

Before collecting his coat and hat Louis went into the men's lavatory. There he sponged his hands and face and combed his crisp hair. He put his hand inside his shirt and moved it across his chest. It came away wet with sweat. It had been hot in the night-club but not that hot.

He looked around. There was no one in the lavatory. He took out his wallet and counted the notes. So far he had only spent four of this lot; they were all unused and with consecutive numbers. That Italian fool would draw attention to the fact. *They* should have thought of that. *They* should have given him used notes which were impossible to trace or notice.

He went out and took up his coat and hat; dropped a coin for the girl, and the doorman let him out into Berkeley Square. No moon up yet; this one was almost spent. Nor any alarm yet, but the sky was alive with searchlights.

Armitage had told him not to be out too late. A nod was as good as a wink. He would afford a taxi if one came along. Otherwise he could walk down to Green Park and take a tube from there.

He went down the three steps and had not noticed in the black-out that two men stood there, one on either side of the steps.

It was the two Polish officers waiting to see him home.

III

They walked together towards Curzon Street.

Stephen said: 'This all so much reminds me of Warsaw – as I have already said. People live with life, people live with death. I remember in Warsaw the children playing in the bomb craters and mothers screaming at them – not for being in danger but because they are getting their clothes muddy. You know. Human nature is very strange.'

'And der blood in der streets,' said Witold. 'The clotted blood in her tramlines, der splash on der wall, der corpses wiz der entrails dangling, yes. Your mother, my mother, who cares?'

'I'm going home,' said Louis. 'Clear off now, both of you. Couple of drunks. I don't want your company.'

'We are thinking of the Lyceum,' said Stephen. 'It is a good place for dancing and finding girls. You would perhaps like to come with us?'

'I've told you,' said Louis, 'I don't want to have to tell you again.'

'Where do you live?' Stephen asked. 'Perhaps we are going near by.'

'No bloody business of yours,' said Louis.

Witold laughed. 'See. Bloody again. Eversink is bloody – just like I said.' He hiccuped.

They turned down Curzon Street. Louis stopped. They stopped.

He said: 'Leave me alone!'

He went on. They went on. He turned down Clarges Street. They turned down Clarges Street, a step behind. A woman came out of a dark doorway; you could only see the glow of her cigarette end and hear the sibilant greeting. Stephen waved her away.

He said: 'You are a new member? Of the Blue Peter?' Louis did not answer. 'I have been a member for a year; but my father was one of the founders in 1936. It is a good club. You pay honest prices . . . My father, alas, is in Poland. I hear nothing from him since last August when a message came. Where do you come from, Mason? And how do you find such pretty girls?'

Louis stopped. 'Look. I'm going home. See? I've got an appointment. I don't want your company, understand? Go off and look for your women if you want to, but don't bother me! I don't speak Polish, but you can understand English well enough to get the message! Clear off!'

'Not Polish?' said Witold, weaving slightly. 'Why not a Polish? Are you a Russian? Or what is it, eh?'

They had come to the corner of Piccadilly. In the wider street the darkness was not so complete, and the searchlights reflected some light back upon the buildings and the moving traffic. From here it was only a hundred yards to the underground. You could see its faint yellow glow.

Although there was an entrance on this side of Piccadilly, Louis was considering a dash across the road to the other entrance; the traffic wasn't heavy and he could make the distance before they could follow him – certainly the big man who looked slow-witted in his cups; not so certain about the slim quiet one.

But then another solution came in sight. The centre of London was always heavily patrolled these nights by Military Police, who kept a firm hand on any misbehaviour on the part of forces personnel on leave and would clap a man into custody at the drop of a hat. Two such were strolling towards them only a few yards away, emerging out of the darkness.

'Hey!' shouted Louis. 'You two. Come here, will you?'

The MPs looked and then came forward, not pleased with the style of summons but ready to investigate.

'These two men,' said Louis, annoyed at the agitation in his own voice; 'they're drunk and they won't leave me alone! Can you get them off my back!'

'On the contrary,' said Stephen, 'we were just escorting our friend home and keeping him company – '

The corporal was a ginger-haired man, square built, moustached, his cap rammed down centrally over his eyes. He looked at the trio with an inflamed expression. One man in civvies, well-dressed, two men from the forces. Triggering off suspicion and worse was the word Poland on the two jackets; the corporal despised and hated all foreigners and knew they weren't to be trusted an inch – it was a crowning pity we'd ever had anything to do with Europe. But curbing harsh words and intemperate actions was the fact that both men were officers. You had to tread careful.

'Well,' he said, 'what's supposed to be the trouble now?'

All three spoke at once; probably they'd all had too much, though even the very big man looked more sober than you'd supposed a minute ago. It was obviously a squabble over damn all. These Polacks were feeling too friendly, the civvy man was fed up with their company. Not surprising neither.

The corporal addressed the slimmer Pole. 'Well, sir, I reckon the gent wants to be left alone – to go off on his own, like. So why not let him do just that, eh?'

Stephen was about to reply when the familiar sound of the air-raid sirens began – low like a gathering of unfriendly dogs, then growing to a high undulating wail, predicting evil. A moment more and you could hear the first ack-ack guns barking in the distance. Extra searchlights began to sweep the sky.

As they stood there hesitating, a taxi drew up near by and discharged its fare. Louis jerked up his hand at it and clutched at the door handle.

'Which way yer going, mate?' said the driver.

'West,' said Louis.

'How far west?'

Louis muttered something as he got in. The square shoulders of the two MPs stood between him and the Poles as the taxi drew away.

Witold spat his disgust in the gutter. The corporal pulled down his tunic and grunted satisfaction at his achievement.

'If I was you gentlemen,' he said, 'I'd take cover. I know I'm going to. Come on, Fred.'

Monday Morning

I

They met in the morning outside her bedroom door.

'Hallo!' he said. 'Up so soon? How's your knee?'

'A bit tricky at first but it's coming on. And your hand?'

'Nothing.'

He found he had forgotten everything about her. This separate individual who greeted him was less flawless of feature but more challenging than he remembered. And the recognition of her, the seeing of her as such a pretty young woman, was at once an allure and an affront. He knew she had been right to turn him down last night, but the knowledge that she was right did not make him feel more friendly about it. Irrespective of rights and wrongs, she'd turned him down.

A waiter hovered about them, vaguely apologetic. Force or prunes or shredded wheat? Sorry, no bacon to follow this morning; bacon was not served on even dates. Scrambled eggs or smoked trout? (Dried eggs of course.) Had they brought their own marmalade? No? Well, he'd try his best to get them a little.

There were few people in the baronial dining hall with its would-be antique pillars, on which the stones were picked out in black cement, and its log fire burning endlessly and heatlessly in the huge hearth. Either the hotel was not so full as they'd thought or everyone was breakfasting in bed.

'Will it take long to get back to London?' she asked as casually as she could.

'Shouldn't be too bad today. But you're limping pretty badly.'

'I'll be all right.'

She poured their coffee.

He said: 'Have we abandoned Birmingham?'

'You mean Aunt Nell?'

'I mean Aunt Nell.'

'It's up to you, Andrew.'

'Don't say, it's *your* leave.'

'Well, what else can I say? It's true.'

'And what about you?'

'Oh, more or less a free agent. I'm not due back at Beaufort's till Wednesday.'

After a minute he said: 'It did occur to me that the trains from Birmingham to London will be better than anything we can manage from here. It might just be worthwhile going there before we go home.'

'Birmingham's a big place. Newmarket Street might take some finding.'

'Do we just cut and run, then?'

She put out her bottom lip and blew upwards as if her face were hot, disturbing her fringe.

'Sorry about last night, Andrew.'

He offered her sugar for her coffee. She shook her head.

'Why should you be?'

'I feel a ghastly prude. Something out of a Maugham short story.'

'At least Maugham's prude hadn't just had a bad motor accident and gashed her knee.'

'It wasn't that. It wasn't that in the very least.'

'OK. I take your point.'

'No, you *don't*. That's absolutely not the point . . . Sorry, sorry. The more I say the worse I get stuck!'

'Forget it.'

'Will you?'

'I'll try.'

She looked at him again quickly. 'I don't even know how to take *that*.'

'Eat your breakfast,' he said, 'it'll do you good.'

'Yes, sir,' she said, but this time the little joke fell flat.

After a few minutes of silence he said: 'Those bastards yesterday . . . I still have a disinclination to cut and run.'

'I'm sure you have.'

'Why?'

'You wouldn't be what you are if you ever wanted to cut and run.'

'Stop making me out the war hero. I'm only in it for the money.'

The waiter came with their trout. After he had served them Andrew said: 'That's funny.'

'What is?'

'I've just remembered something the good doctor said; Norley, I mean, the one I called on yesterday morning. After giving me the usual guff about how brave I must be, he added something like: "Well, I suppose it's a job of work. You get well paid for it."'

'What a sick thing to say!'

'It did seem a bit odd. I suppose he was joking . . .' Andrew stuck his fork in the trout. 'But I suppose he's more or less right.'

'You can't mean that.'

With a streak of perversity he smiled at her and said: 'Of course I want to stop Hitler, and I shall go on shooting down these German Fritzes – at least until they shoot me down; but in a sense it's true; I'm not really fighting for the old ladies of Bournemouth. I *enjoy* my job and get well paid for it. It's exciting, stimulating, a hell of a challenge. One lives on a high. When I'm on leave I drink quite a bit. When I'm with the Squadron I don't *need* it!'

The dining room was filling up. Obviously the clientele were late risers.

She said: 'Yes, but . . .'

'But what?'

'Isn't this a bit more than stopping a German invasion?'

'Go on.'

'Well, I'm not awfully fond of the old ladies of Bournemouth myself, but the other side – is insufferable, insupportable, vile. If England went under . . .' She stopped. 'Wow! What cheek to say this to someone like you!'

'Why not to me? I like to know the views of the people I'm fraternising with.'

'That's pompous, Andrew.'

He opened his eyes at her. 'By God, you're right. Well done!'

She flushed. 'I'm sorry you're not in a good mood. It's probably my fault.'

'It probably is. But never mind. Forget you're talking to a Smart Alec and tell me exactly what you think.'

'I believe,' said Jennifer, 'that you're dodging the real issues just to provoke me.'

'The real issues?'

'Well, people are not just fighting the war for a class, are they? Are they? Or a section of England? They're not fighting for the rich, or the poor, or the good, or the bad. They're fighting just to be able to go on breathing. German conquest, Nazi victory means a victory for brutality, evil, cruelty, oppression, the concentration camp, beatings, terror . . . All the things we really care about will *die*. There's simply no room in the same world for them and for us!'

She tailed off, breathing deeply. He carefully picked a few bones from between his lips.

She said: 'You'd have made a good bullfighter.'

'How come?'

'Trailing your cloak. Go on, hoot with laughter.'

He said: 'No laughter, by request . . . Yes, in the event of defeat England will be run by lots of little Hitlers. All created after Adolf's own image. Yes, I know. They're every bit as evil as you say. A vile thing is stalking through the world. I only wish in fighting it we didn't get quite so involved with a particular image, a sort of propaganda machine of our own. "Our boys." "Our brave lads." "Our noble aims." . . . OK, sourness is all. Let us enjoy the trout.'

They ate in silence but it was not an amicable silence. He knew she was right in everything she had said, and she was right that he had deliberately provoked her. To some extent it was instinctive as well as deliberate – a need to be combative after her rejection of him. He didn't much like himself for being like this even while being so.

The trout was finished but the waiter did not come back. Andrew looked at the girl opposite and found it quite hard to believe that he had been fool enough to take no for an answer. Yet she might have fought and kicked. There was no telling with Miss Ward.

Also that he'd been a fool ever to think of her as actually thin.

Well, he thought, I ought to be a good loser. One of the things the British have always been good at – in sport if not in war.

He looked at her again and was about to speak when he saw that her gentle, sweet expression – deceptive at any time – had hardened. She was looking past him.

He said: 'What's wrong?' and began to turn, but she put a hand across and rested her fingers on his arm.

'Not yet.'

'What is it?'

'Nothing. Do you take salt?'

'With fishbones? Not usually.'

'Can I pour you more coffee?'

'If it would give you an excuse to do something.'

She poured the coffee.

'You remember,' she said, 'Paula's gentleman friend we've been looking for? The one who gave the name of Charles Mason? . . . You remember the presents I told you he gave Paula, and you said if she was short of money why didn't she pawn those, and I said – '

'Yes, yes; got all that.'

'I mentioned a cameo he bought her. I was envious of it. Well, there's a woman in this room, just come in to breakfast, two tables away; she's wearing it!'

Andrew digested this information while the waiter took away their plates.

'How can you be sure?'

'I can't, of course! But near to it. I've never seen a cameo like this before because it's painted – the stones are painted. It's – it's a Roman head on a darkish background, and the crown of laurel he wears round his head is in tiny green and cream and red stones. Paula was thrilled with it.'

'There must be others like it.'

'I've never seen one. And the head is just the same; the size is just the same.'

'She on her own?'

'No, with a short stocky youngish man in a blue suit. In his thirties. He's got hands that he uses for his work, like an engineer or a printer or a carpenter.'

'And the lady?'

'About the same age. She's wearing a very new wedding ring. She's a natural blonde with blue eyes and flaxen hair done in a page-boy bob . . . Her shoes are pinching her . . . She's in blue, and her nail varnish is the wrong shade . . .'

'I get the message loud and clear.'

'Twice she's touched the cameo as if making certain it's there. I'd like to go across and ask her where she got it.'

'Clearly the man doesn't match the description we have of Paula's friend.'

'You mean with another victim? Transferring his presents as he goes. Ugh! No, he doesn't match at all.'

The waiter arrived with a tiny glass saucer smeared with marmalade. Andrew thanked him and passed the dish to the girl.

'You have first lick.'

She scraped a bit off, and he dropped his table napkin and took a look behind while he picked it up.

He said: 'They're not watching us, are they?'

'Seems to me they're only looking at each other.'

'Certainly not the people who pushed us off the road yesterday.'

'No.'

He said: 'It all depends really on how sure you are of the cameo.'

'What depends?'

'Well, what we decide to do.'

'I can't believe there are two so much the same!'

'In that case we could find out how long these people are staying.'

'What difference would that make?'

'I've been thinking . . .'

'What?'

He smiled non-committally at her. 'Let that VAD girl look at your knee. Then we'll come to a decision.'

II

'Stephen? This is Andrew. Can you hear me?'

'Yes, yes. Where are you speaking from?'

'This damn line is crackling. I'm at the Marley Manor Hotel in Warwickshire. With the girl you met on Saturday night, Jennifer Ward.'

'Aha! Congratulations.'

'Not so much aha as you suppose. I took her for a drive yesterday and we were deliberately overturned by another car. My car's a burned out wreck and we had to spend the night here.'

'My God, what is it all about?'

'I can't imagine. Anyway Jennifer has a crocked knee, so we may not be back until tomorrow. In the meantime I shall go to Birmingham today to see if I can find a woman who may have a clue to the whole puzzle. It's an aunt of Paula Krissen's.'

'Paula who?'

'The girl who was murdered.'

'Andrew, do you not think it is time you took me more into your confidence?'

'Sorry. Very sorry. I should have done so on Saturday,

but I didn't realize we were going to run into such deep water. It all began when I drove home after our celebrations on Friday . . .'

When it was told Stephen said: 'Perhaps it would have been better if I had known all this before. For I have found your Charles Mason.'

'What? Did you say . . .?'

'He came to the Blue Peter last night. Henry rang you and could not find you, so he rang me, so I went along to the club and met him. Witold and I.'

'I'm damned. What did you say to him?'

'Not very much. What could I say? I did not know enough. We – exchanged words . . . and I did not at all like him. Then we followed him out of the club and offered to see him home.'

'You . . .'

'He did not appreciate this, and unfortunately was aided by two of your military policemen to whom he appealed and who took his side.'

Andrew shook the telephone. 'Hullo . . . You don't know where he lives, then?'

'Alas no. He went off in a taxi. But we have one valuable clue. Do you know a pretty young blonde called Dot Forrest?'

'No.'

'In the club I hear Mason making an appointment to take her to the theatre tomorrow evening. They are to meet at the Apollo Theatre in Shaftesbury Avenue at 5 o'clock.'

'Tomorrow?'

'Tomorrow. I thought if he could be picked up there he could be followed home. If he has a fancy for killing young ladies he may have such designs on this Dot Forrest girl.'

Andrew stared at the advertisements in the telephone booth. 'Stephen, this chap Mason presumably knows you and Witold well enough by sight now. Can you possibly follow him without being spotted?'

'I have thought of that. Do you know Eric Morsztyn?'

'Vaguely. Wasn't he in 303 Squadron?'

'As a fitter, that is so. But he led a different life before the war – he was in the Polish secret police. Oh, yes, we had them – Colonel Beck was no angel. Eric is on leave; I saw him in the forces club on Thursday. I think he would help.'

'He'd know Mason from your description?'

'Oh yes. And the girl. Together they would be unmissable. I think he could follow them, unnoticed.'

'Well, then. I'll leave that to you. Thank you for all your help. And Stephen.'

'Yes?'

'I have something else to tell you. Jennifer has seen a woman in the hotel and she is wearing a cameo brooch which she is certain is the same as the one the man gave as a present to the girl he murdered. This woman is spending the weekend here with a chap called Filey. We know no more. But if it *is* the same brooch – Jennifer swears it is – then *this* may be the man we want, not Charles Mason at all. I think we have to keep an open mind.'

'OK. Morsztyn will do nothing except find out where he lives.'

'You know my leave ends tomorrow. Yours goes on?'

'Don't remind me. Only until Thursday.'

'I'll ring you sometime tomorrow. It might be in the evening. If you're not in, I'll leave a number where you can ring me back.'

'OK. OK.'

'And thanks again, Stephen.'

Monday Afternoon

I

Actually the VAD girl had had no dire warnings to utter, but the knee was puffy and obviously painful. He could, he supposed, have taken Jennifer home by taxi and train, but a day's rest was a simple solution.

So he went to Birmingham on his own.

Before that a policeman on a bicycle had called and taken particulars of yesterday's accident, and after he had spoken to Radziwill Andrew rang his mother and talked to her for half an hour before setting off.

In fact it was not as difficult as he had expected to find Newmarket Street: a taxi took him direct from Snow Hill. It was on a slope, and No 2 was at the lower end. A shop. This was a poor district with rows of houses in dark brick channels and factory chimneys as sentinels in the distance.

A bell tinged as he pushed open the door. It was a little newsagent's and general store. Sloping shelves carried the newspapers and the cheap weekly magazines; beyond was a dusty, brown-paper-backed lending library; on the counter were clutches of patent medicines and bottles which in peace-time had held boiled sweets; there were socks and handker-chiefs and boot-laces, and above them cards of pencils and india-rubbers and a stained fly-paper still twirling gently in the breeze from the opened door.

A woman came slowly out from the darkness of the room behind. She was old and tall.

'Yes?'

He asked for a pencil. It must be copying-ink. She scrabbled in a box and found one. It was the best she'd got. They weren't making any more like it now.

He could see he hadn't to look any further for the Aunt Nell of the letter. In spite of the broad Midland accent she was not of English descent. She might have been Marlene Dietrich's grandmother.

He paid for the pencil and she gave him the change.

He said: 'I wonder if I could have a word with you in private. I have news for you about Paula.'

The flint-grey eyes flickered.

'I don't know what you mean. Is there anythink more I can sell you?'

'Aren't you Aunt Nell?' he asked.

'My name's Mrs Cromer.'

'I came with a message about Paula Krissen. She's your niece, isn't she?'

'Well?'

For once he wished he was in uniform; it spoke for itself.

'Is there somewhere to talk where we shan't be interrupted?'

She moved one or two bottles around on the counter as if in an intricate but rapid game of chess. She had close-cut, chalky fingernails.

'What's Paula to you?'

'Nothing. I met her – once. But I have news you ought to hear.'

'Did she send you?'

'No. But I have your last letter to her.' The crumpled envelope was passed across the counter. Fingers rustled over the paper.

The lined and faded face, with its wide mouth and high cheek bones and prominent convex forehead, was turned away from him.

'Very well. Come inside.'

II

He remembered afterwards the old-fashioned, overcrowded room with the bone button of the faded blind tapping against the inch-open casement window. That and the kettle singing on the black-leaded open hob, and the smell of cabbage water and bread and dust and stationery. He sat on a Victorian couch whose springs were making grey knuckles in the black horsehair cover; she on the edge of the matching armchair opposite, her face in the shadow while she waited for him to speak.

There might have been kinder ways of going about it, but he didn't find them; and the fact that she was so mistrustful of his motives seemed to make a direct announcement the only way to get under her guard.

It did; but at first he thought the news he brought was only going to make her more tight-lipped and rigid than ever. But as he went on with his tale, telling her everything just as it had happened, he could see her attitude changing. Fear emerged as an alloy in the shock and grief. The first signs that she was going to talk came slowly and reluctantly.

'I didn't think they meant it,' she whispered, and then later: 'Not that way. I told her not to take no more notice of them.' And: 'What've they got, treating her that way . . .'

It was good that he was nothing to do with the police; at any sign of authority she'd have clammed up again. At first she spoke in whispers he could hardly hear, but as she went on her voice grew clearer with a secret desire for revenge, a half suppressed wish to hit back overcoming her fear for her own safety. So it came out, halting, disjointed, while the button of the blind tap-tapped the seconds away.

Afterwards he thought he ought to have known it. Perhaps he'd been fumbling his way towards the truth, and Helen Cromer's dusty confidences only confirmed what he'd begun to suspect. How many spies and fifth columnists, he wondered, had been recruited in the same way as Paula Krissen?

To Aunt Nell, half English by birth and widow of an Englishman, the greater risk when Paula had told her about it had seemed the Old Bailey or the Tower of London for any fatal slip she might make, not the hidden threats of the agents of a rogue nation she hadn't visited for forty-five years. She'd told Paula so and now regretted it. Distant relatives had suffered – of course she knew that – but this was England not Germany, and the longest fingers of danger lay in the Heinkel and the Dornier, not in the SS or the Gestapo. The safety of cousins, like Kurt and Emmy Rusman in Dusseldorf, didn't justify the risking of one's own life and the betrayal of one's own country.

It was of course easy to see why Paula Krissen had been a target. Attractive, vivacious, on and off the stage, in and out of night-clubs, lots of men friends, always meeting someone fresh, not hedged about with tiresome moral prejudices, always short of money, warm-hearted, easy-come, easy-go. Bribery and threats, that was the mixture. What proportion of each? Aunt Nell thought it was all because of Paula's German relations, like keeping Frederick out of a concentration camp. Andrew suspected that the money had been an equal inducement.

Though, to give Paula credit, it seemed it had not been enough in the end.

III

Hell getting back to Marley Manor. Train and train and train and bus: times never seemed to fit. Cool your heels at Stratford and at Repington, cursing the waste of the last free day. Up to now he'd thoroughly enjoyed his leave but today was a bore.

He'd bought a newspaper in Birmingham and read it on the way home. Better news for a change. A British fleet had destroyed a large Italian fleet off a place called Cape Matapan. The Americans had reduced the manufacture of cars and lorries by a million in order to build 3000 heavy bombers for

Great Britain. President Roosevelt had said he did not think public opinion in the US was yet adequately aware of the crisis and its likely impact upon them. American warships were on a good-will visit to Sydney. All the same, Greece was collapsing. The Balkans were lost. Heavy bombing of Belfast and Plymouth. Milk supplies were to be further cut. When he got to the next change he screwed the paper up and left it in a waste bin.

Fuming on stations and in slow rattling trains, he thought of his beloved car, now a twisted wreck. With a car everything could be done in a quarter of the time. Without it you were a lame duck. Flight at speeds not far short of sound; whirring along roads at a lot more than a mile a minute; then walking at four miles an hour or sitting in public transport that didn't seem to go much faster.

Jennifer. And Jennifer sitting up in bed, slenderly naked to the waist but because of her innocence untakeable. Paula with the dreadful eyes and the bloodstains round her mouth and ears, and the very first staggeringly awful creeping smell of corruption. Witold and Stephen in London, finding and losing Charles Mason. Two men in a large black Buick casually, deliberately forcing him off the road. His mother's voice this morning trying not to sound anxious, trying not to sound hurt. Excuses, excuses, my car has broken down. There'll probably be another weekend at the end of the month, I'll come straight over then. The woman with the hard Midland accent and the Teutonic face, the rusty hesitant voice, half vindictive, half afraid, jumping once when the shop-doorbell went, shuffling out and shuffling back, taking the singing kettle off the hob, saying: 'She was changing her mind when she come to see me at Christmas. Said she was going to do no more. She'd been all through the bombing by then. It made a difference to her feelings.'

And the smell of old vegetables and dusty furniture and printer's ink and warm bread. And the chalky finger-nails. That day when the fog came down and you were running out of petrol and there wasn't anywhere to land. Disembodied.

Hardly sure whether you were right side up. 'As Flight Commander on the operation in which your son Henry was shot down over the sea, I am writing to you personally to express my deepest sympathy but also to express the hope . . .' Why has this damned train stopped again? And Jennifer. Thin Jennifer. Not so thin Jennifer. He could feel her body in his hands, like silk but exquisitely better than any silk. 'Things haven't been too good with B Flight recently; Millington was an unsettling influence. Now you are back . . .' Posted missing. Posted missing. Patrolling over the Channel and chasing a Blenheim by mistake. Damn this train. Wonder if there'll be a taxi at the station.

IV

She was waiting for him in the foyer of the hotel.

'I thought you'd missed your train,' smiling her quick-silver smile.

'I had.'

He sat beside her on the settee, suddenly glad after all to be back, to resume something which had broken off this morning.

'Did you find Aunt Nell?'

'In person.'

'Did she talk?'

'She talked.'

He told her all he knew while her fingers moved up and down the corded velvet of the settee and her brilliant eyes clouded at his tale.

He said: 'According to Aunt Nell, Paula had been at this for some time, but it was only in October that she began to kick. She'd been happy-go-lucky about the war till then, and had been too interested in her own life to take sides with any passion; but the bombing of London began to change her feelings, and then a couple of officer friends of hers who'd confided minor secrets to her lost their lives, she said, and she was uneasy as to whether she might be to blame. So she decided to draw out and then found she couldn't. But each time she did anything for them she did it more reluctantly than the last. She even said to Aunt Nell that she was thinking of going to the police and telling them everything she knew, and bad luck to her cousins.'

'D'you think she meant that?'

'Aunt Nell said no. But even if it was there as a possibility she became dangerous to the people who were in contact with her – if they suspected it, and they clearly did.'

She rubbed her knee and he made an inquiring gesture but she said: 'No, it's *much* better. I went for a short hobble this afternoon.'

'Did you see anything of the Fileys?'

'I'll tell you in a moment. But was that all that Aunt Nell said?'

'Unfortunately she hadn't heard from Paula since Christmas. Paula didn't answer her letter. So we're not much further advanced except as to motive.'

'I never thought of her in that way. A sort of love crime seemed so much more natural for her. And she was always saying she hated the Nazis . . .'

'Perhaps she did.'

'But she would say it, wouldn't she, if she was working for them. My God!'

'What is it?'

Colour crept into her face. 'Well, when you come to think of it . . . My friend Christopher Watson – he's about thirty-eight and quite well up in the Foreign Office. A friend of Paula's. Has he given anything away? . . . And it was when Paula knew I worked for Beaufort's, and I probably said they did Government printing for various Ministries, that she said come and share a flat with me.'

'Did you talk to her about your work?'

'I could have.'

'Was any of it classified stuff?'

'Not much. But some. Yes, we talked. One doesn't think . . .'

After a moment he said: 'It's spilt milk. There's nothing to be done now.'

'Except shovel this all over to the police as quickly as possible.'

The dinner gong went. One or two people, who had obviously been waiting around for the summons, drifted off.

'You say you saw the Fileys?'

'I saw *her* – spoke to her . . .' Jennifer glanced round to see no one was near. The flickering light from the artificial fire made her look briefly translucent. 'They'd stuck together all day, but just after tea he went off – left her on her own. I dropped my bag as I was passing and we said a few words. I said – I told her about my knee – said I'd sprained it climbing a fence. It was a useful way to open the conversation.'

'Did it get anywhere?'

'She says they're just married. Honeymoon, in fact. He works for Fordham, making tanks and light carriers. After a bit, I admired her brooch. She said it was a wedding present. I made one or two nice remarks about it, and then said, I hope someone will give me something as nice as that for *my* wedding, and she said it was from her brother.'

'Sometimes people say brothers when they mean lovers.'

'A boyfriend called Charles Mason, for instance?'

'Yes. Well, Paula had no further use for it. Wasn't that how we were reasoning?'

She winced. 'Now that I've started I can't stop speculating.

'Did the Filey woman give you the impression that she was interested in you? Or suspicious of your questions?'

'Not a bit. Very casual. Easy. Frank.'

'Thing is, what more can we do?'

'Their room is on the first floor, Number 18. While they were out I was tempted to slip in, look around, but I funked it.'

'Could you have?'

'Probably not. But their door is the same as ours on the

next floor – they don't automatically lock when you shut them.'

He said: 'You're putting ideas in my head.'

She was silent a while, rubbed her fingers through her fringe. 'I feel so humiliated about what I may have told Paula. I want to hit back in some way. I could kick myself.'

He said: 'Let's eat. I only had a beer and a sandwich for lunch.'

The Fileys were already in the dining room. Madame was wearing her cameo again and talking vigorously to her husband. Her skirt was too tight for her, and Arthur Filey was appreciating the fact.

Andrew said: 'Shall I go upstairs and look now?'

Jennifer looked startled: 'Are you serious?'

'Never more so. Our investigations haven't met with a great deal of success. One might as well go out with a bang.'

'It depends what you mean by a bang. Anyway, don't people usually lock their doors when they come down to dinner?'

'It would be a complication. I had all my best jemmies destroyed in an air raid.'

'Besides . . .'

'What?'

'That bag she's carrying. If there were any secrets they'd be in there, wouldn't they.'

'Her secrets, yes. What about his? Making tanks and carriers? There could be a connection. As you say, once the speculations start, there's no stopping 'em.'

They ate for a while in silence. The embarrassments of last night were not forgotten but they had slipped into the background. All through their time together, except for the one break, they had been able to sublimate their interest in each other by directing their attention towards Paula and the mystery of her death. Only occasionally she looked at him and thought, oh, my God, I'm really in love with him, what can I do? And only occasionally he glanced up at her and wished instead of the knife and fork in his hand he could feel her incredible skin.

He said: 'Shall we try?'

'What?'

'To get in their room. It probably won't work out, but shall we try?'

Her heart began to beat, as if he had made some sexual suggestion.

'If you say so.'

'Why not?'

'All right,' she said. 'Let's try.'

V

Mr and Mrs Filey went up to their bedroom twice after dinner but each time came down key in hand. Andrew prowled round the outside of the hotel, but there were no convenient balconies or drain-pipes. There wasn't even ivy, only Virginia creeper, which could hardly have supported a bush-baby.

Andrew rang home again and this time had a long chat with his father. It eased his conscience. He also rang his squadron and had a few words with Group Captain Quinton. Quinton said he was looking forward to seeing Andrew tomorrow night; there were several matters he'd like to discuss. Andrew hung up, wondering why he'd bothered. Had he supposed in starry-eyed disregard of all he knew, that Quinton would say: 'Nothing important here, old boy; war's in a temporary lull; like another couple of days off?'

At ten o'clock Mr and Mrs Filey went to the bar and ordered champagne cocktails. Mrs Filey was slightly hilarious and Filey perched on a stool opposite her, pink in the face, putting a finger inside his collar from time to time where it rubbed his neck. He found his wife very exciting.

A few minutes later Jennifer, who had been at the bar, slid into the seat next to Andrew.

'They're going to bed soon. I heard her say she wanted to take a bath, and he said he'd walk down to the river to get a breath of air. In that case she's bound to leave the door unlocked.'

'Haven't they a private bathroom?'

'No, the hotel's pretty short of them. There's only four marked with stars on the board. The bathroom is on the opposite side of the corridor.'

'How long does it take a woman to have a bath?'

'Fifteen minutes at least. I can slip up and if I'm caught I can pretend I've opened the wrong door.'

'Oh no, you can't. This is my pigeon. You stay here.'

She touched his hand. 'I can't! I can't just *sit* here! I'll come with you.'

'It doubles the risk. D'you know what you could do?'

'What?'

'Watch for Filey. If he comes back before I've finished, hit the dinner gong.'

She looked at him wide-eyed. 'Hard?'

'Hard enough for me to hear. Say you did it by mistake.'

She giggled, but there was more tension in it that fun.

'All right. Take care. And good luck.'

They waited until the Fileys had separated, then after a couple of minutes Andrew sauntered up the stairs after the bride.

Jennifer watched him out of sight, then stood up and limped to a seat near the dinner gong. She felt hideously uneasy. Even if yesterday's attempt on their lives had not made it clear whom they were dealing with, the news Andrew brought back from Birmingham left no doubts at all. They were not confronting one person, nor even a group of ordinary criminals. With espionage it was kill or be killed, no quarter asked or given. Paula had become unsafe and had been rubbed out. Yesterday a clumsy attempt had been made to silence them. If one or both of the Fileys were implicated and Andrew was caught searching their belongings he could quickly find himself facing a gun.

She bit at her thumb and waited.

Monday Evening

I

Jennifer was right in most of her estimates. Andrew hung about admiring one of the potted palms and only had to wait two or three minutes before Hilda Filey left her bedroom in a peach silk dressing-gown and crossed the corridor to the bathroom, which was opposite, and went in. The bolt clicked home. Andrew walked slowly down the passage looking at his wrist watch. Give her at least three minutes to be sure she hadn't forgotten her bath-essence or her talcum powder. He went to the end of the passage, which had a small window at the end, heavily curtained. He adjusted the black-out and came back. The sound of water running as he passed the bathroom door. Walk as far as the head of the stairs again. He could just see Jennifer's bright head, her taut figure. She shouldn't look so tense.

Back again, try the door of No 18. It opened. Well, well.

The light he switched on showed an oblong room with a divan double-bed and modern off-white furnishings. Three pictures of hunting scenes with lots of men in scarlet coats; a gilt-edged mirror reflecting the walnut wardrobe. Two new suitcases on a folding trestle, a hat box, a valise, a shirt hanging over a chair back, some shoes on a rack, her bag on a chair by the bed.

There isn't time to be careful: open her bag, empty it on the bed. Two letters, a postcard, lots of papers with scribbled notes, some sort of a prescription, a driving licence in the name of Hilda Baker, identity card with the same name, a note case with six pounds ten shillings, kirby grips, compact, lipstick, cigarette case, pills, laxative tablets, nail scissors, a comb, a blue enamel cigarette lighter. Feel all round the bag for hidden pockets, then shove back the things you don't want, keeping only letters, postcard, bits of paper.

Cameo was on the dressing-table, along with a couple of cheap rings. Pick up the cameo, turn it over, nothing to relate it to anything; funny if Jennifer was mistaken and all this was wildly wasted effort and unnecessary risk. He'd be had up for petty theft.

Cases were unpacked, only a few articles of underclothing left in them. The valise with a couple of used collars, a packet of contraceptives, a check cap, a camera — this a 2A Kodak with an F7 lens and nothing exceptional about it. One used spool, which he pocketed.

Drawers next. Clean shirts, cami knickers, pyjamas, vests, stockings. He put his hand into the backs of the drawers but there was nothing hidden. He tried to leave things as he had found them; you couldn't know how fussy she was — or he was — and would or would not notice disturbance.

Books by the bed. Edgar Wallace, Phillips Oppenheim, a book with a brown paper cover called *Wedded Love*. Shake them all: no bookmarks or leaflets.

In the wardrobe a man's overcoat, two suits. One suit had a couple of letters. Her overcoat with a bit of fur round the collar and cuffs. Tailored suit, with pocket; in the pocket a handkerchief stained with lipstick, a marriage licence. So all genuine and above board. 'St Thomas's, Wolverhampton. Arthur James Filey, Engineer. Hilda Mary Baker, Saleswoman.' That covered a lot. Were the addresses worth taking down? He took out his pocket book and copied them in. Then as he put the certificate back he heard footsteps come to a stop before the door.

No time to reach the electric switch. Two swift steps to the dressing table, reach up and take the bulb out. Light flicked away from the room as the door opened.

Hilda Mary Filey, saleswoman, silhouetted, in her dressing-gown, hair tied in bandeau as he had last seen her.

The light from the passage threw her shadow into the room. A clicking of the switch.

'Oh, blast,' she said, coming in and pushing the door half shut behind her with her foot.

The bulb was burning his fingers, was burning . . . He put it down on the dressing-table. The glass made a tiny *tic-tac* sound on the polished wood.

She turned. 'That you, sweetie?'

'Uh-huh,' said Andrew.

'You old silly; that impatient. You said you'd be twenty minutes.' She put her fingers to her mouth. 'Pardon. What's the matter with the darned bulb? I'm not even dry yet. Came straight out to be here before you.'

Andrew moved a few inches towards the door. But she was blocking the way.

She said: 'Has the bedside light gone as well? Really, these hotels.' She hiccuped. 'Oh, pardon.'

'Uh-huh,' said Andrew.

She came towards him. 'I'm still damp, Arty, darling. See.'

She slipped out of her dressing-gown. He could see the pale gleam of her skin.

'Kiss me,' she said.

It was an invitation no reasonable man would see his way to refuse.

When he released her she drew a deep breath and uttered the most piercing scream he had ever heard.

He grasped her bare arm. 'Shut up, you fool! I've a message for you.'

She screamed again, with the sheerest outrage.

'A message from your *brother*,' he hissed. 'From *them*. They – we want you to do a job for us.'

She screamed a shade less fiercely. However, the damage was done. When she drew breath, voices and footsteps could be heard.

'All right,' he said. 'Rouse the place! It'll be the worse for you . . .'

He made for the door and went out. In the passage he

134

came face to face with a sturdy young man in a stiff collar.

Andrew moved past. His arm was seized.

'What the *hell* are you doing in my bedroom?'

'Your wife. She's having hysterics. I heard her and went in. We ought to get a doctor.'

'Hilda!' said Filey. 'How could she? I only left her a few minutes ago . . . Hilda!'

She had appeared in the doorway but had had the forethought to replace her dressing-gown. Her eyes flickered from one man to the other. Split second decisions were in conflict.

'That's him!' she shouted to Arthur. 'That's the man! He was in our room!'

The manager and a chambermaid had appeared at the end of the corridor, and another guest had put his head out of a door.

'What is it, Hilda? Tell me – '

'He was hiding in the room. I just came back and, and –'

'You damned skunk!'

'Absolute rot!' Andrew said. 'I went in – '

'God, I nearly died! I thought it was you, Arthur – '

'Sh,' the manager said. 'Sh, madam. Can we keep our voices down. I'm sure this is an unfortunate – '

'I went into the bedroom by mistake,' said Andrew. 'Quite an accident. For Heaven's sake, I'm sorry; the corridor was dark. These things happen – '

Filey said: 'You've no *right* in other people's bedrooms. Is anything missing, Hilda?'

'I can't see. The light had fused – '

'I've no *wish* to go into other people's bedrooms,' Andrew snapped. 'Let go of my arm!'

'Squadron Leader, please,' said the manager, rubbing his knuckles. 'Mr – r – Filey, I'm sure it's all a misunderstanding. These things can happen. It's always wiser, of course, to lock one's doors.'

Filey let go. The rank of the man whose arm he was grasping had had some effect, and Hilda, although a bit fuddled, was cooling down. It remained for her, of course, to spike Andrew's explanation and start off the commotion afresh. But she said nothing more and simply stood there holding the dressing-gown to her throat and glaring.

'Well, well,' said the manager. 'An unfortunate little storm in a tea-cup, what? An easy mistake and a very natural alarm on the lady's part. I'm sure the Squadron Leader didn't intend to frighten you, Mrs Filey. I hope you'll accept his apologies and consider the matter closed.'

'Well . . .' said Hilda.

'You'd best be more careful in future!' said Filey. 'You fellows in the Air Force seem to think you can do anything you please! Sure you're all right, Hilda?'

'Well, yes . . .' said Hilda.

'Come along in, then. You don't want to catch cold . . .'

The bedroom door closed behind them. The chambermaid moved away, the other disturbed guest had withdrawn his head. Andrew walked down the passage with the manager.

Sweat on your hands, round your collar. Take out a handkerchief and dab your forehead.

'I didn't mention it at the time,' said the manager, 'as I did not wish to make any more trouble for you, Squadron Leader. But as you know, as we both know, your bedroom is on the next floor and in the opposite direction.'

'Quite true.'

'So a word of explanation would not, I think, be out of place.'

'The girl's an awful little tart,' said Andrew. 'She's been making eyes at me ever since we came.'

Jennifer was at the foot of the stairs as they began to walk down.

'In that case,' said the manager, 'why did she scream?'

Andrew put away his handkerchief. 'Good God, man, have you no imagination?'

II

'I feel sure,' said Jennifer, 'that the whole incident must have distressed you even more than you say.'

'Irony,' said Andrew, 'is a bit out of place. And what about the gong?'

'I hit it *three times*. It made a ghastly row. The receptionist came out and snatched the hammer from me. Didn't you *hear* it?'

'No.'

'You must have been deeply engaged.'

He glanced at her, half in comic reproof, half in irritation. All right, he had done his best and it had turned into a stupid bedroom farce: was that his fault? *Yes*, to some extent. But would the woman have screamed any less loudly if he had *not* embraced her? (Probably he had been a fool to tell Jennifer as much as he had, but less, in view of the pandemonium, would hardly have been believable.) *Nothing* had been proved by the adventure, nothing disproved. Husband and wife had behaved in all innocence as an aggrieved husband and wife might be expected to. Except that after the initial outburst – which for God's sake had been piercing enough – Hilda had not accused him in the way she might have. Had his whispered words brought some late caution? If so, it was the only incriminating incident, and by its nature was too vague to build on.

'So what did you find?' she said.

They had gone up to his bedroom, and he pulled out the few bits of paper he had taken during the search. The postcard was from Eire and was from a man called Joe saying how much he was appreciating the lights of Dublin.

One of the letters read: 'Dear Hilda, I'm ever so sorry I can't get to your wedding, but you know, dear, the doctor says not to get up yet so accept this £1 note and I hope you will buy something handy with it. Give my best love to Arthur who I hope to meet sometime and I hope you will be very happy. Mary says you will be comfortable off so that's an important point. You may not think so, dear, but it is. D'you remember Madge and John Dawson that were killed in the Coventry raids? Their two little boys have come to live with their auntie next door but one from us. I will close now with my best love to Mum and all. Your affectionately, Aunt Ida. PS. What is Louis doing now?'

Jennifer was sorting through the bits of paper. One was a shopping list, another a receipt for shoe repairs, on the back of which Hilda had been adding up her expenses. There was a newspaper clipping of Births, Marriages and Deaths; a cloakroom ticket for the Blue Moon Palais de Danse; a memo paper with three telephone numbers. The other letter was an account-rendered for underclothes.

Andrew said: 'I'll have the photos developed, but I expect they'll be snaps of the wedding. These letters of his are valueless . . . What next?'

'D'you think they'll know their things have been searched?'

'They'll surely miss the letters.' As he dropped the papers on the dressing-table he made a disclaiming gesture. 'It was a good idea but a hell of a flop. Never mind.'

She was trying to make the bandage round her knee more comfortable. Hair hid her face and her expression.

He said: 'At least we weren't turned out of the hotel . . . Can you travel tomorrow?'

'Oh yes, thanks, it's tons better tonight. What time does your leave end?'

'Eighteen-thirty. Before that I'll go to the police alone.'

'Why alone?'

'It's my responsibility.'

'I don't see that.'

'I found Paula. I've been cheating on them for three days.'

'Paula was my friend. I shared a flat with her.'

'That's more or less incidental.'

'What happened since hasn't been incidental!'

'Quite so . . . Well, let's see how it goes. I have a feeling

138

that if the police see us together they may think we have
been off on a weekend and have not taken it seriously.'

She suddenly found herself weary. She was drained of
initiative and anxious to be gone. Like a trespasser caught in
a barbed-wire fence, she was anxious to free herself with the
least hurt and the least fuss.

'Perhaps the police will make a better job of it than we
have,' she said, 'but I'm sure they won't have half the fun.
Thanks, Andrew. Good night.'

After a brief hesitation, he kissed her. But there was none
of the latent passion of last night. They had withdrawn
from each other. Her rejection of last night had begun the
withdrawal, and nothing today had brought them as close
again. Their sour exchange of views this morning over breakfast, their meeting when he came back from Birmingham,
then this. Of course it had been a mistake to kiss Hilda Filey
either dressed or undressed. It probably made him seem both
sexy and trivial-minded, so that she related his behaviour
with Hilda Filey tonight with his behaviour towards her last
night.

But *surely*, surely, any numbskull of a girl with any
discrimination, any sense at *all*, would see, must see that his
lark with Mrs Filey had *nothing whatever* to do with his
feelings towards *her*. Hadn't he made it clear, surely to God
he had made it clear beyond all shadow of doubt that he was
taken with her, enormously taken with her, desperately,
deeply taken with her?

Yet in that brief embrace before they separated, such is
the perverseness of human nature that he found her only
marginally attractive to him.

She slipped out through the connecting door. The press of
her shoulders against his palms and the faint taste of her lips
and skin was all that was left.

Monday Evening – Two

I

At eight-thirty pm on the Piccadilly platform of the Elephant-and-Castle to Harrow-and-Wealdstone Underground line, on a seat framed in tiers of as-yet-unoccupied bunks, two men were waiting for a train. On other parts of the platfrom, away from the worst draughts of train and stairs, habitué shelterers were settling down for the night in a certain amount of comfort and in comparative safety, since this was one of the deepest of the tubes. But no one as yet was within hearing distance of the conversation of the two men.

Gissing W, alias Armitage H, in conference again with Louis Baker.

'It's no good!' Louis said in a vehement undertone. 'It's *off*! Out of the question.'

Gissing waited patiently. 'I warned you, Louis. I warned you yesterday. I said there might still be things for you to do.'

'Things for me to *do*!'

'Loose ends to be tidied up. Loose ends for which you were responsible.'

'*How* am I responsible? I tell you I'll not do it! You can take back your award! What do you think I am?'

'Two things. A patriot. And a sensible man.'

'Sensible man! Good God! . . . Anyway, it may not be possible. I think I've been followed.'

'What?' Gissing glanced quickly around. 'Here?'

'No. Last night.'

'When? How did it come about?'

'I was in the Blue Peter – the club in Berkeley Square. Two Polish officers tried to strike up a friendship with me. Then they tried to follow me home.'

'What sort of officers? Naval? Army?'

'Air Force.'

Gissing was thoughtful for a moment. He hitched up the rather greasy collar of his overcoat as if at a sudden draught. 'Did they succeed in following you?'

'No – I got in a taxi, left them in Piccadilly.'

'So what is the problem?'

'I'm sure they suspected something.'

'Why should they? What did they say?'

'Nothing much. It was their manner – insulting and insinuating, as if they knew something about me.'

Silence fell between them as a group of elderly people carrying blankets and thermos flasks passed them on their way down the platform. Grey, orderly, shuffling, nondescript.

Louis said: 'The taxi driver wanted to know my address before he'd take me. The Poles were pressing behind me. So I gave a false address in case they should overhear.'

'Good . . . So there is no real obstacle to your obeying the order if it comes through.'

'Christ, I think there's every obstacle! You don't know what you're asking! I don't even know what the girl looks like!'

'We have a photograph. You will have no difficulty.'

Louis took out a handkerchief and wiped his forehead. 'When d'you suppose I may be asked to do this?'

'Probably tomorrow. If – '

'*Tomorrow*. Christ, it's not a week since last time! Only a week tomorrow! Only a *week*!'

'Control your voice. Remember what I said. If you do this for us you will be acting as a patriot . . . And it will also be sensible because you will be acting not only for the cause but for your own self-preservation.'

Louis laughed. 'Have you any *idea*? Sometimes I think orders come from above and they haven't any *idea*. D'you think it's done like stamping on a beetle or drowning a kitten?'

'Ober-Leutnant, you are forgetting yourself – '

' – And another woman at that! No, by God, I'll swing first!'

'You will certainly swing if you lose your courage. She'll show you no mercy in giving you away to the police. Women have a strong sense of duty.'

'Then why hasn't she been to the police already?'

Gissing fanned his face with his hand, as if dismissing objections. 'At first she did not know of Paula Krissen's death. It appears this young airman told her. But she became infatuated with him and they have spent the weekend together.'

'So it's this airman who found Paula? It was Polish *airmen* who challenged me last night.'

'I am sure that is nothing more than a coincidence,' Gissing said hardily.

'They did mention some other man's name, these Poles,' said Louis, 'but I've forgotten it. Hardingham, I think . . . Anyway, how do we know how much this girl knows? How can you be sure what Paula told her?'

'We can't. But we have to be sure that she does not have an opportunity to pass it on.'

The platform was beginning to fill up with ordinary travellers. People walked past them with the slow, repressed gait of expectant passengers. A rumbling in the distance.

'How much she has by now told the airman,' Gissing said, 'is a matter of conjecture. But he can be dealt with.'

'You'll – '

'If necessary, yes. Provided you do your part.'

Warm air wafted in their faces, preceding a train grumbling in on the opposite platform.

'My part,' muttered Louis.

'What she has told him is probably unimportant, and he

won't have the sense or the knowledge to make anything of it. But as soon as the police know of this they will send expert interviewers from MI5 who will probe every conversation she ever had. Almost sub-consciously she will have retained things in her memory. I know. And Paula Krissen unfortunately knew too much.'

'So I gather,' Louis said bitterly.

'It was a grave oversight on our part that she was allowed to make contact with two of our principals. If their names, or even descriptions . . . It might result not merely in the loss of valuable men but in the crippling of a network that we have been a long time building up. It would be impossible to replace it at short notice and in time of war.'

'Well,' said Louis, 'let those who made the mistakes clear up the mess. Not me.'

'They have tried and failed.'

'What d'you mean?'

'An attempt was made yesterday to clean it up, but it was not successful. We are fortunate to have been given a second chance. Halford and Ward should have gone to the police first thing this morning.'

'How d'you know they haven't?'

'They haven't. So the opportunity of being of signal service to the Fatherland comes to you again. I must say I am rather astonished, in view of the decoration I have brought you tonight . . . Success for you at this stage means everything. By refusing now, by turning tail, you destroy your chances.'

Louis lit a cigarette, and a cloud of the smoke moved erratically away. An irritable smile came and went on his face.

'Think what you're asking me to do. Just think of it, Mr Armitage.'

'Cowardice never lacked excuses – '

'Cowardice be damned! I've given you proof enough – '

'And this is war!' snapped Gissing, showing his discoloured teeth. 'Total war demands sacrifices of us all. If you were an airman who had performed one brave deed, would you expect to be excused from being set to another? If a man proves an adept at dismantling live bombs he is put to it again and again!'

'And I am put to the disposal of – '

'Yes, as many a good man has done before you – and that without the added spur of self-preservation. You are being asked – indeed commanded – to perform this act in the highest interests of the Führer and the State! Heavens, man, by Wednesday it will all be finished and done with!'

'By Wednesday! My God! You're asking me to rush in – '

'This time there is urgency.'

Louis took a deep breath and sucked at his bottom lip. 'Urgency. So no time for preparation, eh? And if it's all done in too much of a hurry and things go wrong, I shall be caught! The laws of England still operate, Mr Armitage. Murder's a capital offence. It won't be any good to me if the war is over next year and I'm six feet underground!'

'I quite agree. It is a risk our soldiers and sailors and airmen take every day of their lives.' Gissing took out a silk handkerchief and dabbed his upper lip, dabbing away the anger that he should not have shown. 'I sometimes wonder about your ancestry, Baker. Your grandfather – your great-grandfather . . .'

'My great-grandfather didn't have to do what I've had to do!'

'And d'you think he would have refused if those had been his instructions?'

There was a subterranean murmuring and muttering in the distance. People stirred on the platform like foliage expecting a wind.

In a much more even voice Gissing said: 'I don't know if you know this, Louis. Not many people in England do. In the early summer of last year, the American Ambassador to Great Britain, Joseph Kennedy, called together a press conference of neutral journalists and told them Hitler would be in London by August 15. That shows what the Americans think of the chance of British survival!'

'But he was wrong!'

'He was wrong – by perhaps a year. But ask any neutral now, any detached observer, and they will all tell you the same – that the Führer will be in London by August 15 of *this* year, there or thereabouts. There is *no* way, simply no way, this island on its own can last very much longer. Just look at a map of the world and see for yourself . . . So we must make preparations accordingly.'

'Preparations,' said Louis, and there was a long silence between them.

Gissing said: 'The girl spent last night out of London and my latest information is that she will do so again tonight. Almost certainly she will return to London tomorrow. There will be a blitz tomorrow night. It isn't necessary for me to tell you where her flat is, but you must leave me with *exact* details as to where you will be tomorrow so that we can make contact with you. Are you working?'

'I'm due at Ferguson's to do my morning stint servicing army radios. In the afternoon I shall put in an hour or so at Ludgrove's. In the evening . . .' He stopped.

'Well?'

'In the evening,' Louis said sulkily, 'I'm taking someone out.'

'Cancel that. Be at some point where we can be sure of finding you. If this is to take place, this thing, it will be in the evening, after dark, to give you the maximum security.'

'How do I know this girl will be alone?'

'You will not be asked to do this if she is not. That is one reason why the decision will not be taken until late. You'd better be home by eight. You'll not be telephoned. A messenger will come.'

Louis bit at his bottom lip. 'I'll have to tell this girl – this other girl – make some excuse.'

'Where were you going?'

'To the theatre.'

'What time? When will the programme finish?'

'Eight o'clock or eight-thirty. They're all timed to end before black-out.'

'Perhaps it's good that you go with this girl after all. As I have always said, it's important to lead as normal a life as possible. If word comes through that you are to do what you have to do we will get a message to you at the theatre. What theatre is it?'

'The Apollo, Shaftesbury Avenue.'

'Is this girl you are seeing just a casual acquaintance?'

'Fairly, yes.'

'If word comes through you will have to leave her directly afterwards. You will make what excuse you can.'

'Christ Almighty,' Louis muttered.

They sat there for a couple of minutes, in a sour companionship of conspiracy and distrust – the one coatless and hatless, gauntly strong, one big hand rubbing at the bristle on his face, the other man, in homburg hat and overcoat, his toes just touching the platform, like a smooth black bear. The enormity of what they planned had somehow become half submerged in the planning. Louis had always believed in the survival of the fittest, and in ordinary circumstances would have felt little more than contempt for a man such as this one beside him. But the man beside him stood for liberation in the most positive way from all that had been worst and most humiliating in Louis' thirty years, he stood for a future full of achievement and self-realization and self-knowledge. This miserable, over-weight, tonsured, elderly businessman was all-important. The future marched behind him.

'All right,' said Louis at last. 'If I have to . . .'

Gissing pursed his lips and let out a little breath. 'There should be one change of plan, though, Baker. Take this girl – your girl – out as arranged, but change the theatre.'

'Whatever for?'

'Take her to the Palladium. One of the doormen there is one of our men – we can rely on him. If there is a message to be given we can be sure he will give it to you . . .'

The train came in, sliding and mumbling like a monster of

the dark, thrusting a warm vitiated breath before it. There was a soda-siphon hiss as doors opened and people climbed aboard. The heart-beat of the monster tacker-tackered amiably.

'Perhaps you will have less difficulty with this Ward girl, because she is, I believe, younger and more attractive than the Krissen woman.' Gissing gave a little shiver of prurient distaste. 'I must say that is a side of the matter that I prefer not to contemplate; but if there is a sexual inducement it may exist in this instance to a greater degree.'

There was another hiss as the doors slid to. The train began to move, gathering speed with unnatural rapidity, disappeared mumbling into the tunnel; the tail light winked and was gone. Warm air rushed after it in adulation; eddies and puffs wafted about the station. Louis's cigarette smoke turned and twisted as if trying to escape.

'The blitz will begin about nine. Be there just before that. I am not aware of the arrangements of the house in the event of an air raid, but in general people are becoming careless and will probably not go to the shelter if they have one. In any case the opportunity is there. Your orders are to make the most of it, Ober-Leutnant.'

A woman with three children trailed past them carrying rugs and a bundle of newspapers. Another woman had arrived and was settling near the two men; bunks were beginning to fill up. The two men still made no move. They were, perhaps, waiting for a later train.

II

Twenty minutes passed before Walter Gissing, having seen his friend off, climbed the flight of steps, paused to get his breath, then walked along the tunnel and took the first escalator. As he went up he read the passing advertisements. There was no sign in his appearance or demeanour that he dealt in life and death and other such primary wares. A rich but shabby stockbroker on his way home from the City to a comfortable fireside. A small but important fragment of the backbone of England, for whom brave men like Andrew Halford were fighting.

As he was nearing the top, a hand touched his arm.

'Evening, Gissing.'

Gissing did not start at the touch; he was not the type. Fraser stood beside him. Luke Fraser. They met at public dinners and the like. Editor of a leading political weekly. Heavy, graven features, greying, receding hair, keen, deep, sensual eyes. Fancied himself as an intellectual.

Gissing stepped off the escalator with the right foot.

'Evening, Fraser. Well met. Are you going my way?'

'West? Yes. What have you been doing of late?'

The fat man smiled with his lips. 'Reading your leading articles and admiring their literary style – sometimes even their content.'

'What particular content?'

'Oh, numerous things. I think your stand against retaliatory bombing was good.'

'That's Penfield – one of my sub-editors.'

'Also your criticism of the Government's handling of the war in Egypt and Cyrenaica.'

'Penfield again. I think perhaps he'd be more at home on the *New Statesman*. But he's a talented fellow and very likeable. You must see him sometime.'

'Delighted.'

More grey-faced people passed them on the way down, drifting down without using their legs. In the dirty yellow light they reminded Gissing of an early Ufa film – shabby dispossessed souls moving downwards on their way to Hell.

'Of course I'm no politician,' he said spitefully. 'Merely a financier – and an amateur philosopher.'

Fraser showed his teeth under his long upper lip. 'With literary talent. I remember that article you wrote for the *Evening News* just after Dunkirk.'

'How flattering of you to recall it.'

'You might even think of writing something for us? Problems of post-war reconstruction, or something of that nature. Might even do a short series with you contributing the first and the last piece.'

'Still more flattering. I must say I do have ideas; but whether they would accord with your own . . .'

'As you've observed, *The Onlooker* is open to all shades of opinion.'

They climbed more steps and emerged by the London Pavilion. Searchlights were making subdued rainbows on the cloud cover, but so far the only mechanized sound was the growl of the traffic. They began to walk up Piccadilly, Fraser adapting his long stride to the less athletic one of his companion.

'You must come and dine with me sometime,' said Gissing. 'What are your best nights?'

'Thursdays and Saturdays. Why don't you come round to my club – '

'No, the invitation was mine. Thursday of this week? Are you free?'

Fraser accepted the invitation. 'Then,' he said, 'you'll be able to offer me constructive advice on my editorials.'

Gissing coughed. 'I deserved the irony. It only seems a pity . . .'

'What?'

'It seems a pity that your journal, with all its editorial talent and financial independence, so often takes what may be called the official line.'

Fraser recalled another article he had seen by Walter Gissing in the *News Chronicle* shortly after the fall of France. Unorthodox sentiments had been expressed, but with enough subtlety to avoid a charge of defeatism.

'Preserving one's independence of judgment in time of war,' Fraser said, 'is a problem. Do you stick pins in a man when he is fighting for his life? Only if by doing so you help him to fight better.'

Gissing tapped the pavement with his umbrella as he walked. It was a muffled, secretive world they had come out

149

into – and menacing in the way Defoe's seventeenth century London must have been. Ominous figures loomed and crouched. A drunken soldier slept in a doorway. The shrill cry of a woman could have been laughter or alarm.

'They should stop these people,' he said abruptly.

'What people?'

'These people selling black-market things. Look, there's one there. And another there. The police should move on them.'

'They try to,' said Fraser good-temperedly. 'But it's a big city. And a big democracy. Perhaps in your ideal state . . .'

'What ideal state?'

'The one you postulate in that article in the *News Chronicle*.' Fraser stopped in his stride. 'Come into my club now and have a drink. Tell me all about it.'

'Thanks no, my dear chap. I have things I must attend to. By the way, this sub-editor of yours, Penfold, is it?'

'Penfield.'

'If he's free on Thursday, bring him with you. I'd like to meet him.'

'Thank you. I'll ask him. Good-bye.'

They separated, Fraser to go up the steps of his club, Gissing to continue on his careful rubber soles down Piccadilly. The two men didn't much like each other; nor did they much trust each other; but they had a reciprocal interest. Fraser's weekly was losing circulation and he thought Gissing's articles might rouse healthy controversy. Gissing found Fraser a useful source of information and it suited his book to give a tactful literary airing to certain combustible ideas.

Gissing mixed in a distinguished company and very much disliked the rough end of espionage. Born in Weissenfels in Saxony, he had graduated from Leipzig University with a law degree and had come to England in 1910, speaking perfect, unaccented English before he ever set foot in Dover, had joined a firm of stockbrokers the following year and had been 'something in the City' ever since. He had never once returned to his native country even for a visit, though in the early days he had sighed for a sight of the Pleisse more than once. His activities on behalf of the Fatherland had been merely routine during the First World War, when he served in the Pay Corps; and it was only later when he became wealthy enough to mix with people of influence that, as a reporter of private opinions held in high places – and in a small way as an influencer of those opinions – he had come into his own.

Inevitably a spy lives a double life, but few succeed in believing equally in both. Gissing believed in both. He had come totally to belong to the routines of English life while taking a special pleasure in trying to undermine them. When the Nazis came to power he had remained what he had always been, aloof from the harsh field work that others undertook; and it was only since the outbreak of war that he had been expected to be active in this way. He did not like it; he intended to drop it as soon as he could; it was not at all his style, nor was it the way in which he could be of most value.

Strolling home now, he tried to brush aside the memory of his recent interview in Piccadilly Underground and to think of Fraser and his magazine and the many famous people he knew, and how such friendships might be manipulated. It was the world in which he operated best, where in a modest degree of comfort he could pursue the more abstract philosophies of deceit and subjugation.

Although he knew there would be no air-raid on London that night he hastened his step as he turned into Down Street. Of itself the anonymous darkness was both a promise and a threat.

Tuesday Morning

I

By mischance they arrived down for breakfast within a few moments of the Fileys. Andrew took the seat Jennifer usually occupied, so that he could face Mrs Filey, but the lady was completely expressionless. At the end of breakfast she opened her bag and peered into it, said something to her husband. He offered her a cigarette and she leaned back and blew the smoke away from her face. It was a silent meal at both tables.

Andrew had ordered a taxi to take them in to Stratford, and after he had paid the excessive bill he went to see if it had arrived. Mr and Mrs Filey were in the doorway, their taxi having just drawn up, and luggage that Andrew knew too well was being put in the boot. Jennifer, coming to the door a moment later, saw that Filey had barred Andrew's way.

'Look here: I want a word with you!'

Not in the best of tempers himself, Andrew stared but did not speak.

Filey stuttered a moment. 'I want to know what the hell you mean by searching our room last night!'

'I don't know what you're driving at.'

'You know damned well! I mean your coming into our room last night.'

'An unfortunate mistake. It was all explained at the time.'

'And I suppose things got turned upside down in our room by themselves, eh? And the bulb got taken out of the electric light? That wasn't explained, was it?'

'Come on, Arty,' said Mrs Filey, plucking at his sleeve.

'No, damned if I will!'

'The trouble with you last night, old boy,' Andrew said, 'was that you had taken aboard more drink than you could comfortably carry and so jumped to ridiculous conclusions – '

'More drink – ' Filey began. 'I'll trouble you to take that back!'

The engineer's voice had been rising with every sentence. Other people were staring. Jennifer detested scenes, but she subdued the impulse to slink away and limped through the door to join the party.

'You may think you Air Force types can do what you please, but you're very much mistaken – '

'Come *on*,' said Mrs Filey.

'Listen to me – ' Filey thrust his pink face forward.

'Go and buy yourself a new collar,' Andrew said, 'or you'll choke.'

'You haven't heard the last of this, I can tell you! I've got your name and I'll soon find the number of your squadron – '

'I know you'd like to sue me for assault,' Andrew said. 'But it's not on. Just let me pass.'

It all hung in the balance; but Hilda Filey's sturdy arm saved the situation, and Filey allowed himself to be dragged away and persuaded into the taxi. Among those watching the quarrel was a little woman in spectacles who stood back to let them pass and then paused to light a cigarette before going into the hotel. Nobody took any notice of her.

Another taxi was now drawing up, and Andrew held the hotel door open for Jennifer to go in and pick up her minimal belongings. When they came out again the Fileys were gone.

'Sorry about that,' she said.

'Why should *you* be sorry?'

'I did suggest searching their belongings in the first place.'

'Maybe you put the idea in my head. But it's totally

unimportant. I trod on his self-esteem last night, and he had to work it off.'

'I suppose it was a natural reaction,' Jennifer said. 'His, I mean. If he'd been hiding something he surely wouldn't have kicked up such a fuss.'

'True enough.'

'So I may have made a terrible bloomer about the cameo.'

'You may,' he agreed. 'On the other hand, *she* was anxious not to bother. Difficult to say whether she was more anxious to avoid trouble than an entirely innocent woman would have been.'

They drove to the station in silence. Andrew paid the taxi and bought the tickets to London. They sat silent on a seat together in the draughty morning light.

After they had been in the train for a few minutes Jennifer said in a rather formal voice: 'Don't know about anything else, but I'm sick that I owe you so much money, Andrew. I can dib up for the watch because I borrowed ten pounds from Mr Lang of Beaufort's. Before we left – '

'Oh, nonsense,' he said.

'Before we left London I was able to pay my rent to Mrs Lawson, but I can still – '

'Forget it,' he said.

'Can't quite. Sorry. And this weekend must have cost you your boots. I know what those places are.'

'It just so happens that I brought you here as my guest. Didn't you notice that?'

Jennifer blew her fringe up. 'I did notice that I haven't been a very satisfactory guest.'

'I didn't stipulate "guest" in inverted commas. Am I complaining?'

'I don't know. It just seems to me it would be fairer if I were able to pay my way. And more satisfactory . . .'

'Who for?'

'Well, for me, as it happens.' She fumbled in her pocket and brought out a purse. 'Even if I could – '

'Put it away,' he said. 'There are few things more squalid than swapping money on a train.'

Jennifer looked at the woman opposite, who had put down her *Daily Mail* and was eyeing them with interest. The soldier next to her needed a shave. The train was crawling through woodlands not unlike those they had walked through after the car crash.

Her knee was very much better this morning. She'd taken the bandage off. 'All the same . . .'

'All the same,' he said, 'let's leave it just as it is.'

'What time are we due in London?'

'Twelve forty-five.'

'And then we go to the police?'

'I take you home. *Then* I go to the police.' He looked at his watch. 'There isn't going to be a lot of time for everything. I left my uniform and some necessary papers at Northcot, which means a long drag out there. And it's a matter of principle not to be late back from leave. I wish I'd known . . .'

'What?'

'I should have left my gear at a hotel in the centre somewhere.'

He thought: a lot of the sparkle's gone out of her this morning. For God's sake, she's on her dignity about something. It surely can't still be because I kissed that bloody girl. If this train is late I'll hardly have *time* to go to the police. Might ring them, check in at Manston, then come back again tomorrow. But the police have to know all the facts *today*. Can't just leave Jennifer without protection. She may not need it, but we can't afford to gamble. I dragged her into this – more or less – and whatever she feels or doesn't feel about me . . . What *do* I feel about her? . . . Wonder if Quinton will wear the idea of my taking a couple more days?

A lot easier just to be a pilot officer – pretty well no responsibility except to your plane and your ground crew. Easier to be rowdy and get drunk, even easier to pick up a bird like Jennifer and drop her again. Must be getting old.

She thought: well this is the end of a beautiful friendship.

155

Would it have been any different if we'd slept together on Sunday night? Only in superficial things: he'd be more affectionate now, patting my hand, stroking my arm, saying, 'It's been wizard, hasn't it, darling,' and really feeling good about me. But quietly just as ready to kiss good-bye and be gone.

Sarcasm aside, it *had* been a good friendship, and she'd not had so much fun and excitement ever before. At least for the first two days. After that it had gone sour.

They'd been fishing for minnows and somehow she'd let her emotions get trawled in. She felt a lot too much; knew when they separated she was going to feel more. She cursed herself for being so damned stupid – like a school kid with her first boyfriend, all set to go off her food and fret herself into an early decline. The only thing absolutely essential at this stage was not to let him have the least whiff of her sickening frailty.

An unexploded bomb was lying just beside the line south of St Albans, and only a single track was being used. They were able to buy some stale buns from a station buffet and two bottles of beer which they scampered back with just as the train was about to restart. Restraint in the carriage had long since broken down and everybody was talking to everyone else. It helped Jennifer a lot, and she chatted with the best, back now to her vivacious mood. Andrew joined in, but eyed the girl with irritation. Was she so bored with him that she had to have other company to restore her good humour?

They crawled into Euston just before three. Then there were no taxis, and it took them twenty minutes to find one and five minutes to drive to 45, Gaskin Street. With the taxi ticking outside, he insisted on seeing Mrs Lawson, and then going up with Jennifer to her flat to see if everything was all right.

It was time to say good-bye.

Andrew said: 'Just for the record, Jennifer, this has been a great weekend – in spite of the occasional hiccup.'

'Sorry you lost your car.'

'So'm I. That's why the police have got to come into it now.'

'Because of your car?'

'I mean the attempt on our lives. Maybe it was your life only. They've got to do *something* about that.'

'What can they do?'

'Come and see you. Establish what's known as a "police presence" – to scare any marauders off.'

'I really don't think I need that.'

'Well, I do.'

'Think they'll come?'

'Who? The police? I think they will, if I put it to them properly.'

'OK, then.'

There was a pause. Her eyes were wide-awake, unblinking.

He said: 'As soon as I get back I shall apply for extra leave.'

'If the police are in charge there won't be much more you can do, will there?'

'Not much. But I want to do it.'

'Let me know . . .'

'Of course. It may be only a couple of days more I shall get, but I'll come straight here.'

'If I'm out,' she said, 'I'll leave a note with Mrs Lawson, saying where I've gone.'

'Where are you likely to go?'

'Oh . . . I don't know.' She transferred her look to him. 'Nowhere very much, I suppose. It's just that I might fancy a walk or something. Keep the knee exercised.'

'OK.'

He kissed her, carefully on the lips, and knew then that for him there were no lips like them.

'Jennifer . . .'

She put her fingers against his mouth. 'Your taxi's waiting. Come back soon.'

Her eyes went darker then. Perhaps it was some shadow of her own danger casting its shadow over her mind, as a

157

man's shadow will be thrown forward by a lamp. Or more probably it was just a feeling that this really was good-bye.

II

A hell of a trek out to Vernon Avenue, and the taxi driver was getting bad-tempered. However, when Andrew told him who he was, the air became much sweeter. But the meter was ticking up, and Andrew could see himself having to indent for more pay as soon as he signed in today.

Odd the feeling you had going up the stairs of No 9, Vernon Avenue. Although the fateful bedroom was a complete avenue away, you found yourself reluctant to open the door and go into the room. It was a gloomy day, though fine; hurriedly grab your clothes and drag them on, throwing tweed jacket and trousers on the bed, emptying the pockets on a side table and thrusting them into your uniform.

He had almost finished when he came on a sheet of paper and realized it was likely to be a spare one he had found in Hilda Filey's bag. He had hastily stuffed it in an inner top pocket of his jacket, and in the hideous row that ensued he had forgotten it was there; the rest of the stuff he had put in his right-hand pocket.

It was a doctor's prescription, that was all.

Miss H. BAKER,
Bismuth. Carb.	Grs XV
Sodii. Bicarb.	Grs X
Pulv. Trag. Co. q.s.	
Tr. Chlor. et Morph.	m III
Tr. Card. Co.	m X
Aquam. Ad.	½ oz
Mitte	8 ozs

One tablespoonful ex. aq., t.d.s., p.c.

The one thing of note was the name of the prescribing physician. 'J Norley, MRCS, LRCP.'

III

He telephoned Scotland Yard from Charing Cross Station. He asked to be connected to the officer in charge of the inquiry into the death of a young woman at No 9 Carlton Avenue, Northcot, on Friday last. After a pause a heavy male voice at the other end asked his name.

'For the moment,' Andrew said, 'that's not important. At this stage I'm anxious merely to give you one or two facts which you may or may not know. The dead woman is Paula Krissen – K-R-I-S-S-E-N – and she lived in a flat at No 45 Gaskin Street, NW1. She shared the flat with a Miss Jennifer Ward, a typist, who works for Beaufort's, the publishers and printers, in the City. Got that?'

'Yes, sir, I've got that,' said the voice. 'Where are you speaking from?'

'A call box, and shall be shortly leaving it. This is not because I want to avoid an interview with you. In fact I hope tomorrow to ring you again and make an appointment to call and see you. The purpose of this telephone call is to alert you to the fact that I believe Paula Krissen was working for the German Secret Service and that, because she was unwilling to go on working for them, she was killed. Got that?'

'Yes, sir. Why do you not come round this afternoon?'

'Because I'm a serving officer and have to report to my base before doing anything else, as my leave is up at 18.30 hours this evening. I'm hoping to extend my leave and see you sometime tomorrow. Now listen carefully. Are you listening?'

'Yes, sir. Please go on.'

'Although Miss Ward is entirely innocent of any involvement in this matter at all, I believe her to be in possible danger. She and Paula Krissen were fairly close friends, and it could be that the people who silenced the Krissen woman

159

may want to silence Miss Ward just in case she too knows too much, just to be on the safe side. Are you with me?'

'Yes, certainly. Where are you speaking from?'

'Charing Cross Station. As a squadron leader in the RAF can I ask you to *make an effort* to get in contact with Miss Ward *this evening* – earlier if possible, so that there shall be *no chance* of her coming to any harm as a result of her friendship with Miss Krissen? Will you send someone round?'

'A squadron leader, sir? What is your name, if I may ask?'

'You've already asked, and I'll tell you that tomorrow. The point is this: I think Miss Ward can be useful to you. It would be a great pity if you ignored this request and she was killed as a consequence. Wouldn't it?'

'Yes. No doubt. Can you give me her address again?'

'45, Gaskin Street, NW1. I have to leave now or I shall miss my train. I'll be in touch with you sometime tomorrow. May I know your name?'

'Green. Inspector Green. Can you just – '

'I know you may feel this may be a hoax, Inspector Green. I know you may feel it's a total waste of time to follow up this call until you have stronger evidence to go on. *Don't do that.* You *can't afford* to risk it. This is a matter of national importance. There could be a chance of uncovering a spy ring. Please act on it. Will you?'

There was no reply from the other end.

'Inspector Green,' Andrew said.

'Yes, sir. Rest assured we will do all we can.'

IV

Manston was the airfield almost on the cliffs which had been so badly strafed last summer that there had been talk of evacuating it. Andrew had been stationed at Biggin Hill then, and had only been moved into East Kent at Christmas.

He reached it in good time after all, and was not altogether surprised to find the affairs of the squadron a little monochrome after the vivid events of his leave – as did the bareness and barrenness of his uncomfortable quarters after the luxuries of the Marley Manor. He was not all that interested to learn that young Bray's enthusiasm had once more outlasted his petrol and that he had damaged his undercarriage in a field in Sussex. Splendid news that Coulson, who had gone down in a blazing kite two months ago was unhurt and a prisoner. Flying Officer Dawson was full of a report that 48 Squadron was to be issued with three experimental Airacobras. Pilot Officer Streit had something to tell him about the peculiar behaviour of a couple of DO 215s. But they soon sheered off when the news got around that Halford was in a monkey about something – a rare enough condition in him to be worthy of respect.

Group Captain Quinton had been called away, so Andrew went round to call on Wing Commander Henshawe, and by way of opening the conversation said he'd be greatly obliged to be given another three days' leave, starting at once.

Henshawe looked his surprise. Hitherto Halford had taken leaves with reluctance; he'd had to be bullied into one last October.

'Beginning tonight, you mean?'

'That's what I'd like. If it can be arranged.'

'You've seen Norris? Everything's all right with him, I suppose?'

Andrew thought of the pile of papers on his desk. 'I'll see everything's all right before I go.'

'Yes, well . . .' Henshawe gazed out of the window at a Lysander moving across the evening clouds like a hover-fly. 'You know, of course, there have been a couple of costly sweeps in your absence. Squadron Leader Hamilton is missing. And we had a bit of a flap doing a diversionary op over Abbeville.'

'Dawson told me. I'm sorry to have missed the fun.'

'I imagine there'll be plenty more,' Henshawe said .drily. 'Can you give me some reason for this application? It would look better if you could.'

'I'm on to something,' said Andrew.

Henshawe raised his eyebrows again. 'To do with the war, you mean?'

'Yes, sir. I telephoned the police this afternoon but I haven't been to see them yet. I need to see them, tomorrow sometime, though there are one or two things I must look after myself first.'

'I gather you don't want to tell me any more. If the police are involved . . .'

'It's to do with a leakage of information. A serious leakage.'

'Ah. Well, take care. Don't get knifed in some mucky little Soho dive. These people have dirty ways, and you're too useful a man to be dropped in the Thames.'

'I'll bear it in mind,' Andrew said, smiling grimly.

'Well, then, instead of fresh leave, let's just issue an extension on, shall we say, compassionate grounds.'

'Thank you very much, sir. My obligation goes deeper than you think.'

'But as I've said: watch your step.'

When he got back to his own barren quarters he again stared at the papers on his desk, but instead of sending for the adjutant he picked up the phone and asked the operator to get him a Mayfair number. Presently he was in touch with a hotel and asking for Flight-Lieutenant Radziwill.

A familiar soft foreign voice came to his ears.

'Hullo, old fellow. Well timed. I was just off out to dinner with Witold and a few others. I was hoping you'd ring before I left.'

'Any news from your end?'

'Yes, but not satisfactory, I fear. Morsztyn has just come back. He waited at the Apollo from four-thirty until six, and no one answering our description turned up. Neither the girl Forrest nor Mr Charles Mason. Very disappointing.'

'Do you think you heard aright?'

'Oh yes. But it is unfortunate. Now we are no further ahead. And you?'

'Some progress all round. I struck a sort of oil with Paula

Krissen's aunt in Birmingham. Paula was working for the German Intelligence Service.'

'Was she, by God!'

'Look, Stephen, I'm back at Manston. I want you to do me a favour.'

'Anything you would ask.'

'I'm only just back here but I've put in for extra leave and shall be in London again tonight. I may need your help. Or Jennifer may. There's a distinct likelihood she may be in danger.'

'What do you want me to do?'

'I've told you on Sunday somebody tried to bump her off, and me with her. That may be the end, but I'm by no means certain. I left her at her flat this afternoon. She'll probably be having a visit from the police this evening, and once she's had that I have a hunch the danger will not be so great. But I can't be absolutely *sure*. I *want* to be sure. I'd like to be there myself to be sure. But it'll take me an hour at least to go through the motions here. The best I can do is catch the 9.05 from Faversham, which should have me in London about 11.13. There's a gap and I want you to fill it.'

'Tell me how.'

'Go round to No 45, Gaskin Street. It's off Eversholt Street, not far from Euston Station. Go round and see her. Tell her I've sent you; and telephone me when you get there; then stay with her until I come.'

'Of course, old fellow. I will do that.'

'She doesn't expect me back tonight. And the police may be there . . . but I'd be much happier if you were too.'

'OK. OK. Will do. That is not a problem.'

'When will you go?'

'It will do after this dinner? I can be there by eight-thirty. Before dark, that is.'

Andrew hesitated a moment. 'I think that should be OK. And Stephen.'

'Yes.'

'I've just come suddenly on something else. So I have a

job for you tomorrow morning as well. Witold too. Could you leave tomorrow morning free?'

'De-lighted. But tell me, what am I to say to the police if they come to see Jennifer? In what way are they involved?'

'Say nothing to them. You have simply come to keep Jennifer company until I return. I especially don't want to become tied in with the police until after tomorrow morning.'

'Very well, then. I will see that she is tucked away safely.'

'And telephone me as soon as you get there. Will you, please? Don't forget that. I think this is all blowing up into something very important. It is very much to do with the war.'

'All correct,' said Radziwill. 'Rely on me.'

There was always one way of being certain that a Pole took things seriously, and that was by mentioning the word 'German' to him. Or possibly, with Stephen, 'Russian' too. There could be no mistake then. Andrew hung up feeling more comforted in mind and prepared to devote the next hour of his attention to Flight-Lieutenant Norris.

V

His incursion into the Fileys' bedroom had been like a delayed action bomb: no result at first, and then a sudden explosion in your face when you think it all defused . . .

An FME, one Robinson, J, had overstepped his leave by four days and police had been sent to fetch him. Norris had given him seven days' CC and stopped him three days' pay, as heavy a penalty as he was entitled to make it.

'Young ass,' said Andrew. 'Did he give an explanation?'

'I believe he got mixed up with some girl.'

Andrew grunted in discomfort. There but for the grace and burden of responsibility . . . Suppose he went to the police tomorrow and told them *all* his supicions? – all the suspicions that had now gathered round him like a swarm of wasps. Would they act? Could they act at all on suspicion alone? Everything was so inferential, facts floating like bits of debris in a muddy pool.

'I see Ferguson is on remand again for me to deal with. Neglect of Duty. What's he been up to?'

'He left the Pitot head cover on Brown's machine. Brown nearly overran the field!'

'. . . We'd better deal with him right away.'

'You don't need any advice,' said Norris, 'but you'll probably remember the way to hurt Ferguson most is through his pocket.'

'I'll more than hurt his pocket if he does that again,' said Andrew. 'If it had been somebody less experienced than Brown . . .'

While he'd been away, Norris said, Dusty Edmonds had turned up. Oh yes? Andrew said; he had never known Edmonds, as he'd been shot down last May. Norris said it was a pity psychologically that Edmonds had come back even for a brief visit. He was between operations and had just been given a new pair of eyelids. He was a pretty frightful sight, and Norris was of the opinion that two or three of the younger fliers had been upset. It was a damned silly error to let him come back, though no doubt undertaken with the best of intentions.

'Like that heap of broken-up old planes we have almost on our back doorstep,' said Andrew.

'Eh?'

'They should be carted away. It doesn't exactly make good viewing. There was an airman's cap on top of the pile this evening when I came in. And an old boot. And a scarf. If we're talking psychology, that's another instance.'

'No doubt you're right. A couple of new chaps are due here from Duxford later this week. Maybe a hint to Henshawe might do the trick – '

'Jack,' Andrew said, 'I've applied for extra leave and am going back to London tonight. I want to snatch a bite and a coffee; think we could do that while we work?'

The adjutant blinked a couple of times. 'Oh, sure, sure. What train are you hoping to catch?'

'The nine o-five. If you can lay me on a car to take me to Faversham.'

Norris looked at his watch, worn fashionably inside the wrist. 'Can do that, of course. Anyway most of the stuff can wait a day or so. Er – nothing wrong with the family, I hope?'

'Nothing wrong with the family,' said Andrew.

Tuesday Evening

I

Dot Forrest had been disappointed when Louis telephoned her to change the theatre. He'd made no attempt to explain why, except to say that 'Applesauce' had some of his favourites in it: Max Miller, Florence Desmond, Vera Lynn, and was supposed to be a smash hit. Dot was too keen to hold him to his promise of Sunday evening to quibble, so they met at the Palladium at five.

They sat in the back stalls; a striking couple; both very tall, Dot with her long synthetic blonde hair and fine dark eyes, her exaggerated eyebrows and bronze fingernails; Louis fresh-shaven, skin mottled where the razor had been, crisp up-growing, up-curling hair, wearing a smart navy suit and smelling of talcum.

All the same Dot wasn't pleased with his looks. He was over-tense, might have had shell-shock, bit constantly at his bottom lip, laughed too much and in the wrong places. People turned round smiling or frowning to look.

In the interval they had a couple of double whisky and sodas each and that seemed to relax him. That or something else. Once or twice he'd lifted his head sharply when an attendant came near him. Now he was becoming much easier. He admired her frock, said why didn't they have dinner after the show, maybe take in a night-club; he knew a better one than the Blue Peter. He went to order another drink, but the girl behind the bar had been told she could only serve a maximum of two drinks per customer.

'When this bloomin' war is over,' said Dot, gazing out of

the window at the gloomy day, 'no more rationing for me. I shall eat and drink as much as I like and get *fat*. Sure I shall get fat. When d'you think we shall beat the swine?'

Louis fingered the programme. 'Not yet, you can be sure. They're every bit as tough as the English. I know them.'

'What? As tough as we are? Go on!' – It was almost 'garn!' – 'Not on your sweet life! They're a lot of dirty cowards. They'll bomb and machine-gun women and children but as soon as we squeeze 'em they'll start to squeal.'

'I know them better than that. My great-grandfather was a German.'

'It's not true!' She was amazed. 'You never told me that! No kiddin'?'

The second bell had gone and they got up and walked back to their seats.

'He was a general,' said Louis. 'An aristocrat.'

'Who was? Your great-grandfather?'

'Yes. His name was Von Langbeim. He served under Bismarck.'

'Crikey, you sound quite *proud* of it!' said Dot. 'More than I'd be. I'd keep quiet about it if I were you.'

'He married – he married the daughter of an English wool merchant. It was much beneath him, of course. Their daughter was naturalized English, and later she married a Bradford man. That's how it happened.'

'Gee, lucky break for you! If you'd been called Von What's-it I wouldn't have been seen out with you! A dirty Nazi. I'll say not! Think what you might have missed!'

The band struck up as they sank into their seats and there was no need to reply. It was just as well, because he might have said more than he should have done – certainly it would have been more than she ever expected.

Tensed up as he was to meet something that he was now hoping to escape, Dot's scorn and challenge had touched a sharp edge, pulled at a raw nerve of pride and arrogance. He found himself despising his own fear and despising the pleasure he had had in her company. A woman who could say what she had just said should be hit violently across the mouth and left sprawling and spitting her teeth in the gutter where she belonged. As the show went on, his contempt for her spilled over into a contempt for the show and the tittering fools about him. He stared blindly, angrily, at the glitter of the stage. He saw Armitage's point of view more clearly than he had done last night. What did one woman matter in the battle for conquest? It was his feeble upbringing which had been responsible for his nervous revulsion. He would show them.

He would show them.

So when an attendant, towards the end of the performance, came cautiously up to him and whispered in his ear, he did not start or move quickly from his seat as he might have done earlier. Anger was his shield. Anger and pride of race stiffened in his mind. He got up without apology to his companion and followed the attendant.

Dot only just noticed him leaving, and turned her head in surprise. He returned in about five minutes.

'Somebody want you?'

'No, I just went to the gents.'

No more was said until the show was over. All through this second half his noisy laughter had been absent. Then as they came out into the fading daylight he said too casually: 'I've got to leave you for a bit now. Shouldn't be long. An hour at the most. Let's meet again about half nine, eh?'

She looked at his hard, furtive face. 'Jeepers, what am I going to do for an hour? Stand on a corner and see who I can pick up?'

He controlled his voice. 'Why don't you go back to your place? You say it's only twenty minutes from Leicester Square. I'll join you there.'

'It's not my idea of an evening out,' she said. 'What's eating you, Charles? Can I help?'

'Maybe.' Maybe after all this woman could be of use, could supply him with an alibi. 'Not yet, though.' He looked her over. 'Anywhere to get supper round your way?'

'I guess so. One or two. If a raid doesn't start.'

'Risk it. I'll call for you at half nine – maybe earlier. We'll go out and have a meal. Then we'll go back to your place. You've got a room?'

'I've got a room,' said Dot. 'It's not the Ritz.'

'Is it private?'

'Oh yes, it's private. You mean . . .?'

'Let's play it as it comes, eh? Just play it as it comes.'

II

After Andrew had left, Jennifer bathed her knee, made herself a cup of tea and then dusted the flat. To a girl like her, total misery came as a surprise. She'd never experienced it before. Something was swelling up inside her and threatened to burst. If it burst, tears would come out of her eyes like an eight-year-old. Cut that out at all costs.

So what had it all amounted to? Young man on leave looking for a bit of fun, finding it in her – then, bang, the chance came up without contrivance and he'd wanted to climb into bed with her. She'd said no, though, God, it would have been good at the time. But she'd said no – her old-maidish instincts had preserved her for some worthier and duller fate. The bus had gone, and that was it. He had promised to apply for extra leave, but it was unlikely he'd get it. If he got it it was unlikely he'd come back here. Why should he? He owed time to his parents. A jolly but painful little episode, sparked off by a nasty and mysterious murder.

She didn't know what would happen to the flat now. She couldn't afford to live here on her own, and she knew no one she wanted to share it with. Anyway, for all you could say against Paula it wouldn't be the same sharing with some dull girl who prattled on about her sweet coupons.

In the bedroom she began to put away the personal things Paula had left around. A comb with two wisps of black hair curling in it, a pink nightdress stuffed anyhow under the pillow of her bed, three kirby-grips on the dressing-table, a badly squeezed tube of foundation cream, a box of loose powder without the lid; Miss Krissen could never be accused of being obsessionally tidy. Jennifer picked up the big bottle of gardenia scent which was on the table between the beds, then put it back again. Perhaps she shouldn't mess things about too much before the police came. If the police came.

Over dinner on Saturday Andrew had described finding Paula in more detail: the dusty room, the dead woman in a chair, the faded flowers, the gardenia scent warring with another smell. She shivered, feeling short of warm blood herself. The bedroom was cold, and she went back into their sitting room, rinsed the cup and saucer in the tiny sink, put away the powdered milk.

Best thing might be to follow Diana into the WAAF. Mr Lang would have a fit but he'd get over it.

And now at this moment, for the time being, she must get *out*; go to the flicks or something, just to break up the sob stuff and the long retinue of weekend memories.

She had discarded the frock which had seen her through all the traumas of the weekend; now she changed again into a green linen blouse and tweed skirt, slipped on her mac – for warmth not rain – and went downstairs. There she found Mrs Lawson intent on talk. Since there was no hurry, she stood at the foot of the stairs patiently listening to complaints about Paula and her behaviour and how she was three weeks behind with her rent and how it was more than a week now since she'd even been back. Jennifer said yes, and no, and yes it does seem a pity, and no I've no idea.

Mrs Lawson said she didn't mind her lodgers going off for a night or two, particularly when a car broke down – well, had an accident then – she wasn't above women having a bit of fun in wartime but she wondered with Paula whether she didn't ought to tell the police about her being away so long. She wouldn't have to bother, thought Jennifer. Any moment now, if Andrew had done his stuff. Should she stay in and wait for them?

'Those two men who called to see me on Sunday,' she said, torpedoing Mrs Lawson in mid-channel; 'did they leave no message at all?'

'Who? Oh, the gentlemen. No, not when they called.'

'Oh, have they been again since?'

'Not been. They phoned this morning and left a message saying they'd hoped to get back to you but there wasn't time.'

'I don't follow. I thought – '

'It skipped my memory when you came back with that young man. I was so surprised to see you with that young man again . . . Now let's see, where did I put it?' Mrs Lawson felt in her pockets, then went back into her room, casting about like an elderly poodle seeking a scent. Jennifer followed her into the room.

The woman found a piece of scrawled paper under a Chinese vase.

'Yes, here it is. It was from a Captain Richardson. He says – '

Jennifer, startled, said: 'Richardson! But that's my uncle! That's – '

'Well, he says – this is the message I was to give you. He says I was to tell you he was passing through London with an artillery draft, and he picked up – picked up Peter at Wembley and they looked you up at your old address and was directed here. He was sorry to have missed you, he says, but that he's leaving for Grange in the afternoon. That's this afternoon, ain't it. He sends his love and hopes you're well.' Mrs Lawson looked up and wafted the bit of paper backwards and forwards in front of her face, as if fanning herself. 'That's all.'

Jennifer took the note and read it for herself. Geoffrey Richardson was her mother's brother, Peter his son. She had not seen either of them since her mother's wedding. Richardson was a successful commercial artist, so when he volunteered for the Army, they had immediately put him in the Royal Artillery; it was about par for the course.

'How awful I missed them!' So the two men calling to see her on Sunday evening were neither the sinister figures conjured up by the attack on the car, nor the more reassuring figures of plain-clothes police. Plain clothes?

'You didn't tell me they were in uniform,' she said sharply.

'Neither they weren't. They was in civvies. When they came to the door they didn't tell me nothing, and I didn't ask them nothing. I thought from the way you spoke on the phone you knew who they were.'

'I was – I just took them to be someone else. Mrs Lawson.'

'Yes, dear?'

'I'm going out now. If anybody should come asking for me . . .' She hesitated. What sort of a message did you leave for a policeman, in uniform or plain clothes? The mischance of Uncle Geoffrey's call left her feeling part reassured, part more alone than ever.

'Yes?'

'Tell them I'll be back about half-past eight.'

'All right, dear. I'd be back before black-out if I was you. It's safer. It's not just the raids. You never know who's lurking about making the most of the darkness.'

The wind was cold as she walked up the street. She forced herself not to limp. Which way to go? You couldn't just loiter, otherwise Mrs Lawson's fears might be realized. A fate worse than death. Funny, that. On Sunday she'd refused a fate better than life. Was *that* it? At least a fate better than loneliness, a written-off girlfriend, a casual cast-off. As she'd said to herself before, things were not likely to have been wildly different if she had allowed Andrew into her bed. He would still have gone back in the same way, maybe protesting his undying affection a bit more earnestly. But how would *she* feel, no longer a virgin, a woman, if not of the world at least of the Marley Manor? No doubt it should have happened, just to jolt her out of herself. And they said pregnancies didn't usually come from the first time ever. (If she had said yes, would he have fished out a contraceptive? God, how awful that sounded! Let it be.) At least I'm walking down the street with my body unbreached, however much my heart is in strips.

She went to a cinema near the station. A re-issue of a French film. No more new French films now. No more Brussels lace, no more Italian gloves.

The film was old and jumpy, but marvellously full of the richness of human nature. Could people such as the French be permanently subdued by conquest, so that their natural genius was choked at its source?

She stayed longer than intended, and came out into the dark street just as the air-raid sirens began. It was not, however, very dark because the sky was a moving fish-net of searchlights. A good deal of ack-ack fire, though this still distant. And, also distant, an ominous drone. She limped along through the emptying streets without that sense of quickening faculties which generally accompanied a raid.

'Better get into a shelter, miss,' said a warden. 'They're coming this way.'

He had hardly spoken when there was a whistle and a heavy crump, and glass blew across the street like pine needles in a wind. Then following it within seconds an ear-splitting crash and a blast of air that stopped her in her stride and sucked away her breath. The heavy crackle of a falling house followed close upon it. She put up her arm to her eyes. The acrid smell of explosives caught at her throat. Presently her breath came back and she went on. She need not pass where the bombs had fallen, could turn down this next street.

A girl of about fifteen with pigtails was walking towards her.

'My back,' she said. 'It feels funny. Is something wrong with it?'

Jennifer saw that her coat was scorched between the shoulders and a dark stain was beginning to soak through. Her round young face was puzzled rather than alarmed.

'Are you hurt?' said the warden, coming up with them. 'God, yes. All right, dear. We'll soon get you fixed up. Here, take my arm. Can you walk as far as the station?'

'I'm OK,' said the girl, sagging slightly.

'Don't go that way, miss!' the warden shouted after Jennifer. 'There's danger from falling masonry!'

But in the side street it seemed safer. It was empty of people; only parked cars loomed in the dark. Another two short streets and she was home. The next crump was distinctly further away. She felt fatalistic. Common sense said get indoors as soon as possible, but it was only a short way now.

Gaskin Street. All dark. There was a brief startling brightness when one of the raiders dropped a flare in the direction of the river.

45. Nine months ago everyone would have jammed into the cellar. Now there would only be the Miss Carters from the third floor and Mrs Allicante and her two children. Mrs Lawson, she'd bet, would be going on with her ironing, swearing to herself when the floor shook. Familiarity with the prospect of death or maiming didn't breed contempt but it bred the same sort of stoic fatalism that soldiers develop under fire.

As she went up she heard the Mackintoshes' gramophone scraping out the Soldiers' Chorus from Faust. Maybe after another cup of tea she'd go down tonight. Just for the company. Just for the familiar things. 'Oh, here comes Miss Ward,' Mrs Allicante would exclaim gratefully, and the two children would immediately be round her asking her to tell them a story. Or the younger Miss Carter would want to recount her adventures when she modelled for an artist. ' "My dear," he would say "a little lower, *if* you please" . . . Well you know how it is with some men . . . Such warm hands . . .' These confidences breathed over her with the smell of stale cigarette smoke. 'Nudism wasn't quite so brazen as it is today.'

Was it worth it, just for the company, to face that? But bed the only other choice, and she knew as soon as she lay down her eyes would open and she would begin to think and think and grieve and think. Knee ache was little; heartache was all.

She went into the flat and picked her way across the dark room to the curtains. First a blind to be drawn, then curtains came across to cut off any chinks of light from the sides.

She had left the outer door an inch ajar so that a glimmer from the dim light on the landing should help her to find her way across. As she finished adjusting the curtains she heard someone quietly close the door behind her.

III

Outside the guns were louder than the bombs. There was one particular battery mounted on the roof of a nearby dance hall which barked incessantly like a dog and made the windows rattle.

She took a step towards the bedroom. The electric light came on.

No introductions necessary. She had never seen him before, but his face and the look in his eyes left no doubt. He said nothing but stood with his back to the door and looked at her and couldn't keep his features steady. His eyes were inflamed and angry, as if she'd done him some terrible wrong.

'What do you want?' Her voice sounded small and hollow as in an empty room. She cleared her throat. 'What do . . . you . . .'

He watched her. He had no interest whatsoever in what she said, so her useless questioning tailed off. She knew the answer, and he knew she knew. It didn't make it any easier for him: he'd have preferred her ignorant. But at least it saved breath pretending. There was nothing to say, only time and nervous energy were needed now. He tried to slip the catch over the door but it stuck. It didn't matter.

Her heart thumping in her throat kept pace with the ack-ack battery outside. She knew what had happened to Paula and she knew it was going to happen to her. There was no way except through the door he barred. The windows were too high to jump. Paula had died in a blitz. Paula had died in a blitz. A cord or something round her throat.

He moved towards her: two light-footed almost apologetic steps as if hoping she wouldn't notice. The gramophone downstairs had changed its tune. She glanced round swiftly, then raced towards the bedroom door.

He'd seen her move coming and in a sharp leap frustrated it. She pulled up, swerved, caught at the mantelpiece to pull herself away as his hand snatched at her sleeve and slipped off again. She ducked backwards and ran round the table.

It might all have been in good fun, a youthful game, with a kiss at the end of it instead of strangulation. He paused, watching her, taking his breath. Her mind fled raggedly over things she might say to delay him. She knew there was no hope of changing his mind.

'I – don't know anything,' she panted. 'I can't do you – any harm.'

She saw he was going to push the table out of the way, and jumped back just before he did it. Behind her now was the bedroom again, and she fled into it, a scream half out of her lips. She had the door nearly shut behind her and her foot against it, but he got his also and his superior weight bulged open the top of the door so that she could not catch and lock it. Now she screamed in real earnest, again and again, but presently stopped because it was taking the vital breath she needed to struggle.

She switched on the light.

At his first heave he had got his foot wedged in the jamb, and there for seconds they stuck, while her shoe bent and twisted under the strain. Then he thrust his hand through the gap and began to grope and weave about for her. She twisted her body out of the way of his blind fingers, but a sudden new jerk and his shoulder was wedged in the aperture. Then it was easy for him. Inch by inch, sobbing for breath and wet with sweat she had to give way.

Then he was through and it was over. She fell back and stumbled across the first single bed – hers – and he followed her still without speaking. He caught her as she fell between the beds and hauled her up by the waist, then he pulled her skirt up over her head.

Then he grunted.

Then his hands grasped at her knickers, tore at them. The elastic held, cut into her thighs. The material tore and with animal hands he ripped it into shreds. He gave another grunt. This was the way to kill.

Mixed with the sound of gunfire were angry shouts; they came through in spite of everything. A shower of stones hit the window, cracking a pane.

'Put out those bloody lights!'

'Put out those lights!'

'Lights! Lights!'

Louis raised his head from staring at the girl's body. The black-out was not up in this room. He turned sharply, leapt to the switch, clicked it out.

She slid off the bed like an eel. Some light still came through from the sitting room, and as his eyes accustomed themselves he could see her behind the dressing-table. She was crouching, quivering. He was just beginning to enjoy himself.

As he grabbed her she hit him across the face with a bottle. The bottle was knocked out of her hand and fell on the floor, spilling its contents. He fell back against the wall but kicked the dressing-table aslant to prevent her getting out of the corner.

He was put off for a space by the intense smell of gardenia which suddenly filled the room. It brought to mind Paula and everything to do with Paula, his courtship, her laughter, her scraping choke as he tightened the last life out of her. It put him off his balance for the length of time a referee could have counted ten. He shook himself. He really fancied this girl, fancied what he saw of her, but he couldn't do what he wanted; he realized that now. There just wasn't time; he might be interrupted by the damned wardens; just finish her off and be gone.

Feeling the blood welling down his face, he went to the door and kicked it shut, cutting off what little light there was left.

IV

Stephen Radziwill stumbled along Gaskin Street, looking for No 45. The raid had delayed him twenty minutes, and then when he was within a short distance of the street he wanted there had been nobody to ask. Everyone had gone to ground while the raid lasted.

He whistled as he walked, for when a man doesn't so much care whether he lives or dies, he becomes still more fatalistic. He came on No 45 at last and pulled at the bell. It took some time to produce Mrs Lawson.

'Good evening, good evening,' said Stephen. 'How are you, Madame? Direct me if you please to the flat of the young lady Ward.'

Mrs Lawson through the narrow gap stared apprehensively at the sky then glared at him. 'Second floor back if she's in. But I think she's out.'

'Very good. Splendid. Do not bother to come up.'

'I wasn't going to,' said Mrs Lawson sourly.

As he went up the stairs Stephen heard her become involved in an argument with an air-raid warden who had appeared from nowhere to shout fiercely, angrily about exposed lights. It soon became a slanging match, but that, thought Stephen, was very much the way of the English.

At the first flight a man was in his shirtsleeves before an open door from which gramophone music was issuing. He was staring up the second flight.

'Hullo, good evening,' said Stephen.

'There's a hell of a row going on up there, mate,' said the man. 'Sounds like they're throwing furniture about or something. Think they'd be satisfied with the bloody raid, wouldn't you.'

Radziwill was off up the stairs three at a time. There were

two doors but by luck he chose the right one. A sitting room, lit, an overturned chair – sounds in the bedroom. Two leaps to the door. Open in darkness, put on light. Man with a woman on the bed. Blood down his cheek, blood on his fingers. Woman with legs drawn up, face suffused, mouth open, dead or nearly.

The man looked up from his throttling, eyes wild, blood-shot, glazed. Charles Mason. Just as predicted. Charles Bloody Mason, as the English would say.

Stephen picked up a chair, swung it. The man recoiled, sat round on the bed, half got up as Stephen broke the rest of the chair over his head. He fell between the beds with a heavy thump. Stephen bent to the girl. Was she still breathing? Air. He turned her a little on her side. A trickle of blood at the corner of the mouth. He rubbed her hand, which seemed he thought to react to his touch. Artificial respiration –

Louis was up, crawling on hands and knees towards the door; Stephen kicked him, numbed his foot with the impact, but Louis grunted and climbed to his feet, swaying, danger-ous, caught Stephen with a savage swinging arm across the throat. They reeled together against the open door as a stone smashed the window and landed on the bed beside Jennifer. Louis was the bigger of the men but no greater in savagery. They fell into the living room; Louis kicking out with his boots, caught Stephen again, then made for the outer door, Stephen in pursuit. They closed again on the landing. Stephen pinned Louis against the wall, hitting him with vicious kidney punches which knocked all the breath out of him.

But Louis had a half-demented strength and thrust away from the wall.

They reeled back against the banister, and the banister, being old and unaccustomed to a sudden violent thrust from more than three hundred-weight, broke apart, and the two men fell through on to the first floor landing below.

Tuesday Night

L ouis at last knew that things were coming right for him.
There had been a crisis not long ago; he couldn't remember details, but everything had seemed in a mess.

Now he knew different. He'd been in a fight, but the right men had gained control of London just in time and he was to have his reward. A position of power and responsibility, as Mr Armitage had promised him – power over lesser people, the responsibility of showing them how to behave in a new and better-ordered world. He'd had a real old set-to, a sheer physical personal fight, and was still recovering from the effects. But soon enough he'd be out of bed and ready to take his place. No more scraping and cheating for a few pounds. No more strangling of women – unless it was from choice, for pure sexual pleasure. It would only be necessary to say who he was – 'Louis Baker, State Controller of this or that district', and people would bow and scrape.

He didn't know how much actual fighting there had had to be in London and in England for this *putsch* to have been so quickly successful. Probably not too much. You got rid of the Old Gang – Churchill and his like – that was all. Now the war would automatically cease. There would be no slip-shod, go as you please, enfeebled democracy now. The country would be properly run by the people best fitted to run it.

Couldn't remember which hospital he was in. Not that it mattered: they'd told him and he'd forgotten. There was a screen round his bed so that he couldn't see a nurse to ask.

All very well to be a favoured patient, but one wanted to talk to people, keep up with things. He wondered how the rest of the country had taken it. That stupid nonentity, Arthur Filey; he hoped Hilda would divorce him and marry someone of *his* choosing. One certainty: the new administration would take no nonsense from Resistance Movements. They'd be quickly and ruthlessly put down, and he and people like him would make sure that suppression was final.

Louis dozed off, and woke suddenly from a disturbing dream. It was last night again and he was getting rid of the girl called Ward. He could still feel the slender neck in his fingers. But somehow Paula had come into the dark room. He could smell her scent everywhere. They had fought. Paula, whom he'd left miles away dead in a lonely house. And a man had come in and they had fought together too.

Well, thank God it was a dream. Or half a dream and half remembrance. He'd killed the Ward girl but it no longer mattered what witnesses there were. He was outside the law. He was above the law.

People were talking. Probably a nurse. He'd ask her the time. Felt pretty tired. Probably they'd given him a sedative. Or was it the remains of an anaesthetic? He was certainly in no pain.

A man's voice. 'I'm not off yet, nurse. There's a case in Number 14 that'll take a bit of time, so I may see you again before I go. In the meantime there's an urgent appendix waiting for this bed.'

'Will Mr Anderson operate?'

'Yes. The new case at the end, the Polish airman, and this chap here – I'm told they're connected. You'll know, of course. As if there wasn't enough trouble about without our people scrapping among themselves.'

'Was it just a brawl?'

'Don't know. It'll be serious for the Pole. It's likely he'll stand for a manslaughter charge when his ribs are mended.'

'Manslaughter? You mean? . . .'

'Oh, not a hope for this fellow. Cervical fracture. If he

recovers consciousness, which I doubt, see if he'll tell you who his relatives are.'

Louis listened with interest, wondering whom they were discussing and waited for the doctor to go so that he could call the nurse.

'How did it happen?' asked the nurse.

'They fell down some area steps. The Pole had had too much to drink and there was a dispute over a girl. Right in the middle of the air raid too.'

The nurse clicked her tongue sympathetically.

The doctor must have walked away then, for Louis' attention wandered. An annoying symptom of his present weakness was that he couldn't concentrate on anything for long. He wondered if Dot was still waiting for him. Too bad. She could cool her high heels. Trumpery creature with her platinumed hair and ugly make-up. True women didn't use make-up; they were natural, healthy, sturdy, fresh-air-loving girls who would become fitting mothers of a superior race. These two that he'd got rid of, they meant nothing to him now. He wouldn't have been surprised if Paula had Jewish blood. And that slip of a thing last night who'd hit him across the face with a bottle and fought like a cat . . . maybe she was Jewish too. If that were so, he'd done them a favour by putting them out of their misery. Extermination.

Thinking of high heels, he remembered how Paula's shoe had dropped off when he was propping her up in that chair. She'd sighed too when he lifted her, just as if she was coming to life again. The girl last night had died quite quietly in the end.

A shaft of pain went through the upper part of his body. He stirred to ease himself. Naturally his injuries would take time to heal. Couldn't be expected to ignore them.

Time and experience fled before his eyes. His father was standing by the bed. 'I always consider,' he was saying, 'that to talk about the equality of man is as ridiculous as to talk of the equality of animals. One is born a lion, another a jackal. Nature never intended that every man should have as much right to the benefits of the world as his neighbour. This is even more true of race. There are only two great peoples in the world, the Germans and the British.'

He was in Munich, on his only visit, just four years ago, visiting the historic scenes of the Party's early struggles, realizing for the first time that all his father had predicted about the rise of a new Germany was coming true before his eyes. And there that man had become friendly with him – he was quite high in the Party – and had recruited him to share in the coming struggle. Then with an ironic switch of scene he was back in the bank handling other people's money, and being ordered about by an arrogant little swine of a manager who had no idea of his true abilities or future importance.

The wedding – his sister's wedding. His sister, who had done a bit of work for the Cause now and then, but had never taken it as seriously as she ought. Pin money for spends was the way she'd looked at it. Well, she'd find out her mistake. The wedding wasn't going as smoothly as it should have done. At the breakfast she took his present and then burst into tears because she said there was blood on the cameo. Silly bitch; she'd learn.

His breath was short. It was all this running – up the stairs after that girl. 'I don't know anything,' she'd said. 'I can't do you any harm.' Well, she certainly couldn't now. When he'd finished, the bones of his fingers were tired with squeezing.

He struggled to sit up. That was better – eased the discomfort. If he could get out of bed and move about a bit . . . He eased his legs over the side of the bed and put his toes to the floor. More pain shivered through him, but he persevered and pulled his body up until he was standing supported by the screen.

He saw the long ward, with its rows of white beds all occupied. All sleeping. Only dim lights were burning and no attendants were about. His coat and trousers were on a chair beside the bed and it was a struggle getting into them. Then awkwardly, every step a trial, he began to walk down the ward, not conscious of any particular objective, but anxious only to be moving again, to leave this damned hospital and see what was taking place in the outside world.

He had staggered as far as the door when it opened and he found himself facing the doctor. They stared at each other.

'Well, what's the meaning of this, eh?'

Louis supported himself against the wall. 'Difficult – breathing. Want to leave – go home. Important things – to see to.'

'You've no business to be out of bed in your condition.' The doctor looked at him closely and his face softened. 'Very well, we'll see what we can do. This way.'

He took Louis' arm and led him up a flight of stairs. Louis struggled up them, panting for breath. On the way they passed the nurse coming down. She looked at them in surprise.

'He's going sooner than we expected,' she said. The doctor shrugged but did not reply.

At the top was a door, and this door led straight out onto the roof of the building. They walked slowly across the leads, and Louis at once realized that this hospital lay in the heart of the City. All the black, sombre city lay about him now, smoking and dirty and powerful. Amid the buildings were the gaps left by fire and explosion. In the distance St Paul's stood out like a great animal, gaunt and alone.

Another spasm of pain; it ran like fire; but he ignored it and stared across the city through the mists of morning. Soon it would be coming light. The grasp on his arm tightened and he saw to his surprise that it was Mr Armitage who was standing beside him.

'This is your reward,' said Armitage.

Louis knew just what was meant: he comprehended it by instinct rather than by reason. They walked nearer to the parapet together.

'Power,' said Mr Armitage. 'Dominion over the City and the Temple. Ober-Leutnant Louis von Langbeim. Here are the kingdoms of the world and the glory of them.'

Louis stared down. It seemed to him that there were great armies of men marching down the narrow blackened streets and that he would take his place at their head.

'It is written,' said Mr Armitage, 'that he shall give his angels charge concerning thee. And in their hands they shall bear thee up, lest at any time thou dash thy foot against a stone.'

Louis impatiently shook off the guiding arm. He needed no sermons or biblical nonsense. His pain had gone and he was ready and waiting to complete his mission. He stepped forward over the parapet and began to fall.

He fell through miles of smoke into a great cold abyss, confident at the last that his future was assured.

'He's gone now,' said the nurse. 'Peaceful enough at the end,' she added.

She covered his face with the sheet and left him alone with his glory.

Tuesday Night – Two

A ndrew arrived at Charing Cross just before 1 am. He had sat fuming and fretting in the dark, with only the tiny blue light in the carriage, the murmur of voices, the inevitable joker complaining he'd be late for breakfast, the occasional flicker of a lighter behind a guarded lapel, the glow of the cigarette end, somebody selflessly passing round squares of chocolate. Now and then impatience almost overcame him and he felt like jumping out on the track and trying to find another and quicker way in.

When at length the train slid furtively into the platform as if trying not to be noticed, his first thought was to ring Jennifer. Presumably Radziwill would still be with her; but maybe nobody would answer the telephone at this hour.

He wound his way in and out of people in the darkness, some of them asking in hushed voices, as if the Germans might overhear, whether there'd been much damage; others called for non-existent porters with a self-confidence no war on earth could shake; men in khaki and air-force blue streamed phlegmatically towards the street. It took a time to find an empty telephone booth. He had put in his pennies and was about to dial the number when he heard a loud rap on the window behind him. The big, reckless, ugly face of Witold Poniatowski.

He opened the door. 'Hallo! Were *you* on the train? I was just going to ring Stephen.'

Witold made a grimace. 'I am waiting for you in all these

hours, and then the train is come in der wrong platform. Stephen is in hospital.'

Andrew's stomach twisted. 'Since when? I rang him this evening!'

'Since this evening. He went on your errand and met a man and fought with him and they dropped downstairs. Now they are all in hospital.'

'All? Who's all?'

'Stephen and this bad man and your little garl – '

'Jennifer?' My turn next, she had said.

'This is correct. Do not pinch my arm.'

'But is she hurt? Tell me, man!'

'If you will hold your voice I will try it.'

With a great effort Andrew said no more. In painful slowness, in his harsh broken English, Witold did his best. He had been summoned from a restaurant in Piccadilly by a landswoman called Mrs Lawful. Leaving his party, as Stephen had left it three quarters of an hour before, he had gone to Gaskin Street and found the police very much in charge, and everyone else gone. They had all been taken to hospital, but Stephen had left this message with Mrs Lawful to ring Witold and say what had happened. He had also left a written message with Mrs Lawful which Witold had picked up when he got to Gaskin Street, telling him to meet Andrew on the 11.13 from Faversham.

'Since then I have been standing over my feet looking at der trains sat never come. At the latest I almost miss you!'

'Jennifer,' Andrew said. 'What happened to her? For God's sake!'

'I do not see her, have not see her. It is only what they say. She have been squeezed about the neck.'

'Christ! Where is she?'

'Stephen and der crazy man are in the Kingsway. Your garl is at der East London. They have no room for her.'

'We'll go there at once.'

'So. It is how you wish. But I think der raid is not yet over . . .'

They had come out into the street. By luck a taxi had just discharged two naval officers who went into the station; Andrew said: 'Can you take us to the East London Hospital?'

The driver cocked a wary eye skywards. 'I can try, sir. I think they're coming back.'

They climbed in.

Andrew said: 'You don't know anything more? Didn't Mrs Lawson say anything? Was Jennifer – conscious, unconscious? Did they bring an ambulance?'

'In Warsaw,' said Witold, 'I once have der acquaintance of a female *pianiste* who recites with her husband who uses der violin. One day they quarrel, and at der concert that night she plays so loud to drown his fiddle. The next day when I see her she is, I think, like your garl will be.'

You could hear the drone of planes again. After a brief silence the guns began to bark.

Andrew shook his head, trying to shake away the sense of sickly guilt. 'And Stephen? I haven't asked about Stephen?'

'They say he shall have cracked ribs, two or three. He has wrote plain in zis note. But it may mean he is off der air for weeks. I would weep.'

'You're not the only one.'

By now they were nearly into Covent Garden. Somewhere close by there was a blinding flash of light followed by a tremendous thump. Everything then was in greater darkness. The taxi slowed. The driver said: 'The road's blocked just ahead. Maybe I can double round, but I fancy I'll be stopped. The bloody bastards, they never let up, do they.'

'Is there a pub around here? . . . That one on the corner. Maybe if we waited there for ten minutes? Come and have a drink with us.'

'Don't mind if I do.'

In the pub everything was light and warmth and cheerfulness. It was a hectic cheerfulness, but it was better than nothing. People were talking fifteen to the dozen and in a corner half a score of young men in khaki were having a sing-song. The air was almost unbreathable with tobacco

189

smoke. When they had ordered and half drunk their orders Andrew said: 'I'll telephone.'

He hadn't much hope because the lines were likely to be down. Out in the aerodromes and airfields of Kent he and his fellows had suffered the strafings of the Luftwaffe, and very hairy they had been. But somewhat different from this. And anyway they were *supposed* to be in the firing line. It occurred to him to wonder who the real heroes of this war were – the men of action like himself who spent their lives, and lost their lives, in adrenaline-pumping combat, or the ordinary citizens of the great cities of England, particularly London, who endured these bombardments night in, night out, stoically, fatalistically, with no hope, no personal expectation, of ever being able to hit back.

He was gone ten minutes and returned to Witold and the taxi driver, who were now well into their third.

'I've got through!' he said excitedly, hardly able to believe it himself. 'She's – she *seems* all right, they *think*. Or going to be all right. Throat injuries and shock. They've given her a sedative, and she's sleeping. She mustn't be disturbed for at least twelve hours, they say. Oh my God Almighty, that's a relief, that's a relief, that's a relief!'

The doctor he'd eventually spoken to had said: 'So far as we can tell there shouldn't be permanent injury to the throat. Shock is sometimes the greater worry on occasions like this. But she's comfortable at present.' But merely the fact that she was *alive*!

He said to the barmaid: 'Got any champagne?'

'Well yes. It ain't exactly vintage, dear, but it's the real stuff. Ex-*pen*-sive.'

'Let's have a bottle,' Andrew said. 'Try to shut out this noise.' And then to Witold: 'Look, are you doing anything tomorrow?'

'I shall be looking at Stephen then, if not before.'

'Right. I agree. I must as well. And *then* if you will help me . . .' He tailed off. To call to see either Stephen or Jennifer would be to bring himself in contact again with the police.

Where the hell the police had been tonight he didn't know, maybe delayed by the raid, maybe they'd taken his telephone call as a hoax. For whatever reason, their absence from No 45 Gaskin Street when they were most needed didn't inspire him with confidence about how they would act – or fail to act – as a result of what he had to tell them.

The champagne came and was opened with a frail pop just audible amid the other noise.

The taxi driver took a good swig and said: 'Reckon we'd all be better in the tube than in this place.'

'We would. But they don't serve drinks there.'

If he told the police all he knew, all he suspected, what could they do? Only if this fellow who'd attacked Jennifer could be persuaded to squeal – and how long would *that* take? No police force in England would move on suspicion alone, and even Defence Regulation 18b would probably be ringed around with safeguards to protect the individual against persecution and false arrest. What about MI5? Where the hell were they and how did you get in touch with them? Not through the average copper on the beat or the average inspector at the local station. And, if the people he suspected got wind of danger, they'd bolt, or else destroy any evidence there might be and sit tight and look innocent and make everyone, himself included, feel a damned fool. It didn't have to be that way. It wouldn't be that way if he could help it.

They were all on their second glass.

'Witold,' he said, or half shouted. The soldiers in the corner were singing, 'Polly-wolly-doodle.'

'An-drew? What is it, old faller?'

'You'll help me? Tomorrow?'

'How is it?'

'I need your help.'

'OK, OK, OK.'

'Are there others you could call on, men you can trust, who'd just do what you'd tell them?'

'Sure. Sure. But many are away . . . There's Morsztyn. I see him siz evening when he come to see Stephen.'

'I think I could get Jenks. Flight Sergeant Jenks. He's on leave and lives in Hammersmith. That might be enough.'

Poniatowski's pale absent-minded eyes were fixed on his glass. 'What enough? What to do?'

Andrew tried in three brief minutes to explain what the situation was. He was not sure how much Witold understood, but when he had finished the Pole pushed his hat farther on the back of his head.

'Whenever I see a German,' he said, 'I feel der itch.'

'Not German in this case, but a Fifth Columnist. Does that mean something to you?'

'OK. Sat means something to me. OK.'

They finished the bottle.

'It's no better,' said the taxi driver. 'I reckon I'd better be pushing off.'

Andrew paid him and thanked him. Then he said to Witold: 'I'm not satisfied about this cut on my hand. It's taken a turn for the worse, and I'm going to see about it in the morning.'

Witold said: 'Sat itch. Maybe he shall be able to do something for sat also, eh?'

'Let's ask him.'

It was while the taxi driver was edging towards the door that they heard it coming. It was as if it was marked for them, named for them, specially aimed for them. Everyone as if by a single barked order dived for the floor. But as they fell, the floor rose up and met them, the windows flew in, thrusting their lethal splinters everywhere. The door fell, the lights went out, the wall of the pub was no longer there; those who were alive could see into the street.

After it, and the constant crackle and rumble of falling masonry and slates, there was a period of almost silence. Then from the floor figures began to raise themselves. Someone spoke, someone shouted, someone groaned. There were no lights. No one could see anything. After the heat and jollity and human noise of the pub, there was a cool air from the street, mingled with a hot air where something burned. It was the taxi, upside down.

After a few more moments, seconds, minutes, other figures in the street began to move again; emerged from cellars, shelters, walls, dug-outs: wardens and special constables and firemen and ambulance men and ordinary people who just weren't anything but survivors of this particular blitz. It was as if this were a parting shot, this final bomb or stick of bombs released as the planes turned for the long and dangerous journey home, because soon after it the terrible crashing abated.

Andrew sat up, found his cap, brushed the rubble out of his hair.

'Witold!'

'Ah yes,' said a voice beside him. 'Sis is making me homesick, yes? Sis recalls me of Warsaw.'

'Are you hurt?'

'No. I think not so. And you?'

'I think not so,' said Andrew. 'But I think the barmaid got it. And some of those soldiers.'

And, they found, so had the taxi driver.

Wednesday Morning

I

Dr Joseph Norley always said that an air raid brought ordinary patients to him in greater numbers, as if the fall of a bomb reminded Mr Brown of his rheumatism or the roar of the ack-ack barrage suggested a new ailment to Mrs Jones. He had been up part of the night too. Considering the weight of the raid, casualties had not been excessive, but enough had come in to the Commercial Dock Hospital to keep him busy for some hours. The pouches under his eyes were heavier than usual.

Miss Harrison, his receptionist, had been up part of the night also, but she didn't show it. Miss Harrison was thirty-seven, tall, slim, neat, fine-featured, pallid, with very good legs and small prim feet. She ushered an elderly woman into the consulting room and withdrew through the dispensary door. Dr Norley sometimes said he didn't know what on earth he would do without Miss Harrison – a statement which was no more than the truth.

'Well, Mrs Knox, how is it with you this morning? Better, I hope?'

'Not much, Doctor. These sharp mornings touch me up. What with the air raid and this cough, cough from half-past four.'

'Medicine cuts the phlegm a little, though?'

'Oh yes. I thought to meself yesterday it might be on the mend. But then this morning early it was just as bad as ever it was.'

'Well, any kind of anxiety will tend to aggravate the condition. Worry is a thing to be avoided. Counsel of perfection in war-time, you may say. But I'm sure we're on the right track. Have you medicine left?'

'Only a drop.'

They talked for a couple of minutes, and then Norley made an entry on a slip of paper. 'Get another bottle made up. Let me see your tongue. Yes, yes. We'll go on like that, and come and see me in another week. How's your husband these days? Good, good. Do these raids upset him? Of course. Well, we must all hope for an improvement now the light days are coming. Good-bye, good-bye . . . Yes, please, Miss Harrison . . .'

The next patient was a middle-aged man in a shiny blue suit. He stood just inside the door, put a bowler-hat on the knob of a chair and wiped the back of his hand across his moustache.

'Good morning, Mr Woods. How's the world treating you today?'

'Oh, not so bad, Doctor.' The man glanced at Miss Harrison, who was filing away the note the doctor had made on Mrs Knox, then he came forward slowly and sat down. Miss Harrison went out. 'I don't get so bilious, but I'm still that tired that I nearly go to sleep at me work. Can't you give me a tonic of some sort, Doctor?'

Dr Norley took out his stethoscope. 'I'll sound you again. Just unfasten your shirt.' He bent over the man.

The little man sat back in his chair. 'Five near the tram depot in Millbay Road,' he said. 'Time bomb beside the gasometer in East Street. Land mine in the Dock Road, killed about ten and started a bad fire that's spread to a paper works. Unexploded land mine caught in the trees on the edge of Millbay Common. Two fires in South Street; top floor of a carpet factory and two floors of an office building: both been put out. A shelter hit, and a church schoolroom in St Saviour's Road.'

'Well, well, quite a busy morning for you, Mr Woods.' The doctor folded his stethoscope and went back to his desk, while the little man glanced furtively round the room and buttoned his shirt. Norley began to write on a sheet of paper. 'Five . . . Dock Road, ten . . . carpet factory . . . Yes, yes, quite a busy morning, Mr Woods. Don't – '

'An' I got a detail. Thompson's old Lutine bell got bust.'

'Lutine? . . . I thought – '

'Lloyd's? Yes. But this is one old man Thompson had put up forty years ago in his office, to ring when one of *his* ships was in trouble. Always called it the Lutine bell. Folk around here know it as Thompson's Lutine bell.'

'Ah, I see. But for our purpose . . .'

'Thought it would do for Lord Haw-Haw. Just the sort of snippet he likes. Comes over the radio tonight, "Pity about the Lutine bell in Thompson & Curry's private office. Won't ring again, I fear." You can just hear him.'

Norley was writing. 'Was it a public shelter?'

'Yes. One of them surface things. Wouldn't be seen in one myself. I always patronize the tubes.'

'Very wise of you.' Norley opened a drawer and slipped something into an envelope. 'Take this prescription and have it made up; it should have a beneficial effect.'

'Damn right it will. Damn right it will.' The little man wiped his moustache again and picked up his hat. In putting the envelope into his pocket he bent it, and the paper inside gave a crackle. 'Just in time for yours truly. Not been this way for some while, have they. Quite like old times.'

'And keep your mouth shut,' said Norley.

'Sure. Trust me, Doctor. I know which side me bread's buttered, don't I. Well, thanks, Doctor, I'll come in again sometime and let you know how I'm going along.'

'Yes, do that,' said Norley. 'Good morning.'

He was about to press the bell for Miss Harrison when he saw her come quickly out of the dispensary.

'Doctor Short is on the phone. I was waiting. Shall I put him through now?'

Norley's square, pouched face sharpened, like that of a dog which has suddenly seen danger or scented a quarry.

'Er – yes, put him through.'

He picked up the receiver.

'Hullo, Norley,' came a voice. 'This is Short. You remember that patient we were interested in, that – er – young fellow suffering from shell shock, who had gone back to Manston?'

Norley was too used to messages couched in vague terms to miss the import of this one. 'Yes?'

'Well, he returned from Manston last night. I don't know if you've been told that.'

'No.'

'For a while I'm afraid he was completely lost sight of. In the black-out it was obviously difficult for our man to keep track of him. He was only picked up again forty minutes ago, outside the RAF Club in Piccadilly, and he told the taxi driver to take him to Dellow Street. The driver did not know where it was, and the airman had to explain.'

Norley traced with his pencil another little £ sign among the many decorating his blotting-pad. 'He came to see me before, you know.'

'Of course I know. But this time there are three other airmen with him. And there's a hint in their manner that suggests they may mean to make trouble.'

'Who located him?'

'Mrs Heather.'

Norley looked sharply up at the ceiling as if afraid it might fall. 'In case of necessity can I call on you?'

'You know how we stand in this matter.'

Norley knew. It was the rule in case of danger that one cut one's losses. 'Very well. I'll ring you again later, Short. Thanks for the call.'

He put up the receiver. Before making any further move he opened a drawer and took from it a cigarette box in which were a number of half-smoked cigarettes and butt-ends. He chose one of the latter, about an inch long, and put a lighter to it. He smoked in silence, then pressed the bell for his dispenser.

'Er – Miss Harrison, have we a fairly full waiting-room?'

'Yes. Twenty or more, Doctor.'

'Do you mind when you call the next patient taking a look round and seeing if there are any airmen among them.'

Miss Harrison's eyebrows came a shade closer together. 'There are three at least. I noticed that. We don't get many of the forces in as a rule.'

The stub of cigarette had burned down until it was a damp crumb glowing against his lips. He took it out with finger- and thumb-tips and dropped it into an ashtray in the drawer. 'Any idea how long before it is their turn to come in?'

'Soon, I should think. They've been here some time.' Miss Harrison took a step forward. 'Trouble?' she said in a different voice.

'Trouble.'

'What is it?'

'Nothing much. Show the next patient in, please.'

A woman in a red hat, accompanied by a small weedy boy, entered the consulting-room.

'Good morning,' said Norley. 'Well, how's the little man this morning? Improvement continuing, eh?'

'I'm OK,' said the boy.

'He isn't, Doctor, reely, he isn't. Wriggle, wriggle all day, that's him. On the fret, you know. I think you're treating 'im wrong. I think it's just nerves, you know. He wants something to make 'im sit still.'

'Let me see your tongue, boy. Bowels in working order?'

'I'm OK,' said the boy.

'It's not natural, Doctor, the way he goes on. His father was saying he didn't seem no better at all.'

'Excuse me a moment,' said Miss Harrison. She bent towards the doctor and in an undertone: 'The one after the next. Can I help?'

Norley raised his head with a slight frown. Then he wrote on a piece of paper. 'No. Keep out of it.'

'I'm OK,' said the boy.

'You must understand, Mrs Page, that one cannot expect

an immediate improvement in a case like this. Diet is as important as anything I can give him. In the meantime continue with the present treatment and come and see me in another week. Oh, and let me see, you didn't settle for your last week's visit, did you?'

'No, Doctor. I've got it with me today.'

Money changed hands, and three minutes later Norley was alone. He didn't at once ring for Miss Harrison to call in the next patient. He was full of little nervous habits as his mind flickered over the difficulties which might confront him. But he had lived so long at the mercy of a single mischance that he wasn't dismayed. Only alert; his mind was tremendously alert as it always was at the approach of danger. It slid in rapid appreciation over what he had done this morning; the boy of seven with the curly hair who'd had a leg blown off – a ticklish job that; the pretty girl with the terrible burns across the mouth; the old man who kept talking about his pension; the new nurse who looked as if she was going to faint. There was ample money in safe securities. All his life he'd stopped at nothing to get money, but ever since the Hatry crash he had always invested it in Swiss and other three-per-cents. Ania had urged him to quit while things were good. Sometimes he wished he could; he had no principles at stake. But it all paid too well to be lightly abandoned.

And really it only meant sticking it out for a few more months. England was pretty well done for – at her last gasp. And Germany wanted peace just as much as England did, peace and the freedom to attack Russia. England would be welcome to keep her Empire in return for giving Germany a free hand in the East. It was all in *Mein Kampf*, plain to be read. Churchill would fall, and then the way was open for a negotiated settlement.

A negotiated settlement. Until then all one needed was a cool head – that and the prestige of one's position.

Miss Harrison came and stood, prim and taut, in the frame of the dispensary door and watched him. He picked up the telephone and dialled a number.

'Hullo. Is that the Elm Street police station? I wonder if Sergeant Chalmers is there. May I speak to him? Doctor Norley. Thanks.'

'What are you going to do?' said Miss Harrison.

'Keep out of this. Hullo, is that Sergeant Chalmers? Good. Doctor Norley speaking from the surgery. So sorry to trouble you, Sergeant, but I wonder if I could ask you to send a man round here, just on a small matter that is disturbing us at present . . . Well, I don't like to complain really, but it's four airmen who I imagine have been out on the spree all night and have come into my waiting-room for a lark. One hates to complain about the Services; God knows, they're doing a grand job, but I'm afraid some of my patients will be upset, and one is afraid these lusty fellows when they've had a drop to drink will smash things. *Do* you mind? Come yourself? Oh, that's so good of you. A weight off my mind. Distinctly, yes. Oh, and Sergeant, d'you mind coming round to the surgery door, and Miss Harrison will let you in. I *don't* want a scene if it can possibly be avoided, and perhaps I shall be able to reason with them and get them to move off quietly. Thanks very much. I'll expect you.'

Norley hung up, and his heavy eyes met the pale, reticent eyes of his dispenser.

'Show the next patient in, will you, Miss Harrison.'

'You're taking risks.'

'Half the battle's to get in the first word. Take it from me. Next please.'

The newcomer, when she was shown in, was a plump, over-dressed young woman with big breasts and bleached hair.

'Morning, Doctor,' she said in a rich winey voice. 'I've just come to report that I'm fine now. Made a good job of me, you have. There was only one thing I wanted to ask you . . .'

Her voice tailed off and she looked over her shoulder.

'What is your report?' said Norley.

'A rare big one on Brownall's Brewery, blarst them. Done no end of damage. Three on the railway sidings that run up behind Moss Lane. Couple of dozen wagons gone west. And the cold-storage place at Carter's End has got a couple of nasty holes in the roof: they wouldn't let me inside to see.'

'That the lot?'

'All in my bit. Isn't it enough?'

'Of course. Any estimate of casualties?'

'None dead but thirty or forty injured, so they say. Thought I was going to be one myself. I was having a quick one in the back room of the White Lion when – '

'Here's the prescription.' Dr Norley had been considering her carefully. 'Look, Mrs O'Hara, I may need your help. If I do, you'll get a further – prescription. D'you follow me?'

'So far. What's it all about?' Her eyes were narrowed and wary.

'When you go, stay in the waiting-room. If necessary I want you to testify that the airmen in there have been creating a disturbance. Understand? I just want you to back up any story I tell. Understand? You're clever at saying just enough.'

'Get off,' said Mrs O'Hara. 'What about the others in the room? They'll swear the opposite.'

'There won't be any. Miss Harrison is going to tell them that I can't see any more patients today.'

'Ah.' The woman took a mirror out of her bag and looked at herself in it. She re-smeared the red on her lips with a small, already pink finger-tip. 'Usual rates?'

'Usual rates, plus a little for inconvenience.'

'All right. Count me in. But I don't like monkeying with the police, mind. Don't let me down, will you.'

'I'll not let you down.'

She went out. Miss Harrison came quietly out of the dispensary and stood again looking at the doctor.

'It is dangerous to use women like that. They are the scum.'

Norley bent to rummage among the papers in the top drawer of his desk.

'It takes a good man to work with shoddy material. That's why I'm here.'

'What are you looking for?'

'Nothing. Only to see all has been put away.'

'Don't you trust me yet?'

'There's no one I *can* trust, except you.'

'Joseph, why don't we get away while there is still time, *if* there is still time?'

'How could we?'

'As I have urged you often before. Each time the danger is greater. Trusting to the help and the silence of a woman like that!'

Norley shrugged. 'The devil drives, my dear. We shall come through, never fear – just as usual.'

'There is more in this house than can be destroyed in five minutes.'

His eyes flickered. 'We shall have more than five minutes, believe me. If the worst comes to the worst there will be time. Has Sergeant Chalmers come?'

'Not yet. He should be here any moment. It is only three streets away. It will be better to wait until he comes.'

'The very opposite,' said Norley. 'Ask the first one in now.'

'How do you know they mean trouble? Have you been told?'

Norley gave her an unamiable smile. 'How does a rheumatic person know it is going to rain?'

'Shall I stay in here?'

'Of course not. Don't lose your nerve, Ania. Get on.'

The tall thin woman turned slowly and opened the door. 'Next, please.'

There was a moment's pause.

'Not two together. One at a time, please,' said Miss Harrison in a sharp tone.

'I wish to go wiz him,' came a deep voice with a strong foreign accent. 'He is my friend, you understand. I come to keep him together.'

'The doctor prefers to see his patients separately. It is a rule we always – '

'Let them in, Miss Harrison,' said Norley mildly. 'Dear me, we have no law against it. Show them – Good morning, gentlemen. What can I do for you?'

The doctor's permission had only just come in time, for a moment more would have seen the two men in without it.

'This hand,' said Andrew. 'I cut it in a motor accident. Perhaps you'd look at it. Don't mind my friend, he's just come to keep me together.'

Poniatowski stood near the waiting-room door, which he had closed behind him, and gazed round with a gape of teeth and wide-set eyes. Miss Harrison glanced at him, then at the doctor; she was white about the nostrils. Poniatowski's gaze settled on her. She turned and left the room by the other door.

'Well, well, let me look at it,' Norley was saying. 'Not a very expert bandage, surely. You've been here before, Squadron Leader.'

'I came on Sunday to inquire about my friend, Paula Krissen.'

'Oh, yes, yes, to be sure. Have you been able to locate her?'

'She's dead.'

Norley's small puffy eyes met Halford's unflinchingly.

'Dead? I *am* sorry. Was it in one of the raids?'

'You might put it that way.'

'A pity. A great pity. I've known Miss Krissen for many years. Please accept my sympathy.'

'Thank you.'

'That's the tragedy of this war; women and children in the front line. Why . . . there doesn't seem much wrong with your hand. Do you feel pain in it?'

'No,' said Andrew. 'There's nothing much wrong with it.'

Norley smiled grimly into the face of his visitor. 'Come, Squadron Leader; what is this farce?'

'No farce,' said Andrew. 'I came to inquire from you about

two other young ladies. A Miss Hilda Baker and a Miss Jennifer Ward. They are not dead – yet.'

'I don't know what you mean,' Norley said impatiently; 'you're wasting my time. I've been up half the night and have many more patients waiting to see me. There's nothing wrong with your hand beyond a half-healed cut of no importance and this older cicatrice. If you have any other business, please state it.'

'I've come to see you,' Halford said, 'because I'm interested in your work in London. I want to know more about it and that is what I've come to find out.'

'I can only suppose you're drunk,' said Norley. 'Please leave my surgery.'

Andrew said: 'Is there a lock on that door, Witold?'

'No.'

'Keep an eye on this man.' Andrew rose and glanced swiftly round the room.

'Is this your idea of a joke?' Norley said angrily. 'How dare you force your way in here and make yourself offensive? Get out at once!'

Andrew had gone to the desk and pulled open a drawer. Norley started forward to intercept him, but Witold put a big hand on the flat of his chest and thrust him backwards into a chair. Norley banged his head.

'Damn your impertinence! Get out of here!' The doctor was up again on the instant and struck at the Pole. Poniatowski grunted and caught the doctor by the shoulders and swung him back into the chair with a crash. Andrew pulled a handful of papers out and began rapidly to go through them.

'Keep a look out for the nurse,' he warned. 'She'll probably scream.'

'Zat will not matter. Morsztyn will not let anyone to enter. Is your Jenks?'

'In the street. But don't let her go out again if she comes in. There may be a separate side door to the street.'

'Help!' shouted Norley. 'Help!'

'Shut your voice!' said Withold. 'Or else – '

There was a movement of the dispensary door; it began to open; Andrew was quicker than Witold; he made the door in two strides.

But facing him was not the tall thin nurse he had seen leave by it; instead a sergeant of the Metropolitan Police Force.

It seemed an unfortunate coincidence, to say the least.

II

A good-looking man in his early fifties, the sergeant, and used to rough and unexpected situations. But not quite used to this. Called by his own doctor who'd treated him for a sprained shoulder, called in to quiet some young shavers from the RAF, who were on the rampage – policeman's uniform would probably do the trick: if not a few hours in the cells, cool 'em off.

But this, he saw at once, was more serious. Not young shavers. Thin, taut, strong-looking young officer – two and a half stripes – facing him, grim-faced, intent; great big fellow standing beside the doctor's chair, another officer but POLAND on his shoulder; Dr Norley, hands gripping desk, spots of red in his cheeks; Miss Harrison, white as a swan, by the other door, clasping a records sheet as if for protection.

You could count the silence before he said: 'What's going on here?'

Norley swallowed and sat back. 'Ah, come in, Sergeant. You've just arrived in time.'

'Just in time,' agreed the young officer, obviously trying to make the best of a bad situation.

Chalmers said: 'What exactly's the trouble, Doctor?'

'These men – '

'The trouble is,' interrupted the English officer, with a real note of authority in his voice, 'we suspect Dr Joseph Norley of belonging to the German Secret Service. We're looking for proof and are very glad to have you here as an independent witness.'

Chalmers saw that the filing cabinet was open and some records pulled out. Thoughts flicked across his mind like disturbed flies.

'Arrest them! Arrest them!' This from Miss Harrison.

Somebody rattled the waiting-room door. Norley made a sudden move to get up; as quickly the Pole thrust him back in his chair, great hand on his chest.

Chalmers said sharply: 'Now then, drop that; let the doctor go! What authority have you for making this disturbance?'

As soon as he saw the English officer hesitate he saw he could now take over. He walked further in and took no notice of what the officer was trying to say.

'First let the docter get up. If you want to explain then, you can explain.'

'These men have been worrying me for half an hour,' Norley said. 'First creating a disturbance in the waiting-room, then in here. I'm very grateful to you for coming personally, Chalmers.'

The two airmen had exchanged glances as the policeman advanced. Andrew made a gesture to Witold, and Witold took his hand off the doctor. Norley got up and stood behind his chair, smiling now, but still white round the lips. He straightened his crumpled lapels.

'I give these men in charge, Sergeant. I really don't like to make a fuss in wartime, but this had gone altogether too far. They should be made an example of.'

'I quite agree, sir – '

'Sergeant,' Andrew said, 'I know the English law doesn't give authority to search houses without a magistrate's warrant – '

'It certainly does not – '

'I don't have any such warrant and couldn't get one, because I've no proof of my suspicions. But I'm personally certain that this man is an enemy agent. I intend to search this house from top to bottom and I'll abide by the result. You can be witness – '

'You'll do no such thing,' said Chalmers, getting heated.

'Not in my presence, you won't. You can come right away with me and make whatever charge you think fit at the station. But you won't worry Dr Norley any further this morning.'

'Thank you, Sergeant,' said Norley with satisfaction.

'I'm sorry,' said Andrew. 'I'm afraid we're going ahead.' He went to the filing cabinet and took out a sheaf of papers.

'No, you *don't!*' Chalmers took out his whistle – a bluff perhaps, though usually effective – but he never got it to his mouth. The Pole caught his arm and pulled it away. At the same time Andrew dropped the papers and jumped to pinion his other arm. The seargeant had had his share of rough and tumble in thirty years in the police force, but one of his assailants was as wiry as they come and the other was three stone over his weight. After a ragged twisting struggle he found himself face down with the Englishman holding him, just holding him, while the Pole leapt after Norley who had run to the waiting-room door and was trying vainly to open it. There was a click like the click of teeth, and the doctor staggered across the room and collapsed near the dispensary door. Chalmers, twisting his head, saw all the easy good-humoured look gone from the Pole's face, his big mouth tight like a trap, and wondered for a moment if he'd broken the doctor's neck. That spurred him to a humped jerk and threw Andrew off his back, whereupon Andrew hit him in the face and threw his weight back on him to keep him down. Chalmers was temporarily winded, and between them the two men got a belt round his middle and tied it and buckled it round a leg of the desk.

In the waiting-room a woman screamed, but the scream was cut off like someone switching off a radio. Avoiding the sergeant's viciously kicking legs, the two men went to the filing cabinet and began pulling out drawers and throwing papers about the floor in a wild confusion. After a very long and tense three minutes Andrew suddenly stopped and stared at a dossier that had come out of the back of the cabinet.

'I think we've got something here, Witold; I really think

so. These are not prescriptions I'm damned sure. Look, if we – '

'*Uwaga!*' shouted Witold, and for a moment everyone paused, even Chalmers who had at last got his whistle to his lips.

A new factor had emerged. Miss Harrison had retreated into a corner of the room and opened a little cupboard. From it she had taken a revolver which she was now levelling at them.

III

Chalmers told it all to his wife later that afternoon.

'I've seldom had a worse morning – or at least a more perplexing one. Not since that fur-coat robbery arrest back in '37. I like to know where I am in a case. I don't like not knowing which side to take.'

'I know you don't, dear,' said his wife.

'It seemed open and shut, right to begin – man you've known for seven years, treated you and your son and your wife, making legitimate complaint against two crazy air-force officers. I could see them in real trouble, those two: common trespass, GBH, and when they got me down I was fighting mad, real mad. Ouch!'

'Sorry, dear,' said his wife. 'Did I hurt? You'll find it easier when it's bathed.'

The sergeant touched his eye thoughtfully. 'It's funny that, you know, the way something's overlooked and the whole case is changed, like. In all this I'd not given a thought to Miss Harrison. Nor had the two officers, I bet. She was just the receptionist, just in the room by accident. But it's like building a wall, isn't it. You build up a whole wall, a house, even, and it all looks ever so convincing, and there's just one weak brick and that lets the whole house down. Miss Harrison was the weak brick.'

'Keep still a minute.'

'You know her as well as I do, don't you? One of those

tidy, over-particular, good-looking sort of women that never get married. Born old maids by temperament.'

'She's been his dispenser for years.'

'Yes. D'you mind when she came to this district? No, neither do I. She probably came when he came, which was before we left Peterborough. Close about her own affairs, of course; but I never thought she'd anything special to be close about. Thought it was just her way. Well, these two airmen have made a fair old mess of the room. The Pole is still at the desk, Halford at one of the filing cabinets, and Halford has been pretty quiet for some seconds. Suddenly he says: "I think we've got something here, Vee-tol," or some such name. "I'll swear these are not prescriptions. It's a – "

'I hear a movement at the dispensary door and then get the shock of my life. There's our Miss Harrison – *our* Miss Harrison! – with a revolver in her hand. It's got a silencer fitted, and she raises it and fires twice before I can take it all in! The Pole gets his in the shoulder, and the Englishman falls behind the filing cabinet as the second bullet ricochets off the wood and smashes the mirror at the end of the room. You know what a nasty sound a revolver with a silencer makes in an enclosed room. No, perhaps you don't, but it's *nasty*. And she was shooting to kill. I could see that by her eyes. They'd a funny sort of glazed look.

'The Pole has gone down behind the desk, holding his shoulder; for a few seconds I can hear the clock ticking on the mantelpiece. It's just twenty minutes past ten. She's watching for either of them to show himself. Then the doctor groans and starts moving.

'She says: "If any of you stir I'll shoot the sergeant. I mean that; keep still. *Can you hear me, Joseph?*"

'Then the doctor grunts and tries to sit up. You can see he'd been right out for some minutes and can't make head or tail of what he found.

' "Get up, Joseph," she says again. "Can you walk?" Her revolver waves up and down. "The dispensary door's open," she says, "and I'll keep them quiet while you get a start."

'It was only just about then, I suppose, that Doctor Norley takes in what has happened: he's been too dazed before. He struggles to his feet and leans against the wall and his mouth gives a sort of downward jerk at the sides. "Oh, Ania," he says; "you fool – "

'She says back at him quick enough: "You wouldn't bluff your way out of this. Go on: there'll be others here soon."

'He says something to her then that I can't catch; he shakes his head like someone coming out of water, dabs a spot of blood from his mouth with a handkerchief, and then he goes – leaving her covering us with the revolver. She'd still got that funny look in her eyes. I've only seen it once before; you remember in '36 I had to go and arrest some people who'd started a Holy Tabernacle in Fourth Street – illegal practices was the charge – one of the women there had that look, the one who when I charged her started talking about "the blood is the life". Only then I hadn't seen it looking at me from behind a loaded weapon. I thought every minute this one was going to fire. Then, to cap all, someone hammers at the door to the waiting-room and shouts, "All right in there?"

'Luckily the squadron leader has the sense to answer, "All right; stay where you are." And then the Harrison woman licks her lips and takes a quick glance round behind her and then slides like a snake through the dispensary door and we hear the key turn in the lock.'

'Phew!' said Mrs Chalmers.

'That's exactly what I said. It was the nastiest five minutes I remember. Of course it didn't end there. Halford rushes to the waiting-room door and hammers on it to be let out. The Pole comes from behind the table, still holding his shoulder, and is for following his friend, leaving me there, if I hadn't shouted myself hoarse at him to let me free. By the way, isn't it tea-time?'

'It's all ready when you are.'

'I'm ready now. The rest can wait till later.'

'Yes, but was it true what the officers said about Doctor

Norley? That's what I can't believe. Did you find any proof?'

'They've not been caught yet,' said Sergeant Chalmers gruffly. 'We don't even know yet. But three Special Branch men were down this afternoon, and everything in the filing cabinets has been taken off to Whitehall. So it looks rather bad for Norley . . . But there's a lot of straightening up to be done before it's settled. That's why I'm going back to the station in an hour.'

'Is the squadron leader going to be charged?'

'With assaulting a police officer? He *has* been charged! I saw to that! However strongly convinced you may be about something, you've no right to take the law into your own hands! Things have got to be done legally and the law has to take its proper course in the end.'

Mrs Chalmers went off to make the tea. As he came into the room she said:

'D'you think he will be prosecuted?'

'Who?'

'This squadron leader. Of course he *ought* to be. And yet . . .'

'It's up to the Super. And it will depend what they find. It was my *duty* to have him charged.'

'Of course, dear.'

'But I bear him no ill-will,' said Chalmers. 'Or shan't once this eye goes down. If it really is what they think it is, then he would have been better to go about it all more quietly. But there you are – that's the way some of these young men go on – still fighting the war in Shadwell!'

Thursday Evening

―――――♦8♦―――――

Walter Gissing rubbed the fine black hair on the back of his hand.

'Fraser, I *admire* your journal. Don't mistake me. But I doubt if I could run to three articles on the financial situation. I know that as a nation we shall soon be bankrupt but there's only so much one can say. Suppose I sketch a rough draft first and let you see it?'

'You mean you want to spill over into political or philosophic protest.'

'Not protest, discussion.'

The three men were standing, whisky glasses in hand, in the book-lined study of Gissing's West End house. By some special dispensation of Providence, or so it seemed to Gissing, this block had so far come through all the bombing without so much as a shattered window. When the sirens sounded he never failed to go into his deep and well-furnished shelter without feeling this time, this time, oh dear, if it should spoil my china, my silver, my books . . . Bombing was a necessary nuisance in the process of winning the war quickly, but it could be very tiresome.

Luke Fraser had just arrived and had brought with him young Colin Penfield, his sub-editor, as Gissing had suggested. Penfield was about twenty-eight, with red hair, a pale skin and a long neck.

Fraser said with a hint of sarcasm: 'You could always do a couple of thousand words on "The Island Pharisees".'

'You mock me unfairly. I complain about faults we all

possess, but naturally I believe our way of life is to be preferred, otherwise I should not be fighting for it. Isn't that so, young Penfield?'

Fraser didn't see that Gissing was engaged in strife on anyone's behalf, but he assumed the claim was meant figuratively.

'Young' Penfield said: 'Well, I suppose if you use success as the criterion, then there's a lot to be said for our present system of values. To date. Whether they'll shortly be superseded by another system is anyone's guess.'

'Which won't be better,' said Fraser, 'only more successful.'

Gissing said: 'The terms are pretty well synonymous.'

'Not morally.'

'Ah, morally.' Gissing took his guests' glasses and went to the bureau with them. 'There'll be nice time for another before dinner . . . Ah, morally,' he continued, coming back. 'That to your liking, Fraser? And you, young man?' They thanked him. 'Ah, morally.'

'Ethically, then, if you prefer it.'

Gissing filled his own glass. 'Some say that spirits before wine spoils one's palate. I hope it's not true because I have some remarkably good Chambertin, made in the year Germany occupied the Rhineland but very forward in character . . . I fear, Fraser, that history, like biology, judges only by results. Ethics or morals are very late runners.'

'But to be considered.'

'I very much follow what you mean,' said Penfield earnestly.

'Well, it's what any *student* knows . . . The subjects of Flavius Honorius were probably neither more nor less admirable in their habits than those of Alaric. One prevailed and the other did not. Can we assume that the dinosaur was a less moral or less ethical creature than *pithecanthropus erectus*? We cannot. I would have guessed the opposite. But victory is to the strong – or the most adaptable – or the more ruthless. History will rewrite the world as we make it. I'm afraid history is not concerned with the failures.'

'Well,' said Fraser, 'there is the case of Jesus Christ, isn't there.'

'Oh my dear chap, I'm sorry, I didn't know I was treading on your corns!'

'Nor are you,' said Fraser, in irritation. 'I'm not a very good Christian. Indeed by many standards I'm not a Christian at all. But your assertion that history is concerned only with success is rather punctured by what might be called his Failure Story. And whatever you may think about him, however you rate him as an influence on civilization, he can never be ignored in any responsible history of the last two thousand years.'

Gissing dabbed the sleeve of his shabby suit, where he had spilt a drop of whisky. 'And you, Penfield? Do you feel the same?

'About Christianity? As a historical fact, certainly, of course. But as a living force nowadays, not at all. It's washed up, finished, on its last legs. I suppose I call myself a humanist. It helps to put this war into a better perspective.'

'Which you think we shall win?'

'I have my doubts.'

'And you, Gissing?' interposed Fraser.

A disclaiming shrug. 'I don't think Hitler ought to be allowed to win. But if he does or if he doesn't, is the difference so very great? He represents a philosophy that's spreading world-wide.'

'From the East.'

Gissing chuckled. 'It depends where you're located. But yes, looking at it from an insular point of view, from the East. Where the Wise Men came from, incidentally!'

'That includes Russia,' said Penfield.

'Of course,' said Fraser. 'Necessarily. I see virtually no difference in the two systems.'

'Oh, *I* do,' said Penfield contentiously, and then, remembering his manners, went on in a more conciliatory tone: 'I think of Russia as following an ideal, experimenting with something totally new and fascinating – '

'Marxism.'

'Yes. Clearly making many mistakes on the way but moving towards a worthwhile end.'

'And Fascism?' said Fraser. 'An ideal too? Equally clear and equally false? Surely it's the other side of the record. A different tune played by the same band.'

Gissing smiled and stared at the gold ring on his finger. This was the sort of conversation he enjoyed. He withdrew a little and listened to his two guests arguing with each other. Penfield was good material and worth cultivating for his own sake. Fraser was on his way out, as were many of his generation and his upbringing. But the theories of life, the principles by which men lived, the political and religious or anti-religious beliefs that drove them on, these were what really interested Gissing.

It was a pity that he had ever had to have any dealings with this man Baker, poor material at best, who had failed yesterday in the second mission given him, and had got himself killed in a brawl which followed. Too close to home to be entirely safe. Full report had not come through yet, and he had not been able to use the telephone today because the blitz had damaged the wires at the corner of the square and repair men had been busy on them all day. But Gissing blamed headquarters for taking on such a man, who fundamentally was unstable, with a thread of fanaticism in him. Of course such men could be useful, and of course he was expendable material, had in fact been so expended. Lucky that he was dead and not injured. Not that he knew anybody but a shadowy figure called Armitage.

'Pray don't think I disagree with what you say,' he interrupted Fraser courteously. 'But these phrases that you've just been using to our young friend, don't you think they belong to an age that is passing?'

'Such phrases as?'

'Well, "sanctity of treaties", "good of the human race", "moral obligations". We're coming back full circle to what we said just now. They may read very well in the leading articles of *The Onlooker*, but they cut no ice with the new men who lead Germany and Russia.'

'Exactly!' said Fraser with a hint of irritation. 'That I agree with totally, and that is why Germany – and if necessary Russia – must be stopped!'

'If they can be. Who's going to do it? We on our own? And always supposing that Hitler and Stalin really *are* the cause of our trouble, and not merely the effect of a change of heart on the part of mankind!'

'You certainly could write about that, Mr Gissing,' Penfield said, picking at a spot on his neck. 'You're arguing that because old-fashioned theism no longer exists, the values that were set by it no longer exist. I see all that. I had a tutor at university who was always complaining about the teachings of the Jewish Christ. Maybe you have to suffer under them to get really angry about them. I never did. But you don't have to be a Christian or an English gentleman to accept a degree of civilized behaviour as the norm, or to know your right hand from your left!'

Gissing said: 'Fraser will tell you that I often play Devil's Advocate. It's a trick I have, to get my guests to respond. But – but let me say, Devil's Advocate or not, there *is* a point to be made, and would be made by at least one man I know. He would ask: what individual has rights which make him more important than the state? He would ask: why should the down-and-out and the weakling be cared for at the expense of the strong? He would say: what treaty is more valuable than the welfare of a nation? It is not right or wrong to tear up a treaty which becomes inconvenient; it is a fair logical choice with expediency as the deciding factor. What is expedient is good. What is inexpedient is bad. It could be the guiding principle in the world today and can be in the textbooks of tomorrow!'

Fraser glanced sidelong at Gissing, whose fleshy, sallow face was a little flushed – less with drink than argument, he was sure. The gangling Penfield was looking down his nose.

'On that count,' Fraser said, 'Hitler and Stalin are good men?'

Gissing shrugged. 'It's not for me to say. I don't think I would enjoy Hitler's company to dinner . . . But eighty odd million people seem to think he's good enough for them. Who is to say they are altogether mistaken?'

'The several hundred million he oppresses, I suppose,' said Fraser drily.

'Oh yes, oh yes; I agree. In other words there are two standards of right: it depends which one you apply.'

'Stalin oppresses no one,' muttered Penfield. 'He wants no war; that's why he has entered into this sad pact with the Nazis. He is trying to lift his people up: he has no aggressive intentions.'

The butler came in to say dinner was served.

'Thank you, William.'

As the men moved into the dining room, Fraser said: 'Would your friend think it wrong to dive-bomb fleeing women and children?'

'Put that way it's a very emotive question. Will the new man of the future think so? I don't know.'

'For whom Hitler is in a way a symbol, a figurehead, eh?'

'If you will. He's certainly in the van. But there's an island race in the Far East, learning quickly, very gifted. To them the Western ethic is only a feeble foreign dogma.'

In the dining room another fire burned, and the table was laid with bright eighteenth century silver, candlelight reflecting off its polished surfaces.

'As you see it, then,' said Fraser, folding himself into the seat his host indicated, 'even if we were able to destroy Hitler – a mammoth task to begin – even then we should only put off for a few years – twenty – forty? – the return of a new Dark Age.'

'If you call it a Dark Age. Yes, that is my belief.'

'Life versus anti-life, eh?'

'Again, it depends how you define life. Life existed long before ethics, you know.'

Fraser sighed. 'Well . . . it's a defeatist attitude to say the least. Whether our public would wear it . . . What d'you think, Colin?'

'It depends how it was put,' said Penfield, sitting down. 'I don't take too rosy a view of our immediate prospects – any more than Mr Gissing – but I wouldn't be as profoundly pessimistic as he is. Nor would I lump the various movements – Nazi, Fascist, Communist, Nationalist – together as being equally anti-human. As I've said, I have great hopes of the Marxist experiment – '

As they began to eat Fraser reflected that not merely was he unsure whether his magazine's public would wear such an argument as Gissing put forward but whether he would do so himself. However, he was in no way committed to publishing what Gissing wrote; one would simply make a new judgment when the time came.

'I shall follow the anchovies with a clear soup, and then very small tender *tournedos* served with fresh tomato sauce,' said Gissing. 'Then roast duck with French salad and stuffed cucumbers. As a sweet I have chosen an iced chocolate mousse with a chestnut purée. It is, I know,' he added, 'parvenue manners of the worst kind to list one's dinner in this way beforehand, but I've discovered that war-time scarcity has turned every man into a *gourmet*. Or at the very least into a *gourmand*.' Privately he had noticed Luke Fraser as a hearty eater at the public dinners they had attended, and he guessed this long thin sub-editor could put it away. It was a little show-off, but it was worthwhile. The impression of the meal would remain in their minds for quite a time.

'I must say,' said Penfield with a nervous laugh, 'it will make rather a change from powdered eggs . . .'

'Yes, what is it, William?'

'Two gentlemen to see you, sir.'

Gissing frowned.

'Their names?'

'They would not give any, sir.'

'Well, I certainly can't see them now. Things will spoil. What do they want?'

'They wouldn't say, sir.'

It was on Gissing's tongue to send back a sharp refusal, but he fancied he saw on his butler's face the faintly disapproving expression reserved for those of his visitors that William classed as 'unsavoury'. It might just possibly be someone with further news of Baker.

'Excuse me, will you,' he said to his guests. 'I'll be back in a moment.'

He ambled softly, with in-turned toes, in his scuffed black patent shoes, into the hall, and as soon as he saw the two men he knew his mistake. They were strangers and wore long waistless grey overcoats and carried bowler hats in their hands. They were broad-shouldered men with keen but unemotional faces and a quiet air of authority.

Gissing stopped, fumbled with the top button of his waistcoat, and his eyes moved from one to the other. He waited for William to leave. Then he said:

'Good evening. What can I do for you?'

'Mr Walter Gissing?' said one.

'Yes?'

'We have a warrant for your arrest.'

Gissing was very quiet for a moment. 'For my – Oh, nonsense! What do you mean, man?'

One of the visitors – they had come nearer to him – produced a paper and handed it to him. Gissing did not read it.

'There must be some mistake.'

'I don't think so, sir. Mr Walter Gissing. Alias Mr Henry Armitage. Formerly Mr Leopold Bauer. I don't think there is any mistake this time. And I must warn you that anything you say may be taken down and used in evidence.'

Gissing thought he had seen the taller of the men before but he couldn't place him. He licked his lips, which were unexpectedly dry. For a moment he felt quite queer as if he were really in danger.

'Really, gentlemen, this is rather a farce, isn't it? What do you suppose you're charging me with?'

'You are charged under the Defence Regulations with being a secret agent in the pay of an enemy country.'

'A secret agent? I?' He laughed briefly and tried to stop himself from vomiting. 'Oh, that's good! That's very good. My guests will be intensely amused. So will the Home Secretary, who happens to be a personal friend of mine. And several other members of the Government!'

'Sorry, sir. If there's been some mistake I'm sure it can all be ironed out at the Station.'

Gissing felt hemmed in. A little air and space were needed, and time and room to think. He would have been convinced this was a genuine mistake – except for that name. Who had discovered a name discarded so long ago? Yet somehow it *must* be a mistake: his whole life was firmly founded on twenty-one years of blameless English residency; his home was here, all his possessions. The obverse side of the coin belonged to somebody else: they could never be allowed to meet.

'As it happens,' he said, 'I'm entertaining important guests and we're about to start dinner. Could you be prevailed upon to wait an hour? I can't disappear into thin air; I'm rather too substantial a person, aren't I? Ha, ha! Or still better, should you be so accommodating, I'll undertake to come to the Station myself later this evening and clear up this unfortunate misunderstanding.'

'I'm sorry, sir. Our orders are to bring you to the Station right away.'

'But for God's sake!' He began to work himself into a state of righteous anger, so that now he *knew* it was all a mistake. 'Am I not permitted – '

'It's no good, Mr Gissing. Perhaps I should tell you that a Dr Joseph Norley and his wife were arrested this afternoon at Folkestone. We have proof – '

The hand on his shoulder. It was not heavy, but psychologically it was like a clamp.

'I have never heard of any such person! Dr Norton, did you say? What possible – '

'We took care that you shouldn't hear of their arrest before. Afraid the game is up.'

For a moment more he went on talking, using indignation as a defence and as a support. The gulf was still a few feet away. 'It's a total mistake, man! D'you realize who I am? I shall certainly complain of your attitude. I shall have the matter raised in Parliament!'

'Get your coat and hat, please. It's quite chilly out. Are they in here?'

'No, they're not. Allow me to call my butler.'

They waited. Gissing's face had lost its usual colour, otherwise he was still composed.

'Ah, William. Will you tell my guests that I am temporarily called away and will you continue to serve them dinner. Is the Chambertin open?'

'Yes, sir.'

'Oh, dear. A pity . . . Very well, then you may as well serve it. I shall be back later, but I don't know quite how long I shall be.'

'Very good, sir.'

They waited again until William was gone. Gissing scratched his nose. 'Ah yes, my hat and coat. What a stupid mistake all this is! At least one doesn't have to advertise it to one's servants.'

He moved towards the small cloakroom and fumbled about among the hats and coats there. Then the taller of the two officers made a swift leap and grabbed at Gissing's hand as it came away from his mouth. He was eating something but not getting it down.

Deprived of this other and less palatable meal, Mr Gissing for the first time in his life struggled, soundlessly, livid of feature and suddenly panting. Even when the second man joined in he kicked and jerked and twitched until they hand-cuffed him. Then the brief fierce protest was over and his heavy flaccid body was limp in their hands. What he had been trying to swallow was not a phial of poison – he would never have thought of carrying such a thing – but a few notes and sentences written on two sheets of india paper.

They half dragged, half carried him out to the waiting car, while Fraser and Penfield, encouraged by William, resumed their interrupted dinner. It was embarrassing for them to carry on without their host, but this he had sent word they should do, and it would have been a criminal waste not to eat such wonderful food in war-time.

In the car Walter Gissing made one last struggling, jerking effort to free himself: it was instinctive, unthinking, an animal not a logical reassertion. Then he stopped and made no further protest.

Protests could be saved for the future. He knew himself to be far cleverer than these two solid men. He knew there would be no one among those who were going to confront him who would be able to match him in subtlety, in shrewdness, in sheer quality of intellect. Therein lay his only hope. It would make a difference.

But as the car drove through the darkened streets came the realization penetrating slowly into his mind, like a knife through a cloak, that cleverness would make no difference. Nor would his knowledge of England and English law, nor all his friendships with people in high places. Inexorably, stupidly, these fools who held him would go about their job, drawing ever tighter the strings of proof until he was netted and secure. After that the end would be just as unhurried, as stupid, as inexorable and as hard. It was true he might be avenged; within six months if all went well he would be avenged; but at present and in this context superior force lay on the other side. It was hard to argue even with himself that it was not to the benefit of his adopted country that he should be quietly and efficiently disposed of.

If, as he had put the point this evening, the race was to the powerful and expediency the final arbiter, he hadn't much more to hope for or consideration to expect.

Friday

After two days Andrew was sick of flat-capped bobbies and earnest magistrates and the pert inquiries of reporters. Discreetly steered in the right direction by dark-suited officers of the Special Branch, the authorities had done their best to hush everything up, but Dr Norley was too public a figure to disappear without trace, and some of the events at the surgery had leaked out. Norley and Miss Harrison had been brought back to Elm Street and officially charged and re-manded in custody, but any trial would be held in camera. Charges brought against Squadron Leader Halford had been dropped.

But it was all very time-consuming and he failed on either day to get more than a few minutes with Jennifer. She seemed to be recovering, but visitors were not encouraged. After-effects of shock, said the house surgeon, were unreliable and hard to predict – otherwise she was mending and now could swallow soft food again.

Her colour the second day was better than the first, and one of the bandages had gone from her neck. All the same she seemed way out from the Jennifer he'd first met, so alert and vivid and bubbling with life and fun. Even her fringe clung to her forehead as if she'd recently been in the rain.

His first words, the first time he saw her, came out in an unstoppable, jerky, flood of high apology. That he could ever have gone back to his squadron and left her unguarded, unprotected, alone in that flat . . . 'The bloody police,' he kept saying. 'The bloody police,' until the lady in the next bed, who'd been pretending not to eavesdrop, took offence and asked him to control his language.

Jennifer whispered hoarsely: 'You couldn't *know*. Nobody could *know*.'

'Well, they could have made a bloody good guess! I still don't know why the police didn't come.'

'Stephen came.'

'Yes, Stephen came. Even he was late.'

'But in time.'

'Thank God. But – '

'I'll be all *right*, Andrew.'

On his second visit she even seemed anxious to tell him about her confrontation with Louis and the five minutes in the flat. He would have tried to divert her, but some female psychologist he'd had a word with on his way in had urged him to let her talk about it as much as she wanted. The lasting damage would be if she *wouldn't* talk.

The police had been to see her twice and asked her a limited number of questions, mainly about Stephen Radziwill's struggle with Louis. Next week she might be called at the reopened inquest on Paula Krissen. Apart from that she could recuperate in peace.

She was obviously still so shaky that he said no more of his personal feelings; instead told her of the fight in Norley's surgery, assured her that Witold Poniatowski had only a flesh wound and was due to return to his squadron today. Stephen's would be a longer job.

Each of his visits broke up with friendly smiles and expressions of good will.

Apart from these short interludes and his sessions with the police, Andrew spent most of his time talking to Stephen. It was a very small way of saying thanks for the obligation he was under. Stephen would have none of it.

'I should have been there in advance, my friend. But the raid just began, and the taxis go off the streets. So I had to go with your underground and change at Leicester Square. If I had been with her half an hour earlier . . .'

'Praise be you were not ten minutes later!'

'Ah yes. Well perhaps we shall have good memories of all this in the end.'

On the Friday morning a meeting at Scotland Yard with an assistant commissioner, some senior official from the Home Office, and two or three other plain-clothes gentlemen from the Special Branch. They were still hoping some other fish might be netted. With garbled reports of Dr Norley's arrest in the newspapers, Andrew thought this unlikely, but clearly they knew their business best.

In the afternoon he went to the hospital again to see Jennifer and found her gone. He stared at the Matron as if he didn't believe her.

'Gone? Miss *Jennifer* Ward? How do you mean, to another hospital?'

'Gone home. She went this morning. A gentleman called for her in a car. Her uncle, I believe. They left about twelve.'

'Was she well enough? I thought she would be here for some days!'

'We thought so too but she was very keen to leave, and of course we were glad of the bed. She pestered Dr Stevenson yesterday to let her leave today. She's not seriously injured, you know. It's largely a matter of rest and quietness – some weeks preferably – and she can do that better at home than here.'

'But I was here yesterday. Why didn't she tell me then?'

The Matron pursed her lips. She hadn't much time for pondering the peculiarities of young women. 'She didn't mention leaving until after visiting hours. She seemed suddenly to take it into her head.'

'Can you let me have her address, please?'

'If you'll ask the secretary . . .'

Andrew asked the secretary.

'Yes, certainly, sir. Hm – Here it is. 45 Gaskin Street, NW1.'

'No, that's the address of her flat, where she – where she met with this accident.'

'We don't seem to have any other. There's nothing here.'

'She must have left a forwarding address.'

'No other. Perhaps she's gone back there.'

'I don't think that's at all likely. Is she coming back for treatment?'

'Not as far as I know, sir.'

'Thanks.' He turned on his heel.

So the hell with it. The more he thought it over, the less he liked it. In spite of what she said, did she still hold it against him that he'd let her down on Tuesday night? Or had he rubbed her the wrong way by something he said yesterday? Or left unsaid? But how could anyone have any natural talk, with that old cow listening in the next bed?

Suppose his visit yesterday had helped her sort out her feelings and she'd made this sudden move in a genuine effort to ditch him? Or was she still in shock and not quite in control of her own impulses? Or were impulses like this a part of her natural temperament? He knew her so little really, could hardly begin to read her character or to hope to understand.

At 45, Gaskin Street Mrs Lawson had her hair in curlers for the first time for forty-eight hours, and was tired of the police and the fuss and everything else; and it had been a thoroughly bad week for her, having a fight in her house and the banisters broken. No, Miss Ward had not been back to the flat, and all her things were still here. The rent was only paid till Saturday. Saturday another week was due, and it was a rule to have it paid in advance too. That Paula Krissen had badly let her down. (By getting herself murdered, Andrew presumed.) No, she didn't have Jennifer's uncle's address; she didn't even know if it was the same uncle who'd called last Sunday. She had Jennifer's mother's address for what it was worth, and he was welcome to it.

He took this down – there was no telephone number – and was about to leave when he had another thought and asked for the address of Beaufort's, where Jennifer had worked.

This too he put down, with telephone number, but Mrs Lawson comfortingly observed that as they had been blitzed she didn't think anyone would be answering *that* number just at present.

He wondered whether Mrs Lawson held him partly responsible for the damage to her banisters.

It was only four o'clock, and he wondered how the hell to spend the next few hours. His extended leave ended tomorrow at six. He couldn't ask for more. He didn't want more.

He had spent the last two nights at the RAF Club, but now went into the Euston Hotel, which was near by, and smiled at the telephone girl and asked her if she could possibly find a number for him. A Mrs Anne Thoroughgood of 12, Edison Lane, Swindon. Five minutes later the telephone girl told him there was a Mr Robert Thoroughgood lived at 12, Edison Lane, but his telephone had been reported out of order. Another smile and could she possibly be an angel and try a local Chancery number he'd been given. It was a firm called Beaufort's. Only three minutes, and the girl said the number was no longer obtainable because of enemy action and the firm had not yet been connected at the new address. Andrew used some of his sweet coupons on buying her a half-pound box of chocolates and then went to have tea in the lounge.

So he had twenty-five hours to spend, looking for Jennifer or in any other activity he waywardly fancied. The one must was to spend most of it with his parents. He'd not even rung them to tell them of his extra leave, thinking it would be all the more fun to appear suddenly on their doorstep.

He could hire a self-drive car first thing in the morning. Swindon was on the way to Bath. He could look up Jennifer – if she was there – before going on to Bath.

But was she there? Who was this uncle who had fetched her from the hospital? Yesterday Jennifer had told him of the identity of the two callers on the Sunday afternoon. That had been an uncle and a cousin. Hadn't Jennifer told him they were only passing through London and were off to Grange? Unlikely he would have returned so soon. Some other uncle, then? Why hadn't her mother and stepfather come? Perhaps they'd sent this uncle instead. Perhaps not.

Andrew swallowed his tea too hot and scowled at an old couple who were complaining to the waitress about the poor quality of the sugar. His mind was full of increasing apprehension. The German cell had been fully smoked out. There could be no further threat to Jennifer. Surely. Even if there were plenty of agents still at large there would be no point in trying to silence Jennifer, for she had nothing more to say.

So it must be a genuine uncle. In any case, had he not been genuine, she would not voluntarily have gone away with him.

Perhaps Jennifer was a member of the spy ring and was anxious to disappear before Norley gave her away.

Perhaps Mrs Lawson was Deputy Gauleiter for North London.

Andrew paid for his tea and got up. He could, of course, hire a car now and be out of London and in Swindon by sunset – if he drew blank there, then he could go straight on to Bath and spend the night with his parents.

It was a week only since he'd dined at the Savoy, gone on to the Bamboo Club and from there to Northcot to find Paula Krissen sitting waiting for him. A hell of a week. As full of incident as the first week of last August when the dog fights for his squadron really began. By rights he should have spent this week hoeing potatoes or sowing lettuce seed. Relaxing, recuperating, taking it easy, instead of on the nose.

He asked the doorman where he could find a good car-hire firm and was told, not surprisingly, Great Portland Street – Mart's, the big firm on the corner of Margaret Street. As he came out of the hotel it was beginning to rain. He remembered vaguely someone had once told him that Guardsmen had carried umbrellas into battle in the Napoleonic Wars. Well, far from having an umbrella, he didn't even have a coat. Not that his weather-beaten uniform would come to much hurt.

There was a taxi at the door and he got in it, gave the driver the address.

'Ain't no good going there, guv. I was down that way an hour ago. Mart's got a stick of bombs Wednesday night so I reckon all you'd be able to hire there would be a couple of loose wheels.'

'Well, find me somewhere, can you.'

'There's a place off the Strand. That do?'

'Lead on.'

The driver made a talkative way through the traffic, his screenwiper clacking noisily.

'Wait a minute,' said Andrew.

'What?'

'If we're going that way. D'you know Salisbury Square?'

'Sure. Off Fleet Street. There's no car-hire firm there.'

'No. I've just had a thought. There's a firm I want to look up. It's been blitzed.'

'Damn right it has if it's in Salisbury Square.'

'They've started up again somewhere close by. I thought I'd look in. Can you spare half an hour?'

'Spare an hour for the likes of you. Sorry I can't do it for free.'

'So'm I,' said Andrew.

They made good speed down Gray's Inn Road and Chancery Lane and into Fleet Street. Then the taxi turned right and came to a stop, its engine tick-ticking while Andrew got out and looked at all that was left of Beaufort's. It reminded him of a Chaplin comedy of the First World War, with a splendid front door intact, leading to nothing but rubble.

But nailed confidently to this door was a large hand-printed notice saying that Beaufort's were continuing business on the second floor of No 12 Cobb's Court.

'Cobb's Court. Where's that?'

'I'll show you. Jump in.'

Five minutes and again they stopped. It was a doubtful hunch, but Jennifer was employed here, paid here. She probably wanted to keep her job and might well have telephoned them giving them her new address.

'Can you wait again? I shall only be three or four minutes.'

'Sure, mate. Take your time.'

The second floor of No 12 Cobb's Court – which looked like a converted warehouse anyhow – was just one enormous, echoing, gloomy room, with lights already on to counteract the rainy day. The firm that had moved here no doubt normally carried on its business in a dozen small, discreet, relatively sound-proof offices. In another couple of weeks some order would probably emerge, but at the moment the manager sat cheek-by-jowl with the office boy, and typist and cashier, draughtsman and director rubbed elbows at two large dining tables borrowed from the restaurant across the street.

Into this dismal and confused scene Andrew came, blinking his eyes to get them used to the unshaded electric lights. No one took any notice of him. There was no inner door to knock on, no counter to rap, no bell to press. Eventually a middle-aged woman raised her head and wandered across.

'Yes?'

'I'm sorry to trouble you, but a Miss Jennifer Ward, who works here, has moved her address, and I'm anxious to trace the new one. She's been in hospital but has just been discharged. D'you think your manager or your cashier might be able to help?'

She was a grey wispy woman with gold-rimmed spectacles and an air of pinched respectability. She looked at his uniform.

'Hadn't you better ask her yourself?' she suggested.

'I would if I knew where to find her.'

'Well, she's over there . . . I expect it will be all right for you to go across to see her. Only of course we *are* in such a state of confusion.'

Andrew looked at the woman, then stared across the gloomy warehouse. At the far end, amid the shadows and the conflicting lights, beyond the tables and the confusion of the centre, he saw a head which he instantly and painfully recognized.

'She – she's no right to be here! She only came out of hospital this morning!'

'It's for her to decide, isn't it,' said the woman frostily. 'Naturally at a time like this Mr Lang was delighted to have her back.' She saw he wasn't listening. 'Perhaps you should see Mr Lang first.'

'No, no, thank you. I quite understand how you feel. I – I . . . Right, thank you very much. I'll go across.'

Once launched on a navigation of that confused sea, he saw that after all there was a certain plan about the grouping of staff. The spatter and tap of voices and typewriters beat over him.

She was standing before some primitive metal shelves on which were already stacked several piles of papers. On two card tables pushed together was a much larger pile, heaped like the lava of an erupted volcano and threatening to overflow onto the floor. Some of the edges of the papers were crinkled and singed. Beside the tables was a chair and beside the metal shelves was a short library ladder she was just beginning to climb. She went up stiffly, stepping up each time with the same foot.

He said: 'I see your knee's still troublesome.'

She turned quickly, stared at him, then sat abruptly on the top of the ladder. Her face flushed up. She pulled down her skirt and put the bundle of papers she was carrying on her lap.

'Hullo, Andrew.'

Dark brown suit, cream blouse, paler belt, shoes matching the belt. Splash of colour, vivid green scarf round her throat.

He said: 'You've had quite a week. You've been knocked about – every since you met me.'

Her eyes seemed even bigger than usual, and darker, lacked the sparkle.

'Obviously it was pretty dangerous meeting you, wasn't it.'

'Seems so. One of those war-time hazards.'

She half smiled. 'Well, I'm OK now.'

'All the same, you shouldn't be here, you know.'

'Why not?'

'Well, a bit sudden, isn't it, to say the least. This time yesterday in bed in hospital, today up a ladder fiddling with a lot of papers.'

'I'm not exactly fiddling. At least not while Rome is burning. That happened ten days ago.'

The reply reassured him as to her general health.

'Couldn't you have told me your plans yesterday?'

'I didn't have any until late in the afternoon.'

'Or left a message?'

'Sorry. Yes, I should have done.'

'They told me at the hospital that your uncle had picked you up.'

'That was a fib. I thought they'd be more likely to discharge me if they thought it was a relative.'

He waited. 'And it was . . .?'

'Mr Lang. The bald man over there. I rang him and asked him to collect me.'

'Right from hospital back to work?'

'I began to feel better yesterday. And I thought I could be of help. The poor dears are still in a hopeless muddle.'

'The poor dears might have given you an easier job.'

She considered him seriously, only the flick of her fingers showing some disturbance.

'I asked for this. I've had most to do with the correspondence. I know nearly all the firms and government departments we had dealings with. You may not believe it, but this "fiddling with papers" isn't as easy as it looks.'

'Come down off the ladder,' he said. 'I want to talk to you.'

A tall man approached them. 'Miss Ward, Mr Lang wants to know if you've come across any of the correspondence from the Arco group.'

'No, Mr Fraser, not a thing. I've half the invoices from Benn's when he wants them. And some of those Ministry of Food leaflets got in here by mistake.'

'Right, I'll tell him.' The man glanced curiously at Andrew as he moved off.

'You ought not to be here,' Jennifer said. 'You're interfering with my work.'

'You're interfering with mine.'

She arranged the papers on her lap and thrust some of them on to the top shelf.

'What time will this place close?' he asked.

'Oh, probably about seven.'

'And are you going home then? To Swindon, I mean.'

'I don't think so. All my things are still at the flat.'

'Can you bear to sleep there after what's happened?'

'I hadn't thought of it that way . . . I don't know. But there's no danger in going back there now, is there?'

'No,' he agreed, 'no danger at all. I suppose. But I would have thought . . . You must be tougher than you look.'

'In some ways, yes.'

He watched her for a few moments.

'These shelves have got no divisions,' she said. 'It's hard to make any sort of lasting order without them . . . I don't know really why I left the hospital so suddenly. It was an impulse.'

'Not the sort of impulse I appreciate. I've been going round in small circles looking for you. I couldn't think what had got into you. Were you trying to shake me off?'

She sorted through the letters. 'I don't know. I thought it might give you . . .' The rest of the sentence, which was muttered, was lost in the clatter of the typewriters.

'What did you say?' he asked. 'I can't talk to you up there.'

She said: 'I wanted to come back here because it was a sort of return to normal – it steadied things in my mind, if you understand.'

'I understand. But that was not what you began to say.'

'It doesn't matter,' she said. 'Can you pass me that other bunch with the string round them?'

He grasped the ladder and shook it. She clutched her papers and the shelf.

'I go back to Manston tomorrow at six,' he said.

She came down the ladder. She had flushed again, a brighter pink.

'You *are* a bully! I shall never live this down. Please go now.'

'What did you think?'

'I thought . . .' She paused. 'Oh, nothing really. I thought if I slipped away from the hospital it would give you the opportunity to – to . . . well, you wouldn't feel under such an obligation to continue coming to see me if you didn't want to. After all – '

'Who said I didn't want to?'

'Nobody. Only . . .'

'Only you thought it might be so. Eh? Is that it?'

'Well, it could be, couldn't it?'

'No, it couldn't. D'you suppose because I said so little in the hospital . . . You needed *quietness*. Besides, I couldn't make love to you with that old hag slavering in the next bed!'

'I never said I wanted to be made *love* to!' she said angrily. 'For Heaven's sake, you say I need quietness, and you come here making a most *awful* scene in front of the people I work with!'

The thick-set bald man had risen from his table and come across to them.

'You'll pardon me, Miss Ward. Is this gentleman annoying you?'

' . . . No. No thanks, Mr Lang.'

'In fact the reverse is the case,' said Andrew. 'It's I who am being annoyed.'

Mr Lang looked him up and down.

'I don't understand you. Miss Ward is only recently out of hospital. I'm very concerned that she should not be upset.'

'I'm really all right, thank you,' said Jennifer. 'Squadron Leader Halford has been involved in all this. He'll be going in a moment.'

'Oh, in that case . . .'

The manager moved off.

'Andrew, you'd better leave now.'

There was a brief interval while the noise of the typewriters was dominant.

'You're such a coward,' he said.

'My God!' Her eyes were angrily bright. 'Don't you think you've insulted me enough?'

'Insulted you by falling in love with you? Yes, if you feel that way, I suppose I have.'

Nobody spoke then.

'All right,' he said. 'Let's face facts. Can you bear to face facts?'

'It depends what they are.'

'In all this business I committed one ghastly mistake, didn't I – I left you alone in London. Right? When I heard what had happened to you I could have been physically sick. I got terrible pains of apprehension in my stomach. Got that? We've been a bit at odds with each other ever since Marley Manor. I don't quite know how it began . . . Well, yes I do, but forget that. Whatever went wrong then, I haven't since had a chance to put it right. I called you a coward because you don't seem willing to face the issue. Once or twice in the hospital I did come round to the point, but always you changed the subject, turned the point away. Well . . . it can't be turned away now.'

Jennifer continued to look at him.

'All right,' she said. 'I'm facing you now. What is it you want?'

'You,' he said.

Outside somewhere a clock struck six.

She said: 'That wouldn't be much good. You've just told me I give you pains in the stomach.'

He ran a hand through hair.

'OK. Have your fun. Maybe I deserve it.'

'Sorry,' she said jerkily, unexpectedly.

'Last weekend,' he said; 'it may have meant nothing to you. I don't know. I thought it had. Maybe it didn't. But it certainly meant something to me. Since then I've thought once or twice I've lost you and thought once or twice I've found you. I want to be *sure*. I'm no longer – complete without you.'

Someone came up behind them again. A woman's voice: 'There's some more stuff here, Jennifer. A few of the bottom ones are charred, but I think you can read them.'

'Thanks,' said Jennifer. 'I'll look through them.'

The clatter of the typewriters again took the upper hand.

'This bloody office,' said Andrew.

'It's quite hard to sort these papers out,' she explained impersonally. 'The heat of the fire was so intense that even things in the heat-proof safe curled up at the edges. Yet other papers that weren't protected have come through quite well. I suppose it was the wind. A strong south-east breeze was blowing off the river and it carried the fire through the building and left one or two corners untouched. Andrew, I'll ask Mr Lang if he can excuse me for half an hour. Perhaps we could go and have a coffee somewhere.'

Andrew looked at her quickly. 'It's up to you.'

'Yes, it is, isn't it. All up to me. Yet not really, not any of it. We – can talk about that.'

She limped across to Mr Lang and presently returned. 'All right.'

Self-consciously they picked their way across the cavernous room.

'You ought to let someone see that knee,' he said.

'I have. Dr Stevenson says there's water on it. What is water on the knee? I thought it was a music hall joke. Like housemaid's knee.'

'I know I haven't got much patience,' he said. 'It's not been part of my training. Maybe I shall learn it, dealing with you.'

'There's a bag here,' she said. 'Just the few things I had in hospital. Mr Lang says I don't need to come back. I've promised to be here prompt tomorrow morning.'

He helped her on with her coat. Her closeness was a magical thing. He followed her and she stopped at the first flight of gloomy, dirty stairs. A silence fell between them that was charged with sudden emotion. It struck at them both fundamentally – went deeper than their feelings had ever gone before. It almost overwhelmed them. Yet words, reason had to come back.

'Andrew, it's not patience I want from you. I don't want you to be patient *about* me or *with* me. I only want you to be sure.'

'*Sure*. I *am* sure; I've just told you. I've never been so sure of anything in my life! But does that mean you are or are not?'

'That's not quite a fair question.'

'Why ever not?'

'We're talking about your feelings, aren't we?'

'Mine only?'

'For the moment.'

'Why should we? This is a joint thing or nothing at all.' He made a helpless gesture. 'Look, Jennifer, I can't prove anything. Nobody can. I know that I love you. I don't want to take you to bed here and now; I want to marry you. To be sure of you, to be sure no one else ever touches you for the rest of your life. Of course, it's a chancy business now, especially marrying somebody like me. But if you'll take the chance I think I can prove something in time. But there's not much more I can say. I'm no poet. I can't talk about the moon and the stars.'

'You're doing very well,' she said.

'Thanks.'

She slipped a hand through his arm. 'You think I'm an awful doubter.'

'Yes.'

They moved on and came to the next flight. Her hand had dropped from his arm.

'You know those who doubt most are sometimes those who most want to believe,' she said.

'Do you want to believe?'

'If you only knew how badly . . .'

He suddenly wanted to shout at the top of his voice but

237

did not. Like a good pilot he knew when to hold his fire.

They had stopped and she was biting at her thumb. He could only see the top of her head, catching coppery gleams of daylight from a distant window.

'You've got me in a corner,' she said. 'Literally.'

He stepped back. 'All right. Come out and we'll fight fair.'

'I don't want to fight any more.'

He took her quietly by the shoulders, just as he had done that night in the hotel bedroom. His hands were not as steady as usual.

'Your fists are still clenched,' he said.

She said: 'Oh, my love, it's tension, not anger.'

'God help me!' he said, shouting now; 'I've got a taxi waiting outside! I've just remembered!'

'Let's get into it,' said Jennifer, 'and go for a long drive somewhere.'